COWGIRL, UNBROKEN

VICKI THARP

COWGIRL, UNBROKEN

Original Cover Design by Designs EE

ISBN 978-1-948798-29-7

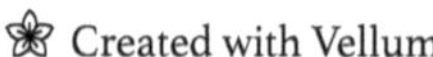 Created with Vellum

1

IF MIA MANN WAS GOING TO DIE TODAY, AT LEAST IT WOULDN'T BE at the hands of the Taliban or her ass-wipe of an ex.

She stretched out the stiffness in her muscles as the sun rose over a frigid, early-November morning. That close to the Wyoming Rockies, she could practically reach out and touch the snow-capped peaks.

She stared up at the flat face of the forty-foot cliff beside the hot spring, pleased it hadn't snowed overnight. Today was the day she'd conquer her free climb over the most difficult route of ascent.

Dangerous.

Potentially deadly.

But something she could control.

She started her climb one grasp, one foothold at a time. Hand over hand, her concentration on each movement and each outcropping or crevice even remotely suitable to use as a hold. The extra chalk on her hands combatted the excess moisture on the rock.

The first twenty-five feet, she climbed steady and true, all the holds memorized and practiced from multiple climbs. Her heart beat strong, her breath puffing out in little clouds of condensation.

Now for the most treacherous part of the climb. The part that would take her across and then up and over the overhang. She rested a foot on the narrowest of edges, the type that would be impossible without her climbing shoes.

She shoved her arm into a crevice, locked herself into place, and shook out her other arm. In her mind, she redrew the map of handholds and footholds needed for the remainder of her climb.

The strain on her foot told her she couldn't hang out indefinitely. She either had to climb her usual route or make the leap, not only to the next hold, but of faith.

Not faith in a higher power, because if there were a higher power, he or she had long ago abandoned her.

But faith in herself. In her abilities.

Reaching behind her, she dipped her hand into her chalk bag one last time. "Here goes nothing."

Moving to her left, she caught the thinnest of edges with her fingertips and stepped over to a narrow ledge. Inch by inch, foot by foot, she ascended, welcoming the strain in her shoulders, the quake in her quads, and the catch in her calves. The discomfort and pain brought her inward, into an almost zen-like blanking of her mind.

Bye-bye world.

Bye-bye problems.

At that moment, nothing else mattered.

Higher and higher she climbed, the earth falling away beneath her. She could do this. She *was* doing this

She clung to the cliff face, her body going past vertical, gravity working against every grip and step. Despite the cold temperature, stinging sweat dripped into her eyes, her muscles shaking from her effort.

For the first time since she'd begun the climb, she questioned her ability to reach the top, as her fingers started to cramp. She glanced above her at the crux of the climb, the most difficult part.

Up and to her left, the only hold on the sheer face was a crimper, a hold just big enough to be grasped by her fingertips. Next came a long, long reach to a bulge of an outcropping she could cup grip. From there she could reach over the top ledge and pull herself up.

She took two deep breaths, psyching herself up and stretching on her tiptoes to reach the crimper. She settled her foot into a divot in the rockface. She didn't waste any time reaching for the outcropping, knowing she couldn't hold the tenuous grip for long.

She didn't have the long legs and massive reach a lot of the taller rock climbers had. The outcropping was a stretch, but she caught it, testing the security of the rock before she transferred her weight and caught the top with her other hand. All she had to do now was haul herself up and over the ledge.

Just when she thought the top ledge would hold, the rock cracked. Adrenaline dumped into her system, her heart rate maxing. Time stopped. Then it slammed back into her with a jolt. Her fingers scrambled for any kind of hold as the rock broke free, thudding and disintegrating on the hard ground below.

In the scramble, her feet cut loose, dangling beneath her. The tendons in her elbow and shoulder straining as she dead hanged above the ground. Her fingers went numb.

She hung from the top of the cliff one-handed like someone in a sappy, motivational commercial.

How the hell had she ended up here?

Not in the physical sense, because her muscles and limbs felt every inch of the climb, but emotionally. Her past had left her shattered like spun glass, literally and figuratively, dangling by her fingertips and wondering if she should try to grab hold with her other hand...

...or just let go.

A forty-foot drop. What people would assume had been the worst mistake of her life. Kicker of it was, they'd be wrong.

She closed her eyes as her fingers slipped free. Her body went into free fall. Her only regret? Not telling Matt that she'd appreciated that he'd tried.

MATT BISHOP RAN DOWN THE TRAIL BEHIND THE CABINS AT THE Lazy S Ranch, the frigid air stinging his nostrils and burning his lungs, keenly aware that Mia never made it back to her cabin the night before.

Usually she returned before dawn, but since they had the weekend off, she might have slept in wherever she'd set up camp.

Matt laughed at the thought that Mia would have gotten any sleep. Hard to sleep in when you've camped out under the stars in near-freezing weather. He'd been there. Done that. And shook all night, not getting a wink of sleep.

But Mia... Mia beat anyone he'd ever known. How much it had to do with her issues since coming back from deployment he had no clue. Because unlike him and Zealand Cross, the other veteran in the Healing Horses program, she hadn't shared shit about her past. And with their time in the program coming to an end, he doubted she ever would.

As he approached the fork in the path, his head told him to take the route to the left, to give Mia the space she so clearly wanted, but his heart forced him to the right and the direction he thought he'd find Mia.

More than capable of taking care of herself, Mia would be

annoyed that he jogged by to check on her. But that knowledge certainty couldn't override his protective streak.

He wouldn't even have to stop and talk. He'd just jog by and confirm for himself that she'd survived the night. He'd stay out of her hair, and if she slept soundly enough, she may never know he'd even passed by.

You know that's bullshit, right? A gnat walking across a feather could wake her.

But he wouldn't let the truth stop him.

As his muscles warmed, the stiffness from the horseback riding he'd done the day before started working out of his quads and inner thighs.

Coming around a bend, the cliff above the hot spring came into view. On particularly cold nights, Mia camped by the spring. The cliff acted as a natural break from the north wind, and the hot spring warmed the surrounding area by a few precious degrees.

Movement on the cliff face caught his eyes. An eagle? The form shifted, and the outline became clear.

Mia.

Dangling from the top of the cliff by one hand as she stared down at the earth below. He wanted to call out, but no words came. Turning on the afterburners, he sprinted for the foot of the cliff.

No. No. No. No. No.

He couldn't take his eyes off her as he ran. Could she hang on? Could he catch her if she couldn't? Could—

She fell, arms and legs flailing.

She didn't call out—which was so fucking like her, always refusing to ask for help.

"Mia!"

He closed the gap at a dead run, his heart tripping and falling with every step.

Too late. No one could run fast enough.

At the last second, she curled into a ball, holding her knees to her chest as she disappeared behind the treetops. Matt waited for the *thud*, the sound of her body hitting the ground. Instead, he heard a splash.

He broke through the trees, the surface of the pool a boiling mass of ripples and bubbles. Matt didn't wait to see if she would pop to the surface. He took a shallow dive off a flat rock by the edge.

He hit the hot water, aiming for the center of the ripple zone. She surfaced at the same time he did, coughing and sputtering as she tread water.

Seconds later, he grabbed hold of her water-logged fleece and spun her around. "What the fuck, Mann?"

She coughed again, her head barely above the water as she struggled against the heavy weight of her soaked clothes. "What are you doing here?"

And yeah, that was more of an accusation than a question. "For fuck's sake, I thought you'd died."

"I should be so lucky," she said as she started swimming for the shore, her strokes short, her kicks weak. To call her progression a dog paddle would be generous.

"Roll on your back. I'll pull you in."

Mia obeyed his command, which told him she had little fuel left in her tank. If she could have made it to shore without his interference, she would have shoved him away.

Maneuvering behind her, he wrapped an arm around her chest and towed her to shore. They lay in the warm water in a sandy spot along the bank, catching their breath. She rolled to her belly and rested her forehead on her fists. Rivulets of water ran down from her short hair.

Since she'd been in the Healing Horses program, she'd

stopped shaving her head, and in the last couple of months, her dark hair had started to grow in.

He wanted to shake some sense into her, but she'd likely clock him with a right cross. If he'd learned anything since he'd met her, it was that she wasn't afraid to defend herself.

As his breathing slowed, he said, "Mind telling me what the hell that was all about?"

She turned her head to look at him. What startled him the most was that she didn't look freaked out about the prospect of almost dying.

"I fell." The *duh* clear in her tone.

"No shit."

Another thing he'd learned working and training horses alongside Mia? She didn't like being handled with kid gloves. Treating her as if she were fragile would only earn you a scowl or a scathing look. And damn, if that didn't make him appreciate and want her that much more.

Now who's the fucked up one?

"I wasn't talking about the fall," Matt said. "I was talking about the 'I should be so lucky' fatalistic part."

She heaved herself to her knees, shoved off the large rock beside her, and ignored his question. He followed, the warm water draining off him, the cold rapidly displacing the heat. The temperature hadn't dropped enough that their being wet would be life threatening before they made the short hike back to their cabins, but it would get hella uncomfortable.

He caught up to her by her sleeping bag and put a hand on her shoulder, turning her around. "You know, you're going to have to open up one of these days."

She glanced at his hand for a pointed second, and he released his hold before she broke his fingers. He wasn't stupid.

One single brow rose as she glanced up at him. "Like you have?"

"I've shared plenty."

The frequent group sessions with Jenna Powell, Healing Horses' program director, as well as the other veterans in and out of the program was all part of the healing process. The more you put into the program, the more you got out.

During his time in the program he'd learned a lot about himself and how to deal with some of his lingering issues post deployment, but...

Mia laughed even as her teeth started to chatter. "You talk. Your lips move. Your stories unfold. But you're all up in your head. You think the rest of us can't see you editing yourself? That you give a version of the truth without slicing open a vein and letting your heart spill out?"

"I—"

The hell of it was, he couldn't argue the point. Not when she saw through him and called him out on his hypocrisy.

Quick and adept, she started packing up her gear. Her mini tirade was the most real that she'd been since they'd started the program, even if it was at his own expense. Maybe if he kept her talking, he could get through to her in a way no one had been able to yet.

He kicked dirt over her smoldering fire. He would have shouldered her backpack and picked up the shotgun, if she would have let him. Instead, he carried her boots as she strode out of camp in her wet climbing shoes.

"Why do you camp out here?"

She kept her eyes on the trail. "Zealand didn't tell you?"

"He wouldn't tell me stuff like that. That's not the kind of guy he is."

The laugh she huffed out sounded more like a cough. They'd both be lucky if they didn't get double pneumonia by the time they reached the cabins.

"You say that, but he ratted me out and told you where I

camped."

"Just the hot spring." By the way her lips flattened—her lips that now had the slightest hint of blue to them—his answer didn't mollify her. "And you sure as hell don't open up. Not when we first got here. Not since."

"What's it to you?"

"You've got to be fucking kidding me, right?" He stopped in his tracks, but she kept going. He jogged to catch up, his socks squishing in his soaked running shoes. "What are you doing here if you aren't willing to do the work?"

"This place. This program. It was never my choice."

———

MIA'S STRIDES GOBBLED UP THE TRAIL, AND MATT HAD A LITTLE trouble keeping up. His breaths came harder and faster, giving her a mental boost.

What was it to him how she spent her time in the program? And she'd be damned if anyone could call her a slacker. "I work as hard as anybody, I—"

"I'm not talking about cleaning the stalls or training the horses. I'm talking about the emotional work. You've got to open up if you want to get better. It's not easy, but it's necessary."

"Who died and made you program director?"

"*Mia*—"

"Stop."

The censure in his voice grated worse than the county judge's had when the judge had remanded her to the Healing Horses program instead of sending her to jail. As if somehow, she'd disappointed him personally. Neither the judge nor Matt knew her well enough to be disappointed.

That singular claim went to her parents.

Maybe if you knocked a brick or two out of that sky-high wall you've built around you, someone could get in and get to know you.

Ha. Fat chance.

The backside of the cabins came into view. As fast as they'd hiked back, she should be sweating, but the chilly air stripped the heat off her faster than she could produce it. Her fingers and toes had already gone numb, and she couldn't wait to take a steaming hot shower.

The shower would warm her on the outside. The inside... well, nothing would thaw that.

Matt followed her up the steps of her one-room cabin and dropped her boots beside the door. He had to be frozen to the bone as well, but he wasn't high tailing it back to his cabin. He stood there, looking at her expectedly.

"Look," she said, trying to make herself clear to a man who sometimes seemed to want more, *demand* more, than what she could give. "All I've got to do is get through the next fourteen days. Then the program is over for us and I'm gone. What about that do you not understand?"

His gaze softened. He reached a hand up as if he were about to touch her cheek but must have thought better of it. "The part where you're willing to give up on yourself."

The gruffness in his voice made her throat tight. She chalked it up to her dropping body temperature and the adrenaline crash, because it had absolutely nothing to do with it sounding like he cared.

Who knows, maybe he did.

But supposedly so had other people in her life, and they'd torn her apart and left her gutted.

Swallowing hard, she opened her door. "I'm going inside before I freeze. You should do the same."

After a beat, he took a step back and retreated down her stairs. She went inside, dumping her backpack on the floor by her bunk and setting the shotgun on the table. She stripped naked on her way to the bathroom, her wet clothes landing in her wake with a *slop, slop, slop.*

Being the first and only woman in the Healing Horses program meant she had the cabin with the two sets of bunk beds to herself. Not that she slept in her bed. No matter how hard she tried or how much she wanted to.

If getting rest meant having to sleep under the stars, it was worth every jagged rock that jabbed into her ribs to get what little shut eye she managed.

Thirty minutes later, she sat at her kitchen table, fully clothed with the blanket from her bed wrapped around her shoulders. Her stomach growled, her shoulders ached, and her fingertips were raw and red. She stared at the vacant bunk on the other side of the room, lacking the will and strength to get up and do anything about her hunger.

Even making a cup of coffee seemed too daunting to attempt.

A knock came at her door.

"Go away."

Any other day, she would have answered, but this being her day off, she doubted the knock had anything to do with the horses or the program.

"C'mon, Mann. Open up," Matt said.

"I'm naked. Leave me alone."

Matt laughed. "Now I know you're lying."

The door opened, and Matt came in with a hand towel-covered plate in each hand. Damn the food smelled good. He set a plate in front of her and one on the other side of the table for himself and headed straight for the coffee pot. Thank God.

She pulled off one of the towels and dug into the bacon. While the coffee brewed, he fell into the seat across from her and slid a fork her way.

"You didn't have to do this," she said around the tastiest piece of bacon she'd ever put in her mouth. Okay, maybe the bacon was only that delicious because she hadn't had to cook it, but still...

"If I wanted to ensure you ate something besides a pack of Pop-Tarts or a bowl of Fruit Loops, I did."

She also had a couple of packs of Twinkies, but they would never win her the argument. When the coffee finished brewing, he poured them both a cup, and she warmed her hands around the mug.

"I could have been naked when you barged in."

"True, but while you don't open up, you're also not modest. You wouldn't have played strip poker with me and Zealand if you were."

Around a bite of scrambled egg, she muttered, "If I remember right, you two were the ones who'd lost most of your clothes."

"And if *I* remember right, you ran out when I lost my last hand." He took a huge bite of his toast and raised a brow at her as if daring her to contradict him. "What's the matter, Mann? Scared to see me naked? Afraid you might see something you can't resist?"

She held his gaze, trying to keep her subconscious from making her nod while at the same time trying to ignore how his all-too-knowing grin made her want things she shouldn't. "No."

Matt laughed and slapped a hand to his chest. "You wound me."

The smile slipped from his face and his expression grew serious. "Will you answer one question truthfully?"

The saliva dried up in her mouth, and she choked on a piece of toast. She washed it down with a swallow of coffee. The word 'no' sat on the tip of her tongue, but when she opened her mouth, "yes" tumbled out.

He set his fork down and wiped his hands on a napkin. "Do you have a death wish?"

2

A knock came on the cabin door. "Come in," she called out. The sly smile on her face said she knew she'd barely avoided having to give him an answer.

Question was, would she have told him the truth? Or would she have skated around the question or, most likely, flat out told him to fuck off?

Definitely 'fuck off.'

He'd never know because the cabin door opened and Pepita, Sidney and Boomer's adopted teenaged daughter, strode through the door decked out in her usual boots, jeans, and Carhart jacket.

"Thank God you two are here," she said. "I really need your help."

Matt gave up his chair, and she plopped down on it.

"Oh, sweet." Pepita took hold of his half-full mug. "Coffee!"

Matt chuckled. "Help yourself."

She flashed him her sweet, innocent smile, but after being around her for most of the past three months, Matt knew the truth. Behind that smile lay a smart, sassy, giant-hearted girl. One who wore her past traumas on her sleeve like a dusty, old tome with the pages thrown open for all the world to see, never ashamed of what she'd survived, who she was, or where she'd come from.

Sometimes Matt wondered if maybe they all should be taking a crinkled page from her book. Perhaps they'd all be better for it.

Mia took the last sip of her coffee, and Matt got the pot and refilled it for her. At least her lips had lost their blue hue, even if she suffered the occasional shudder.

"What do you need, kid?" Matt asked.

"Zealand was supposed to teach my scouting group some first aid stuff, but Taylor needed his help with an emergency."

Zealand had been an Army medic and was Matt's roommate at Healing Horses. But ever since Zealand had gotten engaged to Taylor Foxx, the local large animal vet, he'd been spending as much of his free time off the Lazy S as he could.

"Something about a randy bull and a run-in with a T-post," Pepita added.

That got a hint of a chuckle out of Mia. "*Randy?*"

Pepita leaned in, and in a stage whisper said, "I saw it in a book I had to read for English. Thought it would be better than saying hor—"

Pepita cut herself off when Matt raised a brow at her. "Well, you get the idea."

"Neither one of us know half the medical stuff Zee does," Mia said. "Maybe you should reschedule."

"We can't." Pepita blew out a breath. "I mean we can, but I promised, and they're all going to be here soon, and it's just... I just..."

Matt gave her ponytail a light tug. "What's really going on here?"

Pepita leaned back in her chair and spun the coffee cup

around and around, refusing to meet their gazes. "There's this guy in the group..."

"Now we're getting somewhere." From the corner of the room, Matt pulled up the spare chair he'd dragged in there the night before when he and Zealand had lost their shirts, figuratively this time, in a game of five-card stud.

"Look, you guys know how over-protective my dad is. I can't date, I can't—"

"You're fourteen," Mia said.

"Exactly!" Pepita held out her fist for Mia to bump, but Mia left her hanging.

"I meant you have plenty of time to get your heart broken by some dude. What's your rush?"

Pepita cocked her head, the gears and levers and pulleys all rumbling in her head. "Is that what happened to you? Did a man break your heart?"

Mia choked on her coffee and lost three shades off her complexion as if Pepita had sliced open an artery. Mia stood abruptly, her chair scratching against the wood floor. "When is this thing supposed to start?"

It wasn't lost on Matt how expert Mia had become at avoiding the hard questions.

Pepita checked her phone. "They should be here in thirty minutes."

Mia glanced at Matt as she reached for her coat. "You coming?"

"Yeah, sure. I've got nothing better to do today than help play matchmaker to a teen."

"You have to promise not to tell my dad. He's kind of irrational when it comes to boys. And besides, you're not really a matchmaker if I'm already crushed out on him."

Great. Just what Matt needed to do was wedge himself between Pepita and her father, Bryan "Boomer" Wilcox. A laid-back former Marine who never hesitated to protect the ones he loved. "How irrational?"

Pepita blew out a breath that made her bangs flutter. "Every time the subject of boys comes up, I get the birds and the bees lecture. I mean I get how sex works. I know about consent. I know about STIs and how to not get pregnant. Trust me, none of that has changed in the month since he drilled it into me last."

"At least he'll talk to you about it," Mia said as she zipped up her coat and pulled on her gloves. "The gist of what my mom told me was that having sex before marriage made me a who—well, you get the idea."

By the sour expression on Mia's face, Matt had to wonder about the rest of that story.

Pepita followed her to the door. "Oh, wow, so you mean you've never..."

Mia opened the door, a smile toying with one corner of her mouth. "I didn't say I listened."

Matt started to laugh but swallowed it down when Mia glared at him. He held the door and placed a staying hand on Mia's forearm before she could escape.

"You go on ahead," Matt told Pepita. "We'll meet you up at the barn."

"Don't take too long."

Pepita hustled down the steps as Matt closed the cabin door. Mia shook her arm free. Her chin went up. "What?"

"You never answered my question. About the death wish."

Mia stared down at the floor and scraped the toe of her boot over a nail that had worked its way loose. "Why do you care?"

"Because you scared the hell out of me out there today." Matt didn't even try to keep his voice from rising. He had to pick a battle he could win. "Do I need to get Jenna involved? Do we need to get you outside help?"

She worked her toe back and forth across the head of the nail, before she finally said, "I don't want to die."

Her words came out low, part whisper, part uncertainty. He hooked a finger under her chin until her eyes met his. For a flash, the depth of her despair almost swamped him, before she raised her shields and riveted them back into place.

"Then what is it?" His voice cracked as the words squeezed past the stricture in his throat.

"It's that sometimes I just don't want to feel anymore."

———

In the barn with all the doors closed, the cold became manageable. Though deep in Matt's marrow, he still felt frozen. How much that had to do with getting drenched and having to walk back to his cabin soaking wet and how much of it had to do with watching Mia fall from the sky, he couldn't decide.

Matt stood in the large center aisle and ripped a strip of material off an old T-shirt Pepita had brought for the first aid demonstration and handed it to Pepita.

Charlie, her crush in waiting, sat on top of a folding table. He'd jumped at the chance to be the human guinea pig for the leg splint demo after Pepita volunteered to apply it.

For various reasons, only three of the kids from Pepita's scouting group had showed up. Charlie, Zach, and Xia. But Pepita didn't seem like she cared too much. Charlie was there, and in her eyes, only he mattered.

Mia had already taught them how to bandage an open wound and apply a tourniquet using materials you could find on the trail or make from what you had on you. Like a belt or shoelaces. Then she'd gone back to the cabin and returned with a C-A-T tourniquet.

The military issued Combat Application Tourniquets had

been a normal part of their everyday kit they'd kept on their bodies while they'd been deployed.

Those tourniquets had saved many lives over the years. Just not the one life Matt had so desperately needed it to. Then again, that damage had been too catastrophic for a simple tourniquet.

Pepita's hands shook as she tied the strip of T-shirt around the lower part of Charlie's leg. "That's not too tight, is it?"

Charlie smiled so wide his gums showed, his eyes behind his glasses all mooney. A small kid, you wouldn't know he was fourteen unless he opened his mouth and spoke. That and the dusting of hair on his upper lip. "It's perfect."

Mia glanced over at Matt and rolled her eyes. Those kids had it *bad*.

Matt went to rip another strip, and Zach said, "Let me do it."

Matt underhanded the T-shirt to him. "Have at it."

Zach tossed his head, getting his too-long blond bangs out of his eyes. The jock to Charlie's nerd, he tried to rip the shirt with his bare hands the way Matt had, but it was a no go.

"Uh oh," Xia said, her straight black hair almost obscuring her face as she picked at one of her bedazzled, fluorescent fingernails. "Looks like someone needs to hit the gym."

Zach turned and held the shirt scrap out to her. An hour into the demonstrations and that's the first anyone had heard from Xia since she'd introduced herself to Matt and Mia. "You do it, if you think it's so easy."

She held up her hands like a surgeon already scrubbed and gloved up. "I'm doing an Insta video tonight on water marbling, and I can't afford to break a nail. People can be ruthless online, and I'm just now getting a good following."

Zach pulled harder on the fabric, but it didn't help. "Then why are you here? Why are you even in the scouting group? You don't like to get dirty. You don't want to break a nail. And you have zero interest in what Mia or Matt are saying."

Matt almost jumped to Xia's defense, but Pepita snatched the shirt out of Zach's hands. "Leave her alone."

"It's a valid question," Charlie said, shoving his glasses up his nose.

Pepita cut him a look.

"Seriously," Zach cut in. "I mean, we're trying to learn this so we can go on our winter camping trip next weekend. Call me crazy, but I don't see Xia going to something like that."

"With the snow forecast, I doubt you are either." Xia raised her brows as if waiting for him to argue.

Everyone had been keeping an eye on the weather. Hank Nash, the ranch foreman, had already let them know they might have to go up to the higher elevations and bring the cattle down for the winter before the weather hit. They'd kept the cattle up at the higher pastures longer than normal because the fall had been relatively mild, but it looked like they might pay for that reprieve with the upcoming storm.

Mia said, "Are we going to finish this? Because if not, I've got better things to do."

"Come on, guys. This is cool stuff. It could save our lives one day." Charlie reached into his pocket and pulled out a pocketknife with a daisy chain of blue and black paracord attached to the end. He handed it to Zach. "Get it started with this and then rip."

Pepita took the knife before Zach could and made a series of nicks in the fabric and handed the shirt to Zach to tear into strips. He handed a strip across to Xia. "Here, you do one."

She waited a beat, then took the material from him and wrapped the tails around the sticks on either side of Charlie's leg the way Matt had demonstrated. Looked like she'd been paying attention after all.

"Hey, Xia," Zach said, "I didn't mean anything—"

"Forget it."

She finished up with a knot, and Matt stepped closer to inspect her work. "Nice job. You're a natural."

"If that math degree doesn't work out for you—"

The glare Xia sent Zach shut him up. He probably had a foot of height on her, but that didn't intimidate her. "Are you kidding me right now?"

"What?" Zach glanced around his group of friends. "It was a joke. I—"

"Maybe you should just stand there and look pretty," Pepita said. "That way you can keep your foot out of your mouth."

Mia stifled a chuckle with a cough, and Matt just shook his head.

Pepita took the next strip as they worked their way up Charlie's pretend fractured leg.

"You know, Zach. Just because I'm Asian, doesn't mean I'm good at math."

"I know. I know. I didn't mean—"

"Just like the fact that Charlie looks like Bill Gates' nerdier little brother doesn't mean he can code, or beat everyone at Dungeons and Dragons, or that he stays plugged into his computer twenty-four-seven in the basement of his parent's house."

"*Technically*," Charlie said, "it's not really a basement."

They all glanced around at each other. Xia was the first one who started laughing, and the others followed, the tears streaming out of their eyes.

"Oh, my God," Zach said, holding his hands across his belly, "my abs are killing me."

Mia bumped shoulders with Matt, her voice low when she whispered in his ear. "All I'm saying is Zealand owes us, big time."

"I don't know," Matt said. "They're kind of a kick."

When the kids finally stopped laughing, Zach tapped Xia on the shoulder with the back of his hand. "No hard feelings?"

Xia glanced up at him. "We're cool."

The kids finished splinting Charlie's leg. When done, Matt helped him off the table and let him hobble around with it on.

"Man, this thing isn't going anywhere. You guys rock." He held up his fist, and Xia, Zach, and Pepita bumped his knuckles.

"We done here?" Mia asked.

"Got a hot date?" Matt folded up Charlie's knife and handed it back to him before someone cut themselves and they had to practice bandaging for real.

The kids went up the aisle, goofing off and joking around. Zach lurched into one of the halter racks hanging from the rafters. The kind that looked like a grapple hook. It caught the collar of his shirt, tearing a hole before Pepita could set him free.

Mia shrugged. "Zealand has a friend..."

She let the rest of the sentence drop. Matt had been kidding. How could she have a date? She practically hadn't left the ranch since she came, unless you included the rides out on the range working cattle or the time they all helped Zealand and Taylor, round up some of the wild mustangs that had been set free by an animal rights group.

Which in Matt's mind definitely didn't count.

That she had somewhere to be, with another man, left him with an anvil-sized lead block weighing in his gut. He'd never put any pressure on Mia, even though he'd been interested since day one. And now, he'd missed his chance.

"Why the long face?" Mia asked.

"I don't know what you're talking about." Matt started folding up the table, and Mia threw away the T-shirt scraps and repacked the first aid kit.

He'd just returned from putting the table in the tack room where it belonged when Mia said, "Hey, Matt."

He glanced up. The scowl on his face made his eyebrow muscles hurt, and he tried wiping it away.

"I don't have any plans. I don't know why I said that."

A smile slipped out. "Good to know."

————

THE RELIEF ON MATT'S FACE MADE MIA'S HEART THUMP, THUMP against her ribcage. Two hard beats that would have had her concerned about a heart condition if it weren't for the fact that it only ever happened when Matt Bishop was around.

Fortunately, she'd be out of the program way before she allowed him to draw her in any more than he already had. Attraction was a dangerous game. One she'd lost before.

And look where that got you?

Kicked out of the only career that had ever meant anything to her.

Don't forget the criminal trespass, disorderly conduct, and reckless endangerment charges. And the deferred adjudication that's keeping you out of jail.

Nope. She'd finish her time at Healing Horse and...

Fuck. She had no idea what she'd do.

But sticking around wasn't an option. She had nothing here. No friends. No family—which, truth be told, was a plus. No connections.

Whose fault is that?

A car honked behind her and, through the person-sized gap in the front barn doors, she watched Xia's father pull up.

"That's my ride. Later, losers," Xia teased. She'd almost made it to the doors when she turned around and put her thumb and pinky to the side of her face, the universal sign for a phone, and mouthed to Pepita, "Call me."

"Hey, Mia." Pepita, Charlie, and Zach walked toward her and Matt. Somewhere along the way, Charlie had ditched the splint. "Zach's mom's running late. Can you show them how to start a fire from scratch while we wait?"

She enjoyed the kids, but she also enjoyed her alone time. She glanced at Matt.

"Don't look at me. You're the goddess of fire."

Zach laughed, and Pepita said, "He's not kidding. I bet she could start a fire under water."

"Technically," Charlie said, sliding his glasses up again, "to start a fire under water she'd need a—"

"*Dude*," Zack said. "Can you stop brainiacing for like five minutes?"

Charlie cocked his head at Zach. "Did you just verb 'brainiac?' You're a lot smarter than you look."

Zach gave him a playful shove and Charlie shoved back. Pepita had one of those besotted, ear-to-ear grins on her face. Luckily for Pepita, her father wasn't there to witness it.

"Okay, okay." Mia broke the jostling up, before Zack accidentally broke Charlie. "We'll build a small fire on the back side of the barn. But nothing too big."

She gave them a short list of items to gather and finished cleaning up before meeting them outside. Matt fell into step beside her.

"You don't have anywhere you need to be?" she asked.

"What? And leave you to fend for yourself with the hooligans? I figured you'd never forgive me."

Perhaps. Plus, she actually liked his company when he wasn't prying into her past or trying to get her to open up to him. Not that she would ever tell him that.

They made a small fire ring with a pile of stones Pepita had gathered in her jacket. Charlie had a bunch of small tinder and stray bits of hay. Zach had small and medium size twigs. She showed them how to pack their tinder and stack the twigs in the shape of a teepee on top of the tinder in increasing sizes.

Matt stood back as they all got down on their knees and Mia pulled a ferro rod and striker out of a side pocket of the tactical style pants she wore.

"Hey," Zach piped up, "that's cheating."

"It's still not as easy as you think," Mia said.

Mia demonstrated how to hold the striker at an angle to the rod for a larger spark. She ran the striker down the rod in a series of quick strokes, sparks flying off the end and into the tinder bundle.

The fibers started to burn, but Mia quickly put them out and handed the rod to Charlie for a turn. "You can also use a broken piece of glass or the backside of your knife as a striker if you need to."

Charlie whipped out his knife and, after a few unsuccessful attempts, managed to get the tinder to smolder. They continued putting the fire out and restarting it until Zach and Pepita both had a turn.

They let the last one burn, adding more twigs and small sticks until they had a small fire burning. The kids settled around it, their legs folded, knees practically touching each other, as they poked the fire with larger sticks the way kids and grown men couldn't seem to resist.

Matt shoved his hands deeper into the pockets of his jacket and watched the condensation from his breath rise and disappear. Cloud cover had moved in, obliterating the sun and making the day feel colder than it should, but there was no smell of snow in the air. At least not yet.

Zach's phone pinged, and he checked his incoming message.

"My mom's here." He tossed the stick he had in the fire away and said, "Later, dudes."

He'd walked through the barn's back doors before remembering his manners. He turned around and said to Matt and Mia, "Thanks, that was awesome stuff."

"Let's just hope you never have to use it."

Zach grinned at Matt. "I don't know. Kinda looks like fun."

Mia stood beside Matt and watched the kid walk away. "Kid's got no clue, does he?"

"Fire." Charlie's voice came out strained.

Mia glanced behind them at the pile of used shavings in the bucket of the tractor, waiting to be taken to the manure pile. Small flames danced as they started to spread. Charlie jumped up, grabbed a shovel before either she or Matt could react, and scooped the burning shavings onto the ground and stomped them out.

"Phew." Charlie's smile wavered. "Sorry. Zach's cool, but he's a disaster magnet."

Mia cocked her head. "You think some people are prone to bad things happening to them?"

Charlie grinned, not seeing the dark turn Mia's question had taken. But then again, how could he? He had no idea what she'd been through.

"I tried to calculate it out one time," Charlie admitted, his smile turning shy. "But I think there are too many variables."

Pepita tugged on his arm. "Come on. We should put the fire out and clean up our mess. We leave it like this, and my dad is going to have another reason to kill us."

Charlie followed. "Wait. *Another?* What do you mean another? What did we do?"

"You asked me out on a date and..."

Their voices faded as Mia pushed Matt into the barn ahead of her.

"What are you doing?" Matt asked.

"Giving the kids some privacy. What do you think we're doing?"

"But—"

"Unless Boomer told you to keep an eye on them, it's not for us to worry about."

Even though they had the day off, Matt headed to the first stall. He cut the strings on the bale of hay on the ground in front of it and put a few flakes into the manger for when the horses were brought in later that night.

At the next stall, Matt took the hay Mia handed him. "I guess you're right. I'm sure Pepita can take him if he tries anything funny. Besides, look at that kid. He's not a threat."

"Those are the ones you have to worry about." Mia tried to sound teasing, but it was hard to do when that had been her truth. "They're the ones you think you can trust."

Matt stilled, both of their hands on the same three flake stack of hay. "*Wow*."

Fuck. She'd said too much. "Forget it." She let go of the hay and bent to get more.

Stuffing the flakes in the manger, he quickly latched the feed door on the stall and caught her arm. For once, she didn't shake him off. She didn't know why. "Care to unpack that for me?"

"You my shrink now?"

"No. But I'm your friend."

"Is that what we are?"

Matt let go of her arm. "Fuck if I know, Mann. Every time I think we might be getting closer, building some trust... *boom*. It's gone. Like we haven't just spent the last two and a half months practically living in each other's pockets. So, you tell me."

Matt couldn't or wouldn't hide his frustration. He held her gaze. It wasn't a rhetorical question. It was a challenge.

She regarded him, not sure how to answer.

He shook his head. "There was a moment there, when your shields slipped. But now—"

Door hinges creaked behind them. Mia adjusted her gaze over his shoulder as Jenna, their program director, called out. "Hey, Mia. Can I have a word with you?"

3

———

Something about the barely detectable strain in Jenna's voice when she asked to speak with her made the muscles at the back of Mia's neck bunch even tighter than they normally were. She narrowed her eyes at Matt. Had he told Jenna about that morning? She didn't know when he would have had time to run to Jenna and tattle on her since they'd practically been together the whole time since her fall, but...

Somehow, even that distrusting part of her that had been honed on some very jagged rocks in her life couldn't see him doing that to her. He wasn't the kind of guy to go behind your back if there was a problem. He was the kind of guy who confronted you and your bullshit head on.

She tore her eyes away from Matt's. "Coming."

The walk to Jenna's office couldn't have been more than thirty feet, but Mia's imagination ran wild. She couldn't think what she'd done—besides the obvious—but clearly, from Jenna's tone, she'd done something.

Stepping through the open door, Mia hesitated to take the seat in front of Jenna's desk, preferring to stand the way she had those times when her base commander had summoned her.

Don't be stupid. This could be about anything. You can't go the rest of your life with that stupid monkey on your back chattering in your ear, telling you you fucked up.

Jenna glanced up from her computer. "Can you close the door, please?"

You fucked up.

"What's this about?"

Instead of answering, Jenna bumped her chin toward the door. Mia closed it and leaned against it. Jenna could speak to her from there in an office the size of a twelve-by-twelve stall.

The back wall had a sink and a counter with a coffeemaker. A short run of cheap cabinets ran above. To Mia's right, the wall had a window overlooking one of the stalls they used for observation when it came time for the mares to foal.

Wedge in an old metal desk and a rickety chair and you had the whole office.

Jenna rolled her chair far enough back to cross her away from her desk and crossed her legs, the spurs on her boots clinking. She was younger than Mia, but not by much, but she owned the place. Well, her grandparents, Lottie and Dale Cunningham did, but her and her father Hank ran the ranch and the Healing Horses program.

"I just got off the phone with the judge," Jenna said. She didn't mince words. Or name the judge. The only one relevant to the both of them was the one who'd remanded Mia to Healing Horses.

"And?" Mia unzipped her coat and swiped at the sweat beading on her upper lip.

"He wasn't happy with the last evaluation I sent. Or the one before that. Or the one before that."

Mia didn't say anything because Jenna hadn't asked a direct question. After years in the military, Mia had learned when to keep her mouth shut.

"He said that if you don't pass your final evaluation in two weeks, you failed not only the program, but it would nullify your deferred adjudication."

Why the hell had Mia agreed to this program to begin with? She should have taken her year in jail and been done with it and moved on with her life. Now it looked like she'd wasted nearly three months of a year sentence she could have been serving.

"You want me to lie during the eval? Because I can. I know all the right things to say."

Jenna blew out a breath, rubbing her forehead with a thumb and forefinger. "I don't want you to lie, Mia. I want you to open the fuck up."

Mia held her gaze not knowing what Jenna expected her to say. "Is this the part where you implore me to let you help me?"

"No. This is the part where I ask you to give us something. Anything. Start small. We can work from there."

While her brain said, 'fuck no,' her mouth said, "Yeah, sure." Anything to get Jenna off her ass. In boot camp, Mia had learned really quick to parrot what someone wanted to hear. It had worked well there. No reason why it shouldn't work in the civilian world. "That it?"

Jenna stood. "That's it. Unless you had something you wanted to say."

Jenna waited patiently, but it wasn't like that one conversation would have Mia spewing her life story and revealing all her dark secrets. All her shame. All her pain. All her humiliation. Like some sort of emotional vomit splatting all over the ground.

"I'm good." Though really, they all knew that was a lie.

She stepped out of the office, doing her best not to look like she was running away as fast as she could while she did just that.

Glancing behind her as she walked away, she half expected Jenna would come after her and drag her back. She slammed into something solid. Hands grabbed her upper arms and steadied her.

"Whoa, there," Boomer said. He dropped her arms and rubbed the center of his sternum where she'd inadvertently rammed her shoulder. "Hey, have you seen Pepita? She was supposed to meet me at the cabin after the scouts' thing. She wanted to go to the construction site with me."

A former Marine and amputee, Boomer had married Sidney, the Lazy S's resident horse trainer. He was tall and dark, and the kind of handsome that made the ladies' heads turn. But it was his laid-back charm and a foul mouth he could never quite wrangle that Mia found to be his best quality.

"She was behind the barn a few minutes ago. She and Charlie—"

"Is that the kid?"

"If you mean the kid that *your* kid has a crush on, then yeah. That's the kid."

"What did you think of him?"

Mia took a step back, not knowing quite what Boomer expected her to say. "He's a little too young for me?"

Boomer barked out a laugh. "Fuck, I needed that. I don't know what to do about this kid. They are always on the phone together. She can't put her cell phone down for five seconds worried she's going to miss a text or a meme or whatever the fuck kids are sending each other these days."

"That would be sexts," Mia supplied, but by the furrow that developed in Boomer's brow, that wasn't the fill-in-the-blank answer he'd been looking for. And for a guy so laid back, for a guy with such an enviable relationship with his daughter, this whole growing up thing seemed to have him in knots.

"That was a little less helpful."

"Sorry. But for what it's worth, that kid of yours has a good head on her shoulders. You may not think she's listening, but she's taking it all in. Just, when you find her, you know, don't be a dick."

"Probably good advice."

Mia shrugged. "Dunno. May want to consider the source before you say that."

Boomer pointed out the back of the barn. "That way?"

Mia nodded, picking up a manure fork leaning against the wall. Matt was busy cleaning stalls, even though Jenna was on the schedule for that day. Mia walked over to the open stall door and leaned her shoulder against the support. "You a teacher's pet or something? You think Jenna's gonna give you *atta boy* points for doing her job?"

Matt didn't even break his rhythm—scoop, shake, dump. Scoop, shake, dump. Little clouds of shavings made dust motes in the light shining through the cracks between the rear stall doors and their frames. The heavy scent of ammonia from the disturbed shavings in the closed barn made her nose sting and her eyes start to water. She wanted to open all the doors, because she'd rather freeze her ass off than singe her lungs.

"It's called *not being an ass*, not *teacher's pet*. Jenna works her butt off running a program to help us, and I've got nothing on my plate. Besides, the physical activity keeps me out of my head."

Mia deserved the slap back. She'd had it coming, but after what Jenna had told her... well, she hadn't wanted to be in her head either and had taken it out on Matt. The *last* guy who deserved that.

Where was Zealand when she needed him?

She could verbally spar with him and not feel like a shit. It was how the two of them communicated. But while Matt could dish it out as well as take it, he had his limits and sometimes, Mia didn't know when to stop until it was too late.

"Sorry."

That one word stopped him mid scoop. He dropped the scoop of manure and leaned on the handle of his manure fork. "You want to talk about it?" His eyes flicked to the office and back to her.

"No." She turned and walked into the open stall beside him and went to work. The physical labor wouldn't keep herself out of her head, but if she worked hard enough and long enough, maybe she'd exhaust herself and manage a few minutes of rest that night.

———

"You can't be serious right now."

Matt glanced up from the stall he was cleaning to see Pepita huff through the back of the barn, her hands talking faster than her mouth, her jacket in her hand despite the cold.

"Deadly," her father said as he ushered a red-faced Charlie ahead of him, one hand locked onto the back of the kid's neck.

"It isn't what it looked like, Mr. Wilcox, honest."

The three of them stopped in front of Matt's stall, not even aware that he stood there. He thought about clearing his throat, then thought better of it. He glanced through the bars at Mia one stall over. She mouthed the words, "Uh, oh."

Boomer dropped his hand, and the kid turned to face him. He only came up to Boomer's chest, if that. "Why don't you tell me what it was like, Charlie, because to me it looked a whole hell of a lot like you had your hand up my daughter's shirt."

"Well, I did, but—"

"And are you going to tell me having your lips on hers wasn't what it looked like either?"

The kid swallowed hard, but he didn't shrink back, and he didn't back down. Matt had to hand it to the kid for sticking around and not dissolving into a puddle of fear.

"Can I say something, here?" Pepita pushed in between Charlie and her father.

Boomer crossed his arms over his chest. "You going to tell me you told him to do that?"

"What? No. I mean yes. I mean—*Grrrr*. Dad, you've completely lost your mind."

Boomer glanced from his daughter to the boy and back to his daughter again. If Matt wasn't mistaken, a glimmer of a smile crossed Boomer's lips. "Then help me find it."

"He had his hand up the back of my shirt," she said, emphasizing for her father the word *back,* "because I leaned against that cottonwood tree and a lizard fell down my collar. He got it for me."

Boomer glanced at Charlie, his hands on his hips. "This true?"

Charlie held up his closed fist, his fingers slowly unfurling. A lizard stood in the palm of his hand then jumped, landing on Boomer's pant leg and scurrying away.

Boomer harrumphed. "And the kiss?"

"It was hardly a peck," Pepita chimed in. "There wasn't even any tongue."

Mia stifled a laugh. Boomer cut his eyes toward Mia, then back to his daughter, the defiance and stubbornness something that would work well for Pepita as an adult, but by the exasperated expression on Boomer's face, wasn't something he appreciated now.

And Charlie. He just stood there and took it. He didn't cower, he didn't run. He stood up to a man who could have crushed him if he'd wanted to. Much like another little boy Matt had known—this one in a dusty, war-torn village so very far away.

It was years ago now, but staring at that kid staring up at Boomer, it took Matt right back to that day where the wind whipped the sand against his cheeks until he'd felt sandpapered raw. A place where the grit ground between his teeth and he couldn't remember ever not sweating his ass off.

A place where...

Matt dropped his manure fork and lit out of there. He thought he heard Mia call his name, but he wasn't listening. He had to get out of there before he went full-on meltdown. Many times he could stop it before it got ahold of him too hard, but the way his heart drummed, his lungs seized, and the dark spots dotted his peripheral vision, he was seconds away from a take-you-down panic attack.

He stumbled around the corner of the barn and dropped down behind the rear wheel of one of the big tractors the ranch used for cutting hay in the summer. With his back to the wheel, he held his head in his hands and tried to concentrate on his breathing and not the distant sound of his own voice ringing in his head as he yelled for Yusef to get down, or the sound of the bullets ripping through the air, or the screams, or the smell...

———

Mia shivered as daylight started to fade. She couldn't feel her toes, and the frost in the air made her nose run. She'd given Matt his space when he'd hightailed it out of the barn without saying a word. She hadn't seen him since, and that worried her.

Something had triggered him, but she had no clue what.

In the time that they'd been at the ranch, he'd been the calm one, the steady one, the one focused on helping everyone else, the one people probably questioned why he was there in the first place. But seeing him vanish like that told her he needed Healing Horses as much as any of them did.

Coming around the backside of the two recently completed cabins behind theirs, she stumbled across Matt.

Literally.

He grabbed her arm as her foot caught on his outstretched legs, but still she went down to her knees. She rolled to her side. "Where the fuck have you been?"

Smooth, Mann. Not 'are you okay.' Not 'can I help.' Just anger, frustration, accusation. Why did Matt fight so hard to be her friend?

"Scratch that." She scooted over and sat beside him, her back to the cabin, the chill of the near-frozen ground seeping through her pants. She burrowed deeper into her coat and tried to ignore the cold. "You been here the whole time?"

He shook his head but didn't elaborate.

"You wanna talk about it?"

He met her gaze for the first time, his complexion ruddy. From the cold? Or the emotions? "This from the woman who hasn't given me much more than her name, rank, and serial number since we've been here?"

His direct words weren't cutting, but she felt the nicks just the same. "I don't like to talk, but I'm a good listener."

Before he could say anything, she added, "Though, I can listen better if my teeth aren't chattering."

With a grunt of acknowledgment, he stood and held his hand out. He tugged her along behind him, not breaking the loose connection as their fingers lightly entwined.

The first step in his door, they dropped their hands, their boots, and their coats. He didn't bother turning on the light but walked over to the thermostat on the other side of the room and cranked up the heat.

The other chair to his table was over at Mia's cabin. Instead of braving the cold, she crawled across the foot of his bed and leaned against the wall, drawing his covers over her legs.

"Drink?" he asked as he pulled open the door of the refrigerator. "I've got water, or if you want something stronger, I have sweet tea, or coffee."

Healing Horses sometimes dealt with veterans who had substance abuse problems so in general, the ranch was dry, but since the three of them didn't have problems with drugs or alcohol, occasionally they had beer, but it was rare.

She shivered. "Coffee. Decaf if you have it, otherwise I'll never get to sleep."

"Coffee it is," he said, trying to sound his normal chipper self, but underneath, the emotional tumult of the day still lingered, and it leached out into his words.

When he had the pot brewing, he turned around. "Who are you texting?"

"Jenna. I told her I'd let her know when I found you." She held the phone out and pointed it toward the window and hoped it went. She had one tiny bar when she pressed send.

Matt poured their coffee and handed her a mug. He settled at the head of the bed, handing her one of his pillows. He put the other behind his back while she settled hers in her lap and hugged it to her.

"One hell of a day, huh?" he finally said.

The warmth from the mug seeped into her fingers, and she let the rising steam thaw her cheeks. The cabin lay mostly in shadows now, but she preferred it that way. It made it easier to talk sometimes when you couldn't see the other person's eyes clearly. "I've had better."

Matt scrubbed his hand through his hair. "Fuck, we're a mess."

Mia blew out an exaggerated breath. "Truth."

They sat there on opposite sides of the bed, sipping their coffees and getting lost in their own thoughts. She'd pretty much given up on Matt telling her what happened back at the barn. She got it. As much as the experts said that the talking made things easier, sometimes she thought it would be less excruciating opening up a vein.

"There was this kid named Yusef..." Matt had one leg out in front of him, the other bent, the hand with his coffee resting on his upturned knee. Even in the growing darkness, Mia saw his eyes soften as he thought back.

"I have no idea how old he was," Matt continued, "but he was smart as hell, always watching, taking things in. His mother did laundry at the FOB, forward operating base, where my squad was on TDY. Temporary assignment. She tried to keep him away from us at first, but he always found his way to our rec area. No more than a few weights and a makeshift basketball net under camo netting.

"He taught us how to play this dice game. I still don't know if he was that good at winning or he was scamming us, but he always left there with a few bucks. Kinda became the camp mascot, if you know what I mean?"

She did, but she only nodded, not wanting to say anything that would shut him up. He swallowed hard and threw the last of his coffee into the back of his throat as if he wished it were whiskey. She knew what came next would be like all the other memories people like them carried around, memories that often tried—and succeeded—in dragging them under.

"One night, his mother got killed in their home. A stray bullet came through their window in the middle of the night."

"Shit," Mia said, "I'm sorry."

Matt chuckled, it came out hollow and stripped of all humor. "That's not even the bad part. This kid, he kept coming back. I don't know where his father was, or the rest of his family if he had any left, but he kept coming, sneaking into the camp with the other laundry ladies.

"One day, me and the guys were bitching about this tango, this insurgent, we'd spent the better part of two weeks trying to track down. This guy who was more ghost than man, but he'd done plenty of bad shit. All we had was a name. Nearly lost one of our guys to an IED in the process of finding the guy, and this kid comes up—"

"Yusef?" Mia knew the answer and could tell he was trying to distance himself by not using the kid's name, but if he was going to tell the story, he should own it.

"Fuck. Yeah. *Yusef.*"

Matt got up, poured more coffee for them, and resettled on the bed. "*Yusef* comes up to me and says he knows where the guy is. We took the kid to talk to our CO."

"I don't think I like where this is headed."

He gave her a look that said, 'tell me about it.' "It took a few days, but we made a plan. And like any plan that's devised over there, it goes to shit as soon as we pass through the base's front gate. We know where we're going, but this kid—" He glanced over at her. "*Yusef,* is the only one who knows what the tango looks like. The plan is for Yusef to point him out and scram."

"Uffh." The sound escaped Mia's throat, as her heart sank. She knew what was coming.

Matt set his mug on the ground beside the bed, the tension in the room so heavy it made Mia sweat even though she hadn't completely thawed.

"The little fucker, h-he didn't listen. Kids over there don't mind any better than the ones over here. Go figure."

Matt buried his face in his knees, his fingers grabbing fistfuls of hair. She had the urge to go to him, to offer comfort, but she knew when she was like that, touch didn't take away the pain.

Finally, he raised his head and looked at her. Darkness had almost completely shrouded the room, but the rising moon shone through the window and grazed his cheeks and high-lighted his haunted eyes. "When we captured our target, Yusef came out from wherever he'd been hiding. He had the biggest grin on his face. He was so proud, so... fucking proud."

Matt took a deep breath, and Mia took one as well, bracing for the hit.

"He started running toward us, but... they fucking mowed the kid down. They mowed Yusef down like..."

His voice drifted off. Which was fine with her. She didn't need the metaphor to solidify the picture in her mind. He thumped the back of his head against the solid wall of the cabin, once, twice, three times, probably hoping the pain radiating across his skull would dull the pain in his chest.

Pro tip: it doesn't.

Setting her empty mug on the ground, she crawled over to him. Maybe he didn't need the touch, but for some reason, after that story, a part of her did. Needing that touch unsettled her as much as the story had. She came to rest beside him awkwardly, the side of her head on his shoulder, her fingers linked with his.

He squeezed her hand, and she squeezed back. For a time, the only sound in the cabin was the hitching of his breathing and the occasional sniff.

"Tell me one thing," he said at last, his voice a little rough and slow.

"What's that?" If he asked about the cliff, about that morning, could she refuse to tell him?

"Is this the best Saturday night date you've ever had?"

"It's definitely not the worst."

That wrangled a strangled laugh out of Matt like she hoped it would. He brought their joined hands to his lips and pressed a kiss to the back of her hand.

"Does it feel any better?" she asked. "Getting it all out?"

"No." He held their hands to his chest, and she felt the steady thump of his heart. "Maybe it takes longer for it to get better."

"Or maybe it's all bullshit."

He leaned away a fraction, and she met his eyes, his face mostly hidden in the shadows. "You really believe that?"

"I don't know what to believe anymore. Besides the fact it's late and I should be getting back to my cabin."

Matt grunted, and she couldn't tell if that was in agreement or not. The walls had already started closing in on her. She couldn't stay, even if she'd wanted to.

She stayed until the claustrophobia started gnawing at her bones and she couldn't ignore it any longer. She dropped his hand and climbed out of his bed. What would it be like to lay there all night in his bed and in his arms.

Not that she'd allow it to happen. But she wondered.

He's nothing like Frank. Matt's different.

Yeah, well, she'd thought Frank had been different, too.

She had her stuff gathered and the cabin door open when he came up behind her and closed the door, his hand against the jamb above her head. "Thanks for the ear."

"Thanks for dragging me to shore."

"I guess in a way we're both a little adrift."

Which, besides him running out of the barn, was the first time his *everything is fine here* veneer had cracked, allowing her a peek at the more tender emotions beneath.

He leaned in, his breath warm against her neck. "I really want to kiss you," his low, deep voice came out barely above a whisper.

"Is that all you want?"

"It's a good place to start."

A part of her wanted to say yes, but the rational part, the part that usually kept her out of trouble said, "I don't think that's a good idea."

He blew out a breath. Not out of frustration as far as she could tell, more out of acceptance.

Matt bumped the jamb with the meat of his closed fist and straightened. "Yeah, maybe you're right. If you change your mind, you know where to find me."

He moved to step away, but she reached out and grabbed a fistful of his shirt.

What the hell are you doing?

One kiss. That's all she wanted. What harm could it do?

You know exactly what harm it could do. Don't be stupid. Don't let history repeat itself.

"What the hell are you doing?" Matt asked, his voice even, while echoing the same exasperated recrimination she'd heard in her head.

Releasing his shirt, she slipped her hand behind his head and pulled him in for a kiss. Their lips touched, and he drew back, licking his lips as if he could taste her on them.

He went in for another, just as brief. "Hmmm."

He stepped in closer and she let him, even as her brain set off the warning bells in the back of her head. He kissed her again, the brush of his lips, a light sweeping of hers with his tongue, more touching than timid because Matt Bishop didn't have a timid bone in his body. Or if he did, she hadn't found it yet.

Opening her mouth to his, his tongue swept in, the *hmpfh* it drew out of him something she wanted to explore, but then he broke the kiss and rested his forehead on hers. His breathing rasped in and out like hers.

"Do me a favor. Promise me you'll stay in your cabin tonight. It's too cold. I'll worry."

If only the cold prevented the walls from closing in. If that was all it took to keep the claustrophobia at bay, she would have hitchhiked to the Antarctic already.

But it didn't.

And that wasn't a promise she could make.

"I promise I'll do my best."

4

———

IT CAME AN HOUR LATER. THE SOUND MATT HAD LAID IN BED awake waiting for—the thump of Mia's cabin door closing. It hung just crooked enough that sometimes you needed to kick a boot in the bottom corner of the door to get it to close right.

Hurrying to his window, he caught sight of Mia—her pack strapped across her back, and a shotgun in her hand for protection. As she disappeared out of sight, the first of the predicted snow flurries drifted down. He knew where she was headed, so he didn't hurry as he dressed.

He didn't have a sleeping bag suitable for extreme weather, or really anything suitable for spending the night outside in Wyoming in November, but he'd spent plenty of cold nights out in the higher elevations of the Hindu Kush. This couldn't be much worse, could it?

He layered clothes on top of his thermals before bundling up in his coat. Taking a couple of blankets from the beds, he rolled them tightly and strapped his belt around it to keep it all together. He slung it over his shoulder, the outside air a slap in the face and a punch to the gut as he opened the door and followed her down the trail.

The wind picked up, and he ducked his head into it, hoping he'd be able to find enough of a windbreak to sleep behind. He upped his pace. As fast as he built up body heat from the walking, the wind chill stole it away.

By the time he got within a hundred yards of the hot spring and could see the faint glow of Mia's campfire, his body shivered. His balls drew up so tight he feared they'd take up permanent residence inside his abdominal cavity.

God, he hated being cold.

He'd take being stripped down to his skivvies, sweat pouring into the crack of his ass, his tongue stuck to the roof of his mouth from dehydration over freezing his nuts off any day.

But he'd rather be where he was than warm in his cabin worrying about Mia. Not that she wasn't well equipped or couldn't handle herself. And if she knew he'd followed her out, it would probably break the fragile trust they'd started to build.

But he couldn't *not* be out there. He'd risk the blowback to ensure her safety.

He wasn't dumb enough to get too close. He'd wake up early, get back to his cabin, and she'd be none the wiser.

Which also meant he couldn't start a fire. That would surely give his position away. Instead, he tucked behind some brush and a boulder for a wind break. A place sheltered enough that snow hadn't started to stick. If he could have, he would have made a bed of boughs to get him off the cold ground, but he couldn't do so without risking discovery.

He folded a blanket into thirds and laid it on the ground for padding and insulation, then used the other blanket to cover him.

At first, getting out of the wind felt warm. He stared up and the falling snow. As time went on, his body heat dissipated, and the cold settled in earnest. His teeth started chattering, and even the memory of kissing Mia and the thoughts of all he'd like to do with her couldn't keep him warm.

Despite all that, the rollercoaster emotional day had his eyes drifting closed. He fought it, wondering if hypothermia had settled in, causing the drowsiness. But the pull of sleep, despite Yusef being so prominent in his thoughts that night, proved too strong.

He woke from a fitful sleep with a start as Mia's boot kicked the bottom of his foot. He couldn't see her face, not with her headlamp shining in his eyes. He raised a gloved hand to shield his eyes.

"What are you doing out here?" She clicked off the headlamp, and all he saw were stars tattooed on his retina. She certainly didn't sound happy to see him, but she didn't sound murderous, so he took that as a win.

"I was sleeping." He pushed up ont his elbow. "How did you find me anyway?"

"You sounded like a bear crashing through the woods when you came out here. You're not actually known for your stealth. And I got tired of wondering if something had found you in the night and decided you would make a nice frozen treat, so I came looking for you. Your teeth chattering made you that much easier to find."

"Great." He laid back down and pulled the covers back up to his ears. "Can I go back to sleep now?"

She crouched down and brushed the thin layer of snow off his blanket. "You're gonna freeze out here."

"Does that mean we can go back to the cabins?"

Her hands on her hips, she stood silhouetted against a sliver of moon peeking out from behind a thick, snow laden cloud. "I don't need a white knight, Bishop."

Bishop. She hadn't called him that since their first week together. Was she trying to push him away? Getting to his feet, he got in her face. "I'm not a knight. I'm just a man who sees you, Mia Mann. Who sees through all your bullshit and—"

Mia clicked on her headlamp, turned on her heel, and started down the trail toward her camp.

"Hey, where are you going?"

She spun around and walked backward. "To camp. You coming?"

He threw his blankets over a shoulder and followed. Only a light dusting of snow had stuck, and for the time being, the flurries had stopped even though it felt like the temperature had dropped.

In the distance, a pack of coyotes yipped and yowled, but there were few other sounds beside the crunch of his boots on the trail and the sound of his breathing.

At the hot spring, Mia had stretched a tarp between two trees, staking the bottom corners to the ground. A basic lean-to, but it kept the snow off her bedding and trapped the heat from the nearby campfire.

With a stick, she poked at the fire, then added more fuel from a pile of branches she'd broken and stacked beside the cliff wall. He started to lay his blankets near the fire, but she bumped her chin toward the lean-to and said, "In there."

She dropped her fire poker and helped him set up his bedding. In the end, they used his blankets on the ground and unzipped her down sleeping bag to put over the top of them. Even standing there with the fire to his back he couldn't stop the shakes and the shivers, his body seemingly lacking the fuel it needed to keep him warm.

Mia toed out of her boots and he reluctantly did the same. He went to slip under the sleeping bag fully clothed, but she shook her head and said, "Strip. We'll be warmer sharing body heat."

He eyed her, the glow from the fire highlighting her impatience. "You think you can keep your hands off me?"

"Conceited much?" She unzipped her coat and began stripping down to her thermals.

"It's not conceit if it's true."

She made a noise at the back of her throat that pretty much called him out on his BS, but she almost smiled so one point in the win column for him. He didn't dare continue keeping score, knowing he'd surely lose in the end.

She dove under the covers and he peeled down to his thermals as well. He didn't want to wake up and find his clothes frozen to the ground so he balled them up and put them under the covers with them.

He made a pillow with his coat and crawled into bed, him the little spoon to her big spoon. For their bodies to align, his ass to her groin, her head ended up near his shoulders, her warm breath heating his skin through the fabric.

He shuddered, but not from the cold. She tucked her hands in front of her body instead of draping one across his waist, but he didn't complain or push.

And with the inadvertent hard-on he'd sprouted as she tucked her legs behind his, it was probably for the best he wasn't the big spoon.

———

MIA TRIED NOT TO THINK ABOUT THE LAST TIME SHE'D WOKEN UP with a man in bed beside her, her arm low around his waist, and his morning wood pressed against her hand. Though Matt hadn't shifted, his breathing changed when he woke.

At least he hadn't frozen to death in the middle of the night.

She tried not to read too much into finding him camping not far from her. She knew he worried, but that was the kind of guy he was. A protector. A nurturer. The kind of guy who volunteered first for the shit jobs. The kind of guy who picked up stray dogs off the streets.

The kind of guy who needed to make things better.

This drive in him as much a part of his DNA as his dark hair and brown eyes.

She wasn't special. And the sooner she remembered that, the better.

The early morning sun tried to break through the clouds, but Mia didn't hold out much hope for much of a reprieve. The forecast for the coming week didn't look promising.

Matt rolled to his back. "Can I ask you a question?"

"What's that?"

"What are you going to do when that storm rolls in and dumps a couple feet of snow?"

"I'm trying not to think about it." She rested her head in her hand. A gap formed, allowing some of the excess heat to escape. "I don't stay out here to be difficult, or because I think I'm tough. I'm out here because it allows me to breathe."

"I'm not going to say I get it, because I don't. But I do know sometimes people have to cope they best way they know how. I *do* get that."

His gaze flicked down to her lips for a fraction of a second, but that was all it took for her heart to stumble. She still felt the pressure of his lips on hers from the kiss they'd shared the night before. Could still remember how he'd tasted of rich, black coffee and determination.

I see you, Mia Mann.

Those words he'd spoken stuck in her brain, and she couldn't peel or scrub them away. She didn't want to be seen. She wanted to do her time and disappear.

Do not get involved with this man. Do not get involved with this man.

Thirteen more days to get through. She'd keep that at the front of her mind.

"Maybe we'll get lucky, and the system will bypass us, or at least stay at the higher elevations," she said, returning to the conversation. "Anyway, we should be getting back. I'm on barn duty this morning. If I'm late feeding Eli, he's likely to jump the fence and come knocking on my door."

Eli was Sidney's personal horse. A buckskin gelding with a Houdini complex and the puzzle solving skills of a Rubik's cube champion. He'd hardly met a fence or a stall door that he couldn't escape. He wasn't looking to run away. He was looking for attention.

Matt caught Mia's hand as she went to get up. "Thanks for coming to get me last night."

If Mia stared too long, his sincerity might put a dent in her shield. "Jenna's already looking for a reason to kick me out of the program. Letting you freeze to death wouldn't help my situation."

She rolled out from between the covers and gathered up her clothes.

"What are you talking about?" He quickly stood and started dressing. She tried to avert her eyes, but the tenting of his thermal bottoms was a sight to behold.

He tucked himself into his pants with a grimace and said, "*Mia*, what's going on?"

"The program wasn't my choice." When he looked like he wanted to ask another question, she added, "Jenna has to send in periodic evaluations. I'm failing."

"How do you fail?" He sounded incredulous. But she knew exactly how.

"That doesn't matter. Forget I said anything."

She kicked dirt over the remaining hot coals as he shrugged into his coat. He caught her arm and ignored the glare she shot him. "You can't just drop that on me and then go silent and deep."

She closed her eyes and blew out a steadying breath. "It's not something I'm proud of, okay?"

"You can't let her fail you."

"I'm going to try to not let that happen, but I'm also not going to lie on my eval. That's not me."

He didn't say much after that. He worked hard to get the camp packed up and ready for them to leave, but he wore his emotions on his face, and she could see the problem ruminating in his head as he formulated a plan to help.

"Matt." When she had his attention, she said, "This isn't your problem to fix."

He grunted noncommittally.

Unfortunately, she was the only one who could fix this.

Because really, a year in jail, the thick walls, the high fences... just the thought of being stuck inside tightened her skin and made her want to bolt.

But a life looking over her shoulder after an unhappy judge issued an arrest warrant wasn't any way to live.

So, she'd try.

And God help her if she failed.

———

Sunday night came and the weather continued to hold. It might have even warmed up some, or it could be the roaring campfire in front of Boomer and Sidney's cabin keeping the cold at bay.

This was one of Healing Horses' scheduled nights. A kind of loose group therapy. Jenna expected Zealand back from spending the weekend with his fiancée any minute, and Mia had heard that Mackenzie, aka Mac, was coming as well.

Mac had made an impression on Jenna as a teen, and in a way was responsible for Jenna developing the program. A former Marine, Mac had found herself at the ranch with her last dollar to her name and her own ghosts chasing her tail.

Though Mac wasn't doing much running these days. Not with a couple of twins in her belly, due to pop sometime in the next couple of weeks.

Matt drifted over and dropped into one of the folding chairs. Pepita sat crossways in her chair beside Mia, her brow furrowed and a frown on her face as she thumbed away on her phone.

Mia nudged Pepita. "What's wrong?"

Boomer came out of the cabin with a tray of hamburger patties and headed for the grill.

Pepita watched him walk by and in a voice carefully calculated to be overheard, said, "My dad said I can't go on the scout camping trip with the guys next weekend."

"Only because Ms. Parker had to cancel as one of the chaperons. I don't like the idea of you being the only female out there. At least not without one of us there."

"Then you be a chaperon."

Boomer finished laying all the meat on the grill and set the tray aside. "If it was any other weekend, I could. I told you that."

"Mom, then."

Boomer walked over and squatted down in front of Pepita. "Your mom wants to stick around here. With twins, it's very likely Mac could have the babies early, and she wants to be here when it happens. I promise I'll take you up another time."

"It won't be the same."

He patted her leg and stood. "It will be better."

She shook her head and grumbled. "Not without boys there it won't be."

Leaning down, he kissed her on the forehead. "Hey, kid, don't be in such a hurry to grow up, yeah?"

The flames from the grill shot up as fat from the burgers dripped onto the coals. Boomer rushed over to rescue the meat before it got charred.

"Your father's just trying to look out for you. You're lucky to have someone who cares."

"You agree with him?"

"I don't *not* agree."

"That's the same thing."

Mia shrugged. "A subtle difference, maybe."

Pepita dropped her phone in her lap and gave Mia her full attention. "He doesn't trust me."

Mia leaned in. "I think it's the boys he doesn't trust."

Pepita made a face, but even in the firelight, Mia could tell she was considering what she'd said.

"I guess I get it." Then Pepita raised her voice to be sure her father heard. "But it's not like I'm going to do anything stupid."

Boomer laughed as he flipped the burgers. The aroma drifting their way made Mia's stomach rumble. All that time freezing her ass off in the last twenty-four hours had given her a healthy appetite.

"Sweetheart," Boomer said to Pepita, "every teenager does something stupid. It's the hormones. You can't help it."

Pepita grinned. "Oh, yeah? What kind of stupid things did you do?"

"Nice try, kid. I'm not dumb enough to give you any ideas."

"What about you," Pepita asked Mia. "Did hormones make you do stupid things?"

"Enough," Mia allowed, "but the hormones were easier for me to navigate. It was love, or what I thought was love, that did me in."

Matt perked up, and his eyes bored a hole into the side of her head. He'd been sitting quietly beside her, poking at the coals with a long stick, looking like he was minding his own business. But he'd been minding hers.

She should have kept her big mouth shut.

Pepita opened her mouth, a question on the tip of her tongue. The kid never ran out of questions. But Boomer turned around, a platter of hamburger patties straight off the grill.

"Who's hungry?"

5

Zealand showed up at the cookout in time to claim the last
burger. Hank accompanied Mac down for dinner. After they'd
all eaten, Hank stuffed the dirty paper plates and empty water
and soda bottles into a garbage bag and set it in the back of his
truck to take to the dumpster. Before leaving, he squatted beside
his wife's chair.

Mac sat with her hands on the blanket covering her belly
because her coat didn't come anywhere close to zipping. All
Matt could think was thank God he was a guy.

"Be good." Hank rolled a log under her feet so she could
keep them elevated. "Have Sidney call me when you're finished,
and I'll come get you."

Hank and Mac lived in the old foreman's house a few
hundred yards behind the barn.

"I can take her home," Boomer said. It wasn't like it was far.

"I could have driven myself."

Hank chuckled, the love for his wife sparking in his eyes.

Matt almost looked away, feeling as if he was invading a
private moment. But witnessing them together made him long
for something he couldn't see happening for himself.

"Army," Hank said, using his endearment for her. "You can't even fit behind the steering wheel."

Mac grumbled as Hank pressed a kiss to the side of her head and to everyone around the fire he said, "Night, everyone."

"That's our cue." Sidney tapped Pepita's leg.

"Awh, can't I stay just this once? I promise I won't open my mouth. No one will even know I'm here."

"Go, with your mother," Boomer said. "Besides, I know you still have that English paper to finish."

"All I have to do is type it up." Even as she argued, she stood to go back inside. "You can't protect me from the real world forever."

"Not forever," he allowed, "but maybe for a few more years."

From what Matt had heard, Pepita had become all too acquainted with the real world at a very tender age at the hands of her biological father, the head of a notorious drug cartel that had been running drugs through the Rockies. But Matt understood Boomer's need to protect his adopted daughter from the worst the world had to offer.

While everyone resettled after Hank, Sidney, and Pepita left, Matt leaned toward Mia. "You're really good with her."

"She's a good kid."

"You ever thought about having kids of your own?" As soon as those words left Matt's mouth, he wanted them back. The hesitant smile slipped from Mia's lips, and something flashed in her eyes he couldn't read. But her unconscious shift away from him, he had no difficulty reading. "I'm sorry, I—"

"Jenna asked you a question," Zealand called out to Matt. Mia shot Zealand a *thank you* look for the reprieve.

Matt tried to ignore the cut of Zealand's eyes to his that said, 'don't be a dick.' Matt wasn't trying to be a dick. He wasn't even trying to push Mia's boundaries or buttons. He'd thought it had been an innocent question, not a ticking time bomb he'd tossed in her lap.

Zealand cleared his throat. Oh, yeah. Jenna's question. Matt refocused on the people around him. Jenna with her ever-present tablet for note taking, her dog Dink laying at her feet. Zealand sat on one of the nearby logs, cleaning his fingernails with his pocketknife. Mac tucked up tighter under her blanket, and Boomer removed his prosthetic and rubbed the soreness out of his stump.

"What was the question?" Matt asked.

Jenna leaned forward, her pad of paper in her lap, twisting the pencil over and over again in her hands. "I asked if you wanted to share what happened with you in the barn yesterday?"

The word 'no' sat on the tip of his tongue, but if Saturday proved anything to him, it was that Mia wasn't the only one who needed to open up more. It had been hypocritical for him to call Mia out about not sharing when he'd guarded everything he'd said.

And he didn't have to worry about failing out of the program.

It had been insincere of him to not go all in with the program from the start, expecting to get more out of it than he'd put in.

They didn't have much time before their three months in the program ended, and he wasn't convinced he had much to show for it. Which wasn't Jenna's, or the program's, fault. That was all on him.

Whereas Zealand had embraced the program from the beginning, and he seemed emotionally lightyears ahead of where he'd started. Though finding a woman who loved and supported him unconditionally probably hadn't hurt either.

Maybe Matt should give this group therapy thing more

effort. Fuck, he didn't want to do this. He blew out a big breath and started talking before he could think too hard about what he would say. "Watching Charlie stand up to Boomer, it reminded me of another little boy…"

Matt related the story, much the same way as he'd told Mia, but the memory wasn't as raw as it had been the day before, enabling him to minimize the impact the dark emotions had on him.

These people aren't the enemy. It won't kill you if you allow your-self to be vulnerable.

Jenna nibbled on the end of her pencil. The eraser had already met an untimely demise. He told them almost every-thing. Admitting to the panic attack, but conveniently leaving out the part where Mia had gone looking for him, and the tenderness and understanding she'd shown him. It would have felt like a violation of privacy to share that without Mia's go ahead.

"How did that make you feel?" Jenna asked.

Matt knew Jenna was asking how he felt about losing Yusef. *Losing.* Fuck. He didn't *lose* Yusef. He'd watched the kid get murdered in front of his eyes. Matt tore his attention away from the mesmerizing glow of the fire's hot coals and collided with Jenna's inquiring eyes. "How do you think it made me feel?"

Jenna's brows went up at the open hostility in his voice, but nothing else changed in her demeanor. The animus surprised him as well. Mia's hand lay on her armrest an inch or so from his. She reached out with her pinky, locking it with his. If anyone else noticed, they didn't react, and at that moment, he didn't care. That simple touch grounded him, and the anger flowed out until only the raw anguish remained.

"Like you wanted to take that moment back," Mac answered for him. She *got* it. Hell, of all the people in the world, these amazing humans around him understood. They'd all lived through their own hell on earth. "That everything you'd done, everything you'd said that led up to that moment, you wanted, *needed,* to take back. That if you'd only been a better soldier, a better person, a better *human*, you could have prevented it."

Matt choked up as every bit of that truth hit home. "I—I felt like I failed him. Fuck. I *did* fail him."

"You didn't fire the shots that killed him." Zealand wouldn't let him take the blame.

Boomer stopped rubbing his stump. "Or encourage him to run toward you."

"It's not your fault." Mia added her own two cents, but with emotion weighing her words down, he doubted anyone else heard her.

He absorbed all their words. It wasn't anything he hadn't told himself before, but having the external validation meant something to him. And by retelling his story—it wasn't as if the load had been lifted—it was as if gravity didn't weigh as heavy, and his soul didn't feel quite so black.

It was as if each of his friends had picked up a piece of his grief and helped him carry it.

Matt blinked back the moisture that flooded his eyes, and Jenna leaned back in her chair. "Thanks for sharing. I know that wasn't easy."

Matt nodded, his throat too tight to speak. Jenna turned her attention to Zealand. "Do you have anything you'd like share with everyone?"

Zealand grinned. The fire popped, and the logs shifted and settled. "I have an interview next week with the Bison County EMS."

"Fuck, yeah." Boomer socked Zealand in the shoulder with his fist.

Congratulations were given all around, and Matt couldn't help but smile for his roommate's good fortune.

That's what happens when you do the work.

Maybe Matt needed to follow Zealand's example if it weren't already too late.

"I talked to the fire chief about my previous issues with the sight of blood sometimes sending me into a flashback and explained the work I had done with Taylor and her patients to overcome the problem. He seemed open to discussing it further."

"Taylor will miss having you as her assistant," Jenna said, "but this is great news."

"That new assistant she hired is pretty good, so I'm not sure how much I'll be missed. But that's okay. I know it's time for me to move on. Being a vet assistant was never in my plans."

Working her way around the group, Jenna's focus turned to Mia. Mia's pinky tightened around Matt's, and her breath caught. Mia had to know what was coming next. "Care to share anything, Mia?"

This was the part of the session where Mia usually declined to answer. Where she turned her thoughts inward and let the conversations go on around her.

Mia's phone rang, playing the ring tone from *Psycho*. She grimaced. "It's my family. I have to take this."

Jenna smiled. "That's awesome, we—"

"No." Mia stood. Matt couldn't tell if the light from the fire had washed the color out of Mia's face or if the call had done that. "My family calling is whatever the complete opposite of awesome is, with a couple of circles of hell thrown in for laughs."

Over his shoulder, Matt watched her walk away, the phone to her ear as she went further up the dirt drive where the hill crested, and the cell reception improved. Jenna, Mac, Zealand, and Boomer started talking amongst themselves, something about the babies' nursery and cribs and all things foreign to Matt.

Zealand extricated himself from the conversation and plopped down beside Matt.

Matt squeezed Zealand's shoulder. "I'm really proud of you. I know you're gonna kill it in the interview."

"Thanks. I've got a good feeling about it. If you'd have told me a couple of months ago that I might return to a career I love, I'd have called bullshit on that."

Then Zealand's smile faded as his thoughts shifted. He lowered his voice, not that Jenna, Mac, and Boomer paid them any attention. "You know what you're doing here, buddy?"

"I don't know what you're talking about." Even though Matt knew *exactly* what Zealand had meant.

Matt had made it clear from day one that he was interested in Mia and nothing in the past few months had changed that.

The pinky thing only confirmed what Zealand already knew. Zealand was the type of guy who paid attention to detail. Probably what had made him an outstanding Army medic.

"Don't bullshit me."

Matt had never denied his attraction. Or seen a problem with it. There weren't any rules against fraternization in the program they had to skirt. "And?"

"And she doesn't need another complication in her life."

"Who died and made you her mother, Zee?" The irritation crept in unbidden, maybe more because, on some level, Matt knew Zealand was right. "It's not like you know her better than the rest of us."

"I know enough to know she's bad news and—"

Matt stilled, his eyes narrow and laser focused. "I think you need to walk that shit back."

Zealand dipped his head and blew out a breath, when he glanced back up, the only thing visible was Zealand's concern.

For Mia or him? Hard to tell. "I'm not judging, Matt. I like her. I really do. I'm just saying that out of all of us, she's done the bare minimum of emotional work here and she's probably the one who needs it the most. You keep after her, and one of you will end up destroyed."

"I appreciate the vote of confidence, *friend*."

"I'm not saying anything Jenna or any of the others wouldn't say to your face, and you know it." Zealand tapped Matt on the chest with the back of his hand. "I think you know it in here, too. That's why you're so defensive."

"I'm so defensive because it isn't any of your damn business."

Fuck. He hadn't meant to say it that loud.

The conversation around them dropped, and three pairs of eyes stared back at Matt from the other side of the fire.

"Everything okay over there?" Jenna asked.

Zealand stood to return to his seat. "Sure, Matt was just congratulating me."

Boomer fake coughed into his hand. "Bullshit."

Mia returned and reclaimed her chair. One look at her—at the way her body shook, at the dazed expression on her face, at the way she swiped at the moisture on her cheeks, and Matt wanted to scoop her up into his arms.

He wanted to carry her to the hot spring and lay with her under the stars and hold her and let her know everything was going to be okay, even though it looked like her world had just crumbled.

———

MIA TREMBLED IN HER CHAIR. THE FIRE TOO WEAK TO PENETRATE the chill deep at her center. Her *delightful* conversation with her parents left her emotions as abraded as if someone had taken a cheese grater to them. Why she hadn't blocked their number yet remained a mystery.

The only mystery is why they haven't pulled their heads out of their asses after all these years.

It wasn't the 1950s anymore. Society had changed. Values had changed. But her parents hadn't made that transition. And with each call and each email, they never let her forget that or all the shame she'd brought on the family. The underlying question clear if not spoken: *why couldn't you be more like your sister?*

Sweet, like her.

Obedient, like her.

Smart, like her.

Not a whore... like her.

Would Mia ever get through a day without her sister's ghost haunting her?

Just one day.

Was it really too much to ask?

Mia's pinky sought Matt's almost on its own, but instead of giving her his little finger, he laid his hand over the top of hers, slotting their fingers together. Jenna raised a brow, and Mac and Boomer exchanged a glance. She'd seen those curious looks before, back in a faraway desert when she'd been attracted to another man. Luckily, Mia wasn't that naïve girl anymore.

Mia went to take her hand back. Matt held on, and she was too emotionally drained to fight him.

"You good, Mia?" Zealand asked.

Zealand's simple question pulled her out of her head. Maybe it was the compassion in his tone or the fact that he hadn't taken a stripe out of her hide the way they usually liked doing to each other. It was how they communicated. But every person had their limits and Zealand seemed to know the edges of hers.

"Fuck family," Mia's replied. Then she glanced at Jenna,

anticipating the next words to come out of the program director's mouth. "And no, I don't want to talk about it."

"You don't have to," Jenna said in that reasonable way she had. It took more than a verbal hit to knock Jenna back. "Why don't you tell us how you came to be at Healing Horses."

Mia barked out a laugh and shook her head, the tears rolling down her cheeks again. She sniffed and swiped them away with her coat sleeve. Matt rubbed his thumb over her hand, a physical reminder he hadn't gone anywhere.

"Give us something," Mac said. "You owe it to yourself."

Jenna stopped tapping her pencil on the pad of paper. "Broad strokes. We don't have to do a deep dive if you don't want to."

Again, Mia tried to take her hand back from Matt, wanting to pull into herself, to limit her exposure, to escape. Instead of letting go, he brought their joined hands to his chest and held tight. She couldn't feel the beat of his heart through the thickness of his coat, but she remembered how it had felt the night before. The steadiness. The strength. It pulled her in and drew back on the reins of her own galloping heart.

She blew out a deep breath, knowing Matt would drop her hand once he heard what she had to say. And if he couldn't handle *that* truth about her, then he sure as hell couldn't handle the rest.

"I was dishonorably discharged."

She'd half expected a collective gasp. For the flames to bend, filling the sudden void where the air had been. Neither came. Though she had everyone's undivided attention. Even Jenna wouldn't have known that part of her history, unless she'd looked up Mia's military record.

Saying those words out loud made Mia's chest tighten and her heart beat even faster, squeezing out the space where her lungs needed to expand. These men and women around the fire with her had served their country honorably.

Hell, Boomer would have stayed in if they'd have let him. And here she was, sitting amongst these people who she'd really come to admire, having to tell them that the Marines had kicked her out.

Not her proudest moment.

Not that she would have taken back her actions on that day if she could.

"But that's not why I'm here."

She thought about that statement and amended it. "At least not directly. A judge sent me here. He offered deferred adjudication on some charges I had, which is allowing me to avoid a year in jail if I successfully complete the program."

The dishonorable discharge, and the events leading up to it, had been bad enough. After her arrest, her parents had almost disowned her. Especially after word got around town. Mia, always the wayward daughter. The troubled one. The disobedient one.

Only the good die young.

In Mia's sister's case, that had been true. But then again, her sister hadn't lived long enough to raise any kind of hell.

Zealand chuckled. "I didn't expect any less than that from you, my friend. What the hell did they nail you for?"

What was wrong with these people? Where was the judgement, the sour expressions, the inability to look her in the eye without shaking their head in disappointment?

She glanced at Matt. He hadn't dropped her hand as if he'd suddenly found himself linking fingers with Jack the Ripper. And like Zealand, he also had an amused turn to his lips.

"It's not funny," Mia said, though she couldn't help the grin from spreading on her face. "Okay. So maybe the story is a little funny."

As humiliated as her parents had been over the years about her exploits, a part of her had been proud for using her minor notoriety for something good. And if she told everyone about *this*, maybe they'd forget to press her about her dishonorable discharge.

"Free climbing has been in my blood for a long time. Once I got out of the military, I was at loose ends, chasing that adrenaline. I wasn't into drugs, so it was the most legal high I could find.

"But where I lived, there were only man-made objects to climb. I didn't let that stop me." Mia shrugged. What else was a climber to do when there was nothing around to climb?

Zealand leaned forward in his chair. "Like what?"

"Like water towers. The five-story bank building. Which, in our town, was the highest building around. You can't get away with much in that town. I surely couldn't. But because of my father's social status, I got little more than a few slaps on the wrist and written about in the police blotter in the local paper."

"Weren't you afraid of falling?" Jenna asked. "You could have been killed."

"I wasn't exactly in a place at the time that I cared."

That knocked some of the smiles off everyone's faces. Mia didn't bother telling them that there wasn't a whole lot that had changed in that department. She refused to go into all of that.

She switched tacks before Jenna could grill her on that. "I kind of dug the notoriety, so I had little incentive to stop. And then one day, I heard that one of the local judges—a lay minister at the church and a homophobic piece of shit—sided with the high school on a dispute with a male student who wasn't allowed to bring his boyfriend to prom. I protested by climbing the church steeple and hanging a pride flag from the spire."

Matt chuckled and squeezed her hand. "I'm thinking the judge didn't take it too well."

"I got a fine, that time. But, instead of paying, I decided to leave the good judge a message. I scaled the side of the county courthouse and scrawled 'love is love' on his window in rainbow colors of shoe polish."

"Fuck, yeah." Boomer leaned across Zealand, and she gave him a high five.

"Why doesn't any of this surprise me?" Matt leaned away, looking her up and down with what looked like approval on his face.

Her stomach unwound several knots. Not everyone thought the way her parents did. Mia knew that. But she sure as hell hadn't expected this reaction. No reproach, no disapproval, no *tsk-tsk*, no wringing of hands, no threats to kick her out.

"To be fair," Mia said, "I thought he was in court that day and never expected he'd walk into his office as I wrote it."

"Oh, man." Zealand hooted with laughter, and it looked like Jenna had tears running down her face from holding her laughter in.

"The judge was at his wits' end. It was either a year in jail, or here. I chose here."

Matt leaned in and whispered in her ear. "Thank fuck for that."

Mac held her belly as she tried to catch her breath from laughing so hard, though in her condition, just walking across a room got her winded. When she'd finally caught her breath enough to speak, she said, "I wanna be you when I grow up."

Matt chuckled and kissed the back of her hand. "That's amazing."

"Amazing?" Who were these people? "I'm practically a jailbird."

Jenna leaned back in her chair. Mia couldn't tell what had made Jenna look so proud, the fact that Mia had shared with the group, or Mia's act of defiance. "You stood up for what was right.

You spoke out—in an unorthodox way—to protect those who were powerless to protect themselves. There's no shame in that."

"Way to kick ass," Zealand said.

"Don't you dare tell Pepita," Boomer said, though he sounded as if he were kidding. "I don't want to give the kid any ideas. She's a lot like you in that way, sticking up for the underdog."

For the first time since she'd been arrested, that sense of shame and humiliation didn't weigh so heavy. Her heart settled into a near-normal rate, and air slipped more easily into her lungs.

Matt winked—and fuck if that didn't gouge her bomb-proof shield. As dangerous as Matt was to her sense of self-preservation, a return smile spread on her face.

"What about the dishonorable discharge? Care to share?" Jenna never let up.

Mia's heart dropped faster than it had when she'd fallen from the cliff. She opened her mouth to say 'not on your life' when Mac stiffened and grabbed her belly. "Oh, shit, oh shit, oh shit."

Zealand knelt at her feet a second later, his hand going to the pulse on her wrist. "What's going on? What are you—fuck, your pulse is high." He turned to Boomer. "Get Hank down here."

"It's okay," Mac said. "It's just Braxton Hicks contractions. They just hit a little harder than normal and took me by surprise."

"Uh, huh." Zealand didn't sound like he was agreeing with her. "I still think you need to get checked out. At least call your doctor and let him know—"

"I'm not calling my doctor on a Sunday night for—"

Boomer must have made the call to Hank.

The rev and growl of Hank's diesel truck starting up could be heard across the expanse of the ranch between the cabins and the foreman's house. Within seconds, the bounce and flash of Hank's headlights came into view as he gunned the truck, plowing through the potholes.

"Oh, shit," Mac said. "I'm in trouble. I'll be lucky if he leaves my side now until the babies are born. Lord knows I love that man, but a girl needs her space."

Hank skid to a stop near the fire, the dust he'd kicked up floated through the flames.

"What's wrong?" Hank dropped to his knees beside Zealand, while the rest of them loosely gathered around. There wasn't anything they could do to help, and Mia hated feeling like something was beyond her control. "I knew I should have made you stay in bed."

"Hank, I'm fine. And I already have the mattress pattern permanently embedded on my ass. I can't stare at those four walls, binge-watching reality television without going cr—"

Mac grunted and doubled over in her chair, the pain stealing her breath.

As the pain subsided, Hank snatched her up in his arms. "I'm taking you to the hospital."

"I'm f—" The protest caught in her throat as another wave of pain hit. "Yeah. Hospital."

Hank strode to the passenger door and buckled her in.

"You think she's in labor?" Jenna asked. "Grandma and Grandpa wanted me to call when it was time so they could catch a flight back from Florida."

Dale and Lottie had decided they were too old to take another Wyoming winter and had decamped to the Keys for six months. Mia had barely gotten the chance to get to know them before they'd left.

"It's too early," Hank said, as if his denial could keep his babies from making a surprise appearance.

The headlights highlighted the worry, the fear, the panic etched in every line on Hank's face.

Mia couldn't breathe, remembering back to a time when her womb had revolted against her. She almost hadn't survived the outcome. Now she paced in front of Hank's truck, feeling the walls closing in on her even though miles and miles of open land stretched out all around her.

Emotionally, she flailed. This wasn't a feeling she could outrun. She cradled her arms around herself, the phantom pains making her legs weak.

Hank bolted for the driver's side door, Zealand hollering after him that he'd meet them at the hospital as he ran for the beater of a truck he'd bought a couple of weeks before.

"I'm right behind you," Jenna said to her father. "I just need to—"

Hank closed his door and rolled down the window. "Stay here. I'll call you if the babies are coming, but otherwise, everyone needs to get some sleep. We still have to bring the cattle down tomorrow before the bad weather closes in."

"Go," Boomer said. He hobbled over, using a long, sturdy stick as a makeshift crutch. "We'll worry about the livestock."

Hank nodded once, backing up and heading down the dirt road with a little more care than when he'd come.

Please let the babies be okay. Please let the babies be okay.

Mia felt the hollowness in her gut, in the womb where no baby lay.

Matt put a steady hand on her shoulder. "Hey, are you okay?"

"Why wouldn't I be?"

"You tell me."

She blinked at him as her thoughts and emotions swirled, twisting up the here and now with what had been.

The rage.

The flying fists.

The bruises.

The bleeding.

The cramping...

"*Mia.*" Matt's voice came out soft, but firm. He held onto her shoulders and caught her unfocused gaze. "You've been staring down the road for five minutes. Everyone's already gone inside. Come on. Let's go back to your cabin before you freeze."

She didn't remember agreeing, but it wasn't long before she found herself standing on her porch.

"Would you like me to stay with you for a while?"

Yes. Say yes.

He must have sensed her hesitation because he said, "I'm not looking for anything to happen. You've made your position clear, as I have made mine. I just want to help, if I can."

That part of her that wanted to lean into him, the part that wanted to wrap her arms around his waist, the part that wanted to share her body with him...

That part rose up on her tiptoes and kissed the dark scruff on his cheek. She kept her hands to herself to prevent her from grabbing him by the coat, hauling him into her cabin, and doing everything to him she'd fantasized about. Did she dare?

She wanted him. He'd made it clear he wanted her. What could it hurt?

Ha. You're not that stupid anymore.

Matt smelled of smoke and horses.

Not sand and gunpowder.

Matt isn't Frank.

"I'll keep that in mind." She had her hand on the doorknob when she glanced back at him.

With her porch light on, the disappointment in his eyes couldn't be mistaken. He took a step back and hitched his thumb over his shoulder toward his cabin. "I'm twenty feet away if you need me."

She wanted to slap back and say, 'I won't.' But there wouldn't always be a body of water to break her fall. Was it so terrible knowing that if she fell, she had a safety net? "Thanks."

His smile brought a warmth to her chest that the cold couldn't penetrate.

Fuck. If she was anyone else...

"And if you decide to camp out tonight, knock on my door."

She didn't want him to have to sleep out in the cold. It had taken him forever to warm up the night before, even with her at his back and the fire at his front.

If you go, he'll just follow.

"Okay," she said, not knowing if she really meant it.

His smile grew and somehow pulled a matching one from her. "Okay."

Once inside, Mia lay on the top bunk, hoping that not having another bed over her head would make the cabin less confining. It had helped, but now, more than an hour after she'd crawled in, that itch was back under her skin. To get out, to get away before the walls and the ceiling crushed her.

Closing her eyes, she imagined herself dressed in superhero garb standing in the middle of the room, holding the encroaching walls at bay.

They stopped moving and held. But her virtual muscles strained, and she wouldn't be able to hold out for long.

Knock on my door.

Matt's words came to her.

I just want to help.

She needed a distraction to get Mac, and her own past, out of her head. A short-term reprieve. A type of satiated exhaustion only sex had brought in the past. Even though Matt had made it clear that he wanted her, when he said he'd help, he hadn't been talking about sex.

But sex with Matt hadn't been far from her mind these past

couple months. And after last night when they'd shared their bedroll, their bodies nearly naked...

She knew as well as anyone that sex wasn't a cure or an antidote for what ailed her.

But sometimes, it managed as a well-placed Band-Aid.

6

THE SOFT CREAK OF THE PORCH BOARDS DIDN'T YANK MATT FROM a deep sleep. He laid awake in his bed, his hands behind his head, staring up at the underside of the bunk above him, worried about Mac and the babies, and Mia and her demons.

He'd focused on every sound he'd heard, trying to make sure Mia didn't sneak out without him knowing. At this rate, he'd be sleeping in the saddle on the way up to the high pastures to bring the cattle down in the morning.

The door latch clunked, and Matt rose to his elbow and watched as Mia stepped into the cabin, a rush of cold air following her in. In the near darkness, he could make out her general shape as she closed the door.

He almost said, 'hey,' but something about the cautious way she carried herself had him biting back the word. She toed out of her boots and unzipped her coat, draping it across the table.

Step by step, she dropped a layer, her shirt and then her pants, until she stood in front of him in only her long johns.

"What—"

She held a finger over his lips, and he swallowed the rest of his question. Stripping off her remaining layers, she stood naked before him. Moonlight glanced off the swell of her breasts and hid in the valley along her midline.

Lifting the covers, she crawled on top of him, straddling his hips and sitting on the tops of his thighs. He reached down and adjusted himself in his underwear, the movement not lost on her. He had so many questions.

But he wouldn't voice them. At least for now. Still, he wondered...

Did she not want him to talk her out of it?

Or did she not want to have to tell him why she'd come?

The tip of his hard cock stuck out of the waistband of his boxer briefs, dripping precum onto his lower abdomen. She fell forward, her hands on either side of his chest. His hands went to the lean, powerful muscles of her thighs, the ones that either could propel her up the face of a cliff or wrap around his neck and choke him out.

If only you could go out that way.

"This doesn't have to mean anything." In the quiet, her nearly whispered words had an ethereal life of their own. "Sometimes sex helps to exorcise the demons. At least for a bit."

She removed his hands from her legs and wrapped his fingers around the wood spindles at the head of his bed. "Are you in?"

He was almost glad that she forbade him to talk, because any answer would have come out nothing more than a croak. He nodded once and felt some of the tension leave her body.

"Two rules," she said. "Hands to yourself. And you can talk if you want to revoke your consent."

He almost laughed. *Like that was going to happen.*

But he still had questions. And that tiny piece of him that retained a sliver of sanity almost stopped her. She was upset. Hurting perhaps. Between the call from her parents and Mac's distress, sex may not be in her best interest.

"I can see you thinking," she said. "Stop. Yes, I know what I'm doing. And yes, I can do this without regret."

He'd have to take her at her word. After all, she was a grown woman.

Now, the biggest question swirling around in his head was how he'd manage not to put his hands on her.

She ducked down, kissing her way across the stubble on his jaw. He tilted his head back, loving the way the tip of her tongue traced down the length of his neck, her breath warming his exposed skin.

Her short hair tickled, sending goosebumps racing over his skin. She smelled of fresh air, lodgepole pine, and escapism. With infinite skill, she worked her way down his body, her fingers scrunching through the hair on his chest. The flat of her tongue worked his nipples into peaks, sending rapid-fire lightning strikes to his groin, and the light scrape of her teeth over the sensitive tips had his balls drawing up tight.

Coming prematurely didn't concern him. There was plenty of pleasure they could give each other without a hard dick if they had to work their way through his refractory period.

They'd worry about that if and when the time came.

In the meantime, he'd enjoy her hands on him and the way they teased and tortured his nerve endings. She hitched her fingers into his waistband and slipped his underwear off him, his cock straining between his thighs, waiting for a touch that never came.

The anticipation had his heart rattling in his chest and his breath coming faster as his arousal built. Her touch like no other he'd felt before. Purposeful, bold, teasing, and worshipful all at the same time. His grip tightened on the headboard's spindles. If he could see his knuckles, no doubt they'd be blanched white, his need to touch her a battle he might not win.

She settled between his thighs, pushing his legs wider, her

tongue tracing the crease of his leg and around the base of his balls. The amount of precum dripping from his slit could have floated the Ark.

With a measured, methodical swipe of her tongue, she licked him clean, teasing the crown and following the sensitive ridge around. A little more of that and he could have come without any stroking. Then she took him deep, this long, slow slide to the back of her warm, wet throat.

One of the spindles cracked, sounding like a shot in the dark. He considered loosening his grip, but it was the only thing keeping him from reaching for her.

He didn't know the reason behind her rules. And didn't care. Not when her mouth and hands brought him to the brink. He tried to hold back. Just when he was about to say, 'fuck it' and let himself come, she pulled back. The sly, mischievous smile sexy as hell.

He liked her like this. Opening up, her shields inching down.

There was a joy in her movements, an emotion he hadn't witnessed in her before. Easing her way up his body, she kissed him on the lips. He opened for her, their tongues tracing the other, his saltiness making the kiss hotter.

She broke the kiss. If his night with her ended here, he would be more than fine with that. But instead of getting up and leaving, the way he half expected her to, she said, "Condoms?"

Fuck. Condoms. Yeah. Um…

He let go of the headboard long enough to point toward the bathroom.

She gave him one last heated kiss before padding away, with Matt praying that Zealand might have kept a few in the cabinet under the sink.

He let go of the headboard and worked out the stiffness in his fingers as she ransacked the bathroom. She returned a few minutes later and straddled him.

He stroked himself as she tore the packet. *Best sound ever.* When he reached for the condom, she held it out of reach. She might have given him the stink-eye, but in the dim light, he couldn't be certain.

She rolled the condom down his cock and got into position above him, his tip at her entrance, her mouth by his ear. "You want out?"

He couldn't help the chuckle that escaped, but he caught himself before he said 'no.' Playing by her rules, he shook his head.

Without having had his mouth or hands on her, he'd expected some resistance as he entered her, but she was wet and ready and sank down to the hilt. He pulsed inside her, on the brink of orgasm. Gritting his teeth, he groaned. His hands went to her hips of their own accord. As she started to grind against him, her head fell back, and her hands braced on his chest.

A low groan escaped her.

He wanted to let his hands roam over her bare landscape, over the ridges and the valleys and the multitude of brightly colored tattoos she had that ran up her arms, over her shoulders and down her back. He wanted to kiss each and every one. He wanted to hear the stories and connect with their meaning. Maybe if he understood them, he could understand her.

But he didn't dare move his hands from her hips, knowing he was already bending the rules.

She lifted her head, her hands running down his arms to her hips. Her eyes opened. He sensed it more than saw it. She stilled. "You're not very good at following orders."

He rubbed his thumbs over the points of her hips in answer, and she started moving again.

"Fuck, you feel good," she said.

She didn't know the half of it. He'd been fantasizing about this moment for weeks, never expecting it to come true. But as fantastic as it felt being buried deep inside her, the sex felt more like something they exchanged rather than shared.

But he'd known that going in. That he was there for a purpose and that purpose alone.

He accepted that.

But that didn't mean he didn't want more.

At least the sex was a start. If he let her use his body to skirt her shields, he could do that.

She held his hands over his head and clamped her internal muscles around him. He hissed, and her breasts flattened against his chest as she leaned in and whispered, "Get out of your head and let yourself feel."

She had a point.

Bending his legs, he braced his feet on the mattress, and she met his thrusts, her grip tight in his, their breaths coming in the same rapid puffs. The heat they generated chased the cold away. Sweat slicked their bodies, and the base of his spine tingled with his impending orgasm.

"Faster." She released his hands and sat up, bracing one hand on his upturned knee and pleasuring herself with the other.

With his hands free, he held her hips again, using the leverage to pound deep inside. She moaned, her head falling back, but that was all the warning he got before she tumbled over the other side, clamped down around him, and took him with her.

She collapsed on top of him, her forehead resting on his shoulder, most of her weight on her elbows. He didn't know if the *hands-off* rule remained in play, but he took a chance and skimmed his fingers up her back and hugged her to him. Instead of pulling away, she relaxed against him.

Which seemed more of a victory than the fact that she'd come to him for sex.

Her heart thumped against his chest, and he wondered how much of that rapid beat stemmed from exertion versus her fear of exposure. Of allowing herself to be vulnerable for a few seconds. A minute.

And as much as he wanted to lay there all night, soaking her up, absorbing her weight, and allowing his body to offer her what comfort it could, he needed to take care of the condom. An unplanned pregnancy would not make things better.

"I need to get up." He reached between them, holding the condom in place as he pulled out. If he asked, maybe she'd stay, at least for a while.

She moved off him, and he left the warm bed to find a trash can. It took less than a minute, but when he came out of the bathroom, she'd already managed to pull on her thermals and had one foot in the leg of her pants. He stood there, hands on his hips watching her dress, wanting to ask her to stay. A pipe dream. He knew better.

"What?" she asked as she pulled a sweatshirt over her head.

"I didn't expect you to stay. But I didn't expect you to leave so soon either."

"We both knew what this was." She paused as if considering what she'd said. "At least I thought we did."

"I didn't do anything I didn't want to, if that's what you're asking."

"Okay." She stomped one foot into her boot and then the other, not exactly in a hurry, but not taking her time either. "We good then?"

He didn't quite know how to answer that. The sex, he couldn't complain about, and the memory of her riding him to completion had him starting to grow hard again. But he wanted more, and he knew she wasn't in any place to hear that. Not now. More than likely, not ever.

"Yeah, Mann, we're good."

He watched her go, the door latch clacking loud in the otherwise silent night. He still hadn't gotten used to how quiet it was on the ranch after sunset, besides the occasional yip of a passing pack of coyotes or the braying of Boomer's donkey in one of the far pastures.

As insane as it sounded, sometimes, he missed the explosion of mortar rounds in the distance. At least they had kept his mind in the present and not locked in the past.

As soon as she stepped off the porch, he threw on his clothes, not wanting to miss her when she left. He had no doubt she'd leave her cabin that night.

After cinching his belt around the rolled-up blankets, he pulled on his coat and leaned against the jamb of his open door, his arms crossed over his chest, trying to maintain some warmth. He waited five minutes, maybe ten, before her door opened, and she stepped outside. Her looking first to his cabin made him want to smile. At least he weighed on her mind.

"You weren't going to come get me were you." He left out the upward inflection at the end of his sentence. It wasn't a question. A bit of his annoyance with her slight crept in without him meaning for it to. He'd known this would happen. That's why he'd dressed quickly so he'd be ready when she left.

She glanced to her left, the direction she normally went to sneak out of her cabin because it took her away from his cabin before the trail doubled back on itself and veered toward the hot spring.

Turning back, she locked eyes with him. "You coming?"

———

BESIDES THE CRUNCH OF THEIR BOOTS ON THE ROCKS AND DIRT, they walked in silence. Clouds, thick and heavy with snow, blocked much of the light from the moon and stars. Mia broke out her headlamp.

She probably could have made it to the hot spring in the dark with her eyes closed, considering the number of times she'd trekked that trail, but she didn't want Matt to stumble in the dark and land his ass on a cactus. She wanted to get some sleep if she could, not spend the rest of the night picking cactus spines out of his butt.

By the time they made it to the hot spring, her eyes had grown droopy, the emotional and physical exertion made her want to curl up under the shelter of her tarp and sleep for the next week with a smoldering fire at her back.

Inviting Matt along turned out not to be all bad. He set up the tarp and the bedding while she started the fire. When the flames grew large enough, she added bigger branches then stripped to her long underwear. He did the same.

He slipped under the covers first, his back to the tarp and held open the unzipped sleeping bag.

"You don't want by the fire?" she asked.

"Your turn."

She collapsed on the ground beside him, and he snuggled up behind her, his arm loosely over her waist, not so tight it confined her, but just enough to let her know he hadn't left. If she'd had any energy and had thought to bring another condom, she might have jumped his bones again so that post-orgasmic sleep would quickly claim her.

But she was too tired to move, much less have sex again. She thought about scooting back, about molding her body to his, of taking his hand and joining it with hers and holding him in tight, but as much as she wanted that, she knew it would be too confining. She needed her space, as much as she resented that at times.

Even in her exhaustion, her brain fought sleep, her eyes

flicking open as the fire cracked and popped, and the embers floated skyward.

Matt's breathing evened out, but his body remained too rigid for him to be asleep. "Did it help?" he asked at last.

She knew he was referring to the sex. "It was just sex, Matt."

"Yeah. Sure." She didn't detect any petulance in his voice, but maybe it held a hint of frustration. She didn't know what he expected of her or how he thought the sex would have changed things. It wasn't that simple.

Her *issues* weren't that simple.

If they had been, that wide swath of men she'd hooked up with after her discharge would have healed her many times over.

"Despite what a lot of men think, dicks aren't the magic cure."

"Of course not." Amusement laced his words. "For it to be truly magical, I need to be able to use my mouth and hands, too."

Mia chuckled, loving that he could make her laugh after the day she'd had. She ran her hand down his forearm and twined her fingers loosely through his. Against her better judgment, she confessed, "It didn't help, but it was what I needed."

They lay there, both lost in their own thoughts.

Don't do this to him.

Don't drag him into your life when you have no intention of letting him stay.

Stay for what, she didn't know. What she did know was Matt had feelings for her. How deep those feelings ran, she had no clue. But sneaking into his room and searching for relief hadn't been fair to him.

He didn't exactly push you away.

But sex with Matt also wasn't the same as a nearly anonymous hookup. Nobody expected anything out of NSA, no strings attached, sex beside the physical release.

"This doesn't change anything." She didn't say it too loud, more of a reminder to herself than to him.

"You've already made that perfectly clear." His voice was thick with sleep, but clear. He grunted and rolled up onto his elbow and pressed a kiss to the exposed skin near her neck. "What do you think you're protecting me from?"

"Me," she managed. And all the bullshit and messiness that entailed.

A smart woman would pack up her gear and find another place to sleep. Somewhere where Matt couldn't make her want things she knew she couldn't have. After all, if he got to know her, *really* got to know her, he'd realize he couldn't love her.

She would fail him the same way she'd failed her parents. And if her parents couldn't love her unconditionally, how could anyone else?

"You think you're going to break my heart?"

The amusement in his voice had her rolling onto her back. He stared down at her, his face lit by the dying flames. He'd have to fall in love with her for her to break his heart. "I'm just trying to manage expectations."

"Consider them managed." He leaned down and kissed her. The briefest touch of his lips to hers, but it made her chest tight with its tenderness.

Fuck, she was in trouble here.

"And I think you need to let me worry about my heartbreak, okay? You've got plenty of other things to worry about without adding that to your list."

———

THEY FOUND ZEALAND STANDING IN FRONT OF THEIR CABIN DOOR

early the next morning as the sun started turning the black of night into a dark gray. The scowl on Zealand's face was unmistakable. The clouds still hung low. But weather reports claimed the worst of the weather should hold out until the end of the week.

Matt walked up his set of steps and Mia walked up hers as she and Zealand gave each other a nod.

"How's Mac?" Mia asked.

"The babies are fine for now, but her blood pressure is elevated, and the doctors are concerned about her developing eclampsia. They're keeping her for observation."

"But she's going to be okay?" Matt didn't know much about eclampsia, only that it could be dangerous for the mother and the babies if it went untreated.

"Should be," Zealand allowed. "They can deliver the babies early if they have to. She's far enough along that their lungs should be fully functional."

Matt didn't miss the way Mia sagged against the door, the information coming as a relief. She jerked her chin in the direction of the barn. "I'm going to grab a quick shower. I'll meet you guys up there as soon as I'm done. It won't take me long to saddle up."

"Sure." Matt watched her disappear inside. A hot shower sounded like heaven. And as much as he loved Mia's scent on his body, he couldn't go all day smelling her on him and remembering what she'd done to him and not get a hard-on. Riding horses all day with an erection wasn't his idea of fun.

He went to shoulder his way past Zealand, but his roommate didn't budge. Matt outweighed him in muscle, but he didn't kid himself that Zealand would be easy to take down. Matt glared at him. Zealand's scowl only dug deeper, drawing Zealand's thick brows together and wrinkling his forehead.

Matt crossed his arms over his chest. "What's wrong with you?"

Zealand shifted enough for Matt to scoot by. The door slammed behind him, and Matt spun around. "*What?*"

"What's going on with you and Mann?"

"That's none of your business."

"If it affects her ability to finish the program and her ability to stay the fuck out of jail, then I think it's everyone's business."

"You going to run to Jenna? Is that what you're saying? Lay out your suspicions."

Zealand set his hands on his hips and blew out a breath. "I just want what's best for her. That's all any of us want."

"And I don't?" If Matt didn't keep his voice down, Mia would hear their argument without having to leave her cabin.

"That's not what I'm saying."

Matt crowded Zealand's personal space. "Then what are you saying?"

"I'm saying I'm concerned. I'm saying I don't think you or she are thinking clearly."

Zealand stepped back, his stare unwavering. Matt stared back. They didn't have all day to spend in a pissing contest, not with the bad weather moving in and a bunch of cattle to bring down.

"We kissed."

Maybe admitting a little of what happened between them would get Zealand off Matt's ass. "But she's made it perfectly clear it's not going any further. Stop worrying."

That little confession didn't mollify Zealand the way Matt thought it would. If anything, it only pissed him off more. Zealand started pacing, but within the compact cabin, he only made it about three or four long strides before he had to turn around again.

Zealand stopped abruptly, with near murder in his eyes. The

table standing between them came as a relief. Zealand would have to go over the top of it to get to Matt if it came to a fight.

"I found the used condom, dumbass."

"Oh." A lungful of overheated air whooshed out of Matt. He rubbed the back of his neck, the muscles there hard as high-tension steel. A headache started radiating around his skull.

Zealand pulled out a chair and dropped down into it. Matt took the chair across from him. "It's not what you think."

"Why do people always say that when it is always exactly what people think?"

Matt cut him a look, but it bounced off Zealand like a rubber sword against a steel shield. "I didn't force her into it if that's what you think."

"Fuck, Bishop. If that's what I thought, this conversation would have started with my fist to your face."

"You're pretty protective of—"

"Somebody has to be." Zealand held his arms out wide, his incredulity nearly making the windows clatter in their frames.

"She came in here. On her own volition."

Zealand stood, his palms flat on the table as he leaned across. "But you didn't stop her."

Matt scrubbed his hands over his face. "No... I didn't." Then he met the heat of Zealand's gaze head on. "Am I the asshole, here? Fuck. I don't even know anymore. She matters, Zee. Much more than I ever expected she would. The last thing I want to do is hurt her."

He wasn't blowing smoke. Zealand must have sensed that because his expression softened, and he sat back down. "I just wanted to make sure you weren't just thinking with your dick. From the sound of it, she hasn't had enough people in her life that have made her a priority."

"We're on the same team here."

A knock came at the door, and Mia walked in without

waiting for a reply. "You girls done gossiping? We've got a long, cold day in the saddle ahead, and I'd rather get back before nightfall."

She stopped in front of the table, the door open, the freezing air rushing in as she glanced from Zealand to Matt and back again. "What's going on here?"

"Matt and I were just coming to an understanding."

"About me." She glanced between the two of them again. Neither one of them were brave enough to lie to her. To Zealand, she said, "I don't need a big brother to protect me."

"Too bad." Zealand stood and looped an arm around her neck and pressed a chaste kiss to her cheek as they walked toward the door. He chuckled when she shoved him away.

"Ewh, gross." With a crooked smile, she made a show of wiping off his kiss. "Boy spit."

Matt laughed and fell into step behind them. Mia had a family here, whether she wanted one or not.

7

———

THE WEEK FLEW BY IN A SERIES OF RIDES UP INTO THE HIGHER pastures bringing cattle down. By Friday, they'd also distributed round bales throughout the large pastures for the cattle, prepped the barn to keep the horses inside during the worst of it, and made sure they were stocked up on all the feed and groceries they'd need in case they were snowed in for a while.

The heavy blanket of gray clouds hung so low Mia thought she could reach up and rake her fingers through them. They'd be lucky if they were only snowed in for a few days.

Mia sat backward in one of her chairs. Matt took the chair on her left and Zealand took the one on her right. They ate their lunch and played a couple hands of poker, soaking up the warmth of the cabin. Between the days in the saddle out on the range and the nights out by the hot spring, Mia thought she might never thaw out.

What the hell was she going to do when the snowstorm came? She'd likely freeze if she camped out. But staying inside meant she'd likely have a panic attack.

Matt had accompanied her every night, and she felt guilty as hell that he braved the cold for her.

Matt bumped his knee against hers. She glanced up, and he bobbed his chin at the battered stack of cards in front of her. "Your deal."

She stuffed a grape into her mouth and started shuffling the cards. A knock came at their door.

"Come in," Zealand said.

Pepita stepped in, all wrapped up in her heavy coat, gloves on her hands, and her backpack slung over one shoulder. "Can I play?"

"What are you doing here?" Matt gave up his seat for her and liberated her of her heavy backpack. The backpack hit the floor with enough force to make the floor shudder beneath their feet. "Jesus, girl, how many dead bodies did you pack in there?"

Pepita rolled her eyes and stole a handful of Matt's pretzels. "No bodies. Though that would be much more interesting than a pile of biology, algebra, and social studies books. The school sent everyone home early because they didn't want the school busses on the road when the snow started. The teachers piled on the homework to make up for it. I can't wait until I'm grown up and can do whatever I want."

Mia scoffed. "Don't be in such a hurry. Adulthood isn't all it's cracked up to be."

"I'll take bills over solving for 'x' any day."

Matt handed Pepita a soda before she started drinking his.

"Plus, when I'm an adult," she said, "I can eat cake for breakfast, and no one is going to tell me no."

"She's not wrong," Zealand said.

Mia glanced up at Matt. "Want me to deal you in this round?"

"Sure," he said as he headed for the door. "I'll grab the other chair from our cabin."

He opened the door and found Jenna standing on the porch,

her hand raised, the color gone from her face. She stood, "What's wrong?"

Jenna's eyes landed on Pepita. "Good, you're here."

Pepita stopping eating Matt's lunch and said, "What is it?"

"The babies are coming."

Pepita and Zealand got to their feet, but Jenna held her hands up to stop them. "Mac's having some kind of problem. Hank didn't have time to go into it. They need to do a c-section, but they're going to have to fly her to Idaho for the surgery. The hospital there has a higher rated NICU, neo-natal intensive care unit."

———

"HANK ASKED YOU TO COME," JENNA TOLD ZEALAND. "THEY'RE already prepping Mac for the flight. Quinn says he can hold the chopper for you if you hurry."

Zealand put on his coat and grabbed his truck keys.

"We should go, too," Mia said.

"Hank asked if you two could stay here with Pepita. Sidney was already in town with Alby and Santos getting more supplies."

Alby and Santos were the Lazy S's two ranch hands.

"They dropped her off in Murdock, and Boomer is meeting her there. They're hoping to be able to drive through the pass before the snow starts falling. I was going to call my grandparents and head that way myself."

"Go," Matt said. "Between the four of us, I'm sure we can handle one precocious teenager."

"You going to be okay, here?" Jenna asked Pepita "I could stay—"

"I'm not a kid. I've stayed home alone before."

"But not overnight.'"

"How much trouble can one girl get in?" Pepita asked.

Zealand was already out the door. Matt eyed Pepita. "I hope that's a rhetorical question and you're not taking that as a challenge."

Pepita rolled her eyes. "I'm just going to curl up on the couch and watch movies and eat popcorn. I can't even Facetime my friends. The crappy internet is even crappier when the weather is this bad."

"Okay," Jenna said, though she didn't seem completely convinced. "You have my number in—"

"Chill. I've got everyone's number. I can take care of myself."

Matt glanced pointedly at Mia. "She sounds like someone else I know."

"Go." Matt shooed Jenna away. "We've got her. She's in good hands. Right, Mann?"

Jenna was already out the door when Matt glanced back at Mia. "Ri—"

"What's wrong with her?" Pepita scrambled to Mia's side, her hand raised but too afraid to touch her. "Why is she shaking like that?"

"Mann." Matt sat her down and went to one knee, his hand on her leg. "Do I need to call someone?"

His heart rate ramped up, even though deep down he knew she was okay. She had that faraway look in her eyes he'd seen before in other veterans who'd bumped into a situation that took them back to a time they'd rather not remember. He'd been there too many times himself.

Afraid Mia might devolve into a straight-out panic attack in front of Pepita, he turned his attention to the teen and said, "Why don't you head back to your cabin? We'll come by in a bit and check on you."

"You don't have to protect me from this," Pepita said. "I've seen it before with my dad. It doesn't happen very often anymore, but..." She let the rest of the sentence drop off and started gathering her stuff. "But I get it. Nobody likes it when others see them like that."

Matt helped Pepita with her backpack. "You've seen a lot. Understand a lot."

"Enough," Pepita allowed. She bumped her chin toward Mia. "Take care of her. You don't have to worry about me."

Before she left, Pepita said, "Come by later. Let me know she's okay?"

"Count on it, kid."

After Pepita left, Matt leaned back against the door. A few tiny flakes of snow had blown in. They stuck to the floor for a few seconds before melting. At the table, Mia shook, her arms crossed tightly across her abdomen.

He knew she'd be embarrassed for him to see her like that and thought about going back to his cabin and giving her her space. He was pretty certain that's what she'd want.

But what she wanted wasn't necessarily what she needed.

"Come on." He took her hand and led her over to the bed. He slid out of his boots and scooted against the wall.

She curled up beside him, her thoughts turned inward. As she laid her head in his lap, her shaking eased and her breathing didn't have that hitch to it anymore.

Wherever her mind had taken her, she was coming back to him. He wasn't going to pressure her to talk. But he was there to listen if she needed it.

He considered it a win that she hadn't shoved him away.

They stayed that way until the light started to fade, ice began to build against the window frames, and the panes of glass started to fog.

Mia's sweatshirt had ridden up, and Matt traced tiny circles on the inch of bare skin near her hip.

"You think the babies are going to be okay?" Mia asked. Her

voice came out no louder than a whisper, but he heard every word over the hum of her refrigerator and the intermittent whirr of the heater's fan.

Matt didn't want to sugar-coat it. If the hospital in Murdock needed to fly Mac to a hospital with a higher level NICU for the babies following an emergency c-section, things were probably looked a little tenuous.

He thought about texting Jenna to see if she had an update, but with the way the weather had moved in, the single bar of service he normally had at the cabin had vanished. And with no landline except up at the Big House, he didn't expect an update anytime soon.

"I'm sure they're doing all they can." Which was as truthful as he could manage.

She shifted again, rolling to her back as she looked up at him. The sweatshirt rode up higher, exposing one of her many vibrant tattoos. He skimmed a finger over her flank and decided to ask a question to take her mind off Mac and the babies.

"What's this a tattoo of?"

She trapped his hand against her skin.

"It's all right if you don't want to show me. I get it. Tattoos can be very personal. They all tell a story. Sometimes that story is that you were drunk and an idiot."

For the first time since Jenna had left, light returned to Mia's eyes. "This should be good."

He shrugged, though he couldn't hold back the smile. God, he'd been such a stupid, naïve kid back then, full of hormones and cum. He'd had way too much time on his hands, hanging with a bunch of kids as equally shiftless as him.

It definitely hadn't been his finest moment. But there had been worse.

"Wanna see?"

Mia rolled over, bracing an arm across his legs and resting

her head in her hand. The fact that the tattoo he'd questioned her about was now hidden wasn't lost on him.

"Show me."

He started unbuckling his pants.

She stopped him with a look. "Is this a trick you pull on all the girls so you can show off your dick?"

He chuckled. "No. It's just an unfortunate choice of locations... among other things."

She made a get-on-with-it motion with her hand. He unfastened his jeans and pushed the waistband of his underwear down, exposing the strip of skin just above his pubic bone.

She barked out a laugh then reached out to touch it. He willed himself not to go hard as her fingers ghosted over the amateurish lettering. He mostly managed.

"Wow... You really thought a lot of yourself."

She couldn't keep the laugh in, and Matt found himself laughing along with her. She had the most amazing laugh when she allowed herself to feel joy. It did funny things to Matt's chest, making it tight and hot all at the same time.

He let go of the waistband, hiding the tattoo as well as his teenaged indiscretion. "I was young and dumb. I've got no other excuse."

Mia waggled her brows. "Though there's something to be said for truth in advertising."

Matt threw back his head and laughed. "You don't think I should get it removed?"

Mia sat up. "Are you kidding me?"

Matt sobered. "No. I've gotten a lot of push back from women I've dated in the past."

"But that's what bad tattoos are for. To remind you of a time... you know..." She shrugged. "Before." Her mood shifted a fraction. "My vote says you keep it. If a woman can't appreciate your journey and how far you've come in your life, then she doesn't deserve you or what you've got going on below that tattoo."

He couldn't argue with that logic. Bumping his chin toward her body, he said, "Come clean, Mann. As tatted up as you are, you've got to have a few tattoos you regret."

"Don't laugh."

"No promises."

She rolled onto her belly and lifted up the back of her sweat-shirt just enough to expose the base of her spine. "Classic tramp stamp. My dad went off the rails when he saw it."

At the base of Mia's spine was a butterfly with flowering vines flowing around it. The line work looked like something a toddler scrawled with a crayon they'd gnawed on. "Please tell me you didn't pay for this."

"A friend did it with India ink and a sewing needle." She rolled onto her side again to face him.

Matt hissed in a breath. "You're lucky you didn't get leprosy, or Mad Cow disease, or whatever the fuck you get when you do stupid shit like that."

"I'm pretty sure that's not how those diseases work."

"Still..."

He liked the easiness between them. If only it could stay that way. "Which one is your favorite?"

"That's easy." She sat up and turned around on the bed, her back to him. "It's my back piece." She lifted her sweatshirt, exposing her back and shoulders.

The head of a magnificent dragon lay in the center of her back, its scaled body curving up and down and around on itself as it blew flames from between razor-sharp teeth. The attention to detail, the vibrant colors, the lines, the shading was some of the best work he'd ever seen.

He sat there stunned, unable to put words to a piece of art as beautiful as what lay before him. The amount of time she must have lain on the tattooist's table was more hours than he cared to contemplate.

She glanced at him over her shoulder as his dumbfounded silence dragged on. "You hate it." Reaching back, she started to tug her sweatshirt back into place, but he reached out to stop her.

"I don't hate it. I'm speechless."

"You don't think it's gross, or tacky, or unladylike, or—"

"I think it's *you*. Amazing. Beautiful. Captivating. Vibrant. *Original*."

He pressed a light kiss to her bare shoulder but didn't push it any farther. He wasn't trying to get into her pants, he was trying to get around her shields.

"Can I touch it?"

"You want to touch it?"

"Is that so surprising?"

"Most guys want me to keep my shirt on and pretend it's not there."

"Most guys are idiots."

Mia huffed out a laugh. She'd shown more true emotion in the past couple of days than she had the whole time they'd been on this ride together. Was he finally getting under her skin? Was she finally realizing he wasn't the enemy here?

"I'm glad you're not most guys."

"Careful, Mann. Someone overhears that, and they might think you like me."

She hung her head for a moment as if she hadn't heard the teasing in his tone. He traced the fine lines of the artwork from the intricate scales, to the sharp talons, to the billowy puffs of smoke coming from the beast's nostrils.

"You know," she said, her voice low so that only he could hear even though they were alone. "I wouldn't have come over to your cabin the way I did if you didn't mean something to me."

He met her eyes over her shoulder, her gaze unwavering as if she had a lot more she wanted to say, but when she glanced away in that heated moment, he knew she wouldn't voice it. Not yet anyway.

"I know," was all he said.

He continued his appreciation of her dragon—down her ribs, and over to her left side where it skirted the tattoo she'd hid from him earlier. Her hand went to her side again, blocking his view. He put his hand over hers, her skin almost superheated beneath his.

"Let me see." He kept his voice gentle, not a demand. More of a soft ask.

A whoosh of air escaped her lungs, and she slipped her hand from beneath his.

Before removing his hand, he said, "If you don't want to share—"

"It was the worst day of my life. It's not something I show people."

"Fair enough." Matt wouldn't push her boundaries any further. She'd already opened up more than he'd ever expected.

"But…" She held the hem of her sweatshirt up higher, fully exposing the tattoo on her flank.

The tattoo stole his breath, shredded his heart, and left a hollowness in his chest.

Above a date, instead of the typical fallen soldier cross with a helmet on the stock of a soldier's rifle with the barrel inside a pair of combat boots, there was an infant's knitted cap on top of a rattle set in a pair of baby booties.

———

"Jesus Christ," Matt choked out.

Breathe.

One long breath in. One long breath out. Once. Twice. Mia could get through this. Matt's fingers traced the outer edge of the tattoo as if afraid to touch it.

"This was while you were deployed."

Mia had to clear her throat, but it didn't keep her voice from cracking. "Yes."

He lay down in front of her, and she had to blink rapidly to keep him in focus.

"It was the same night my convoy was ambushed, and the building we sought cover in collapsed under RPG fire. We were stuck for hours in the dark before rescue came. Not all of us made it. I've never gotten over the claustrophobia that night brought on.

"Earlier that day, the baby's father took his anger out on me when he found out I was pregnant. He wasn't stupid enough to hit me where it would show. Turns out, he wasn't as divorced or as unattached as he'd said he was."

The muscles in Matt's jaw worked, and Mia had no doubt Frank would not have survived an encounter with Matt.

"Later that day, he assigned me to a resupply convoy. We were ambushed."

"Let me get this straight..." Matt's eyes turned to flint, though Mia knew that he didn't direct that anger on her. "Your superior officer, *the father of your child*, sent you on a mission when he knew you were pregnant—"

"To be fair, he had no way of knowing about the ambush."

"*To be fair?*" Matt sat up. "He had no right sending you out there when—"

Matt cut himself off before she could. She didn't want to debate what Frank should or shouldn't have done. Not that what he had done was right, but there had been a lot of things that had gone down in the desert between the two of them that never should have happened.

Talk about young and dumb.

But if she could talk to her younger self now...

"I don't know why I lost the baby. Whether it was from the punches he'd landed, the cave-in, or if it was something that would have happened anyway. But as soon as I'd found out I was pregnant, I'd wanted the baby. There was no question. Even if it affected my career."

"But you were dishonorably discharged."

"For confronting Frank after I'd been treated and released by the medics. I punched him in the face in front of a bunch of witnesses."

"What happened to him?"

"He's still in as far as I know. He got a slap on the wrist after the Secretary of Defense stepped in on his behalf. Apparently, the Secretary and Frank's father go back to West Point."

"Surely, you had other recourse."

She sat there, incredulous. Not only had she spilled all of her deepest, darkest, and most shameful secrets, the most unbelievable thing was that Matt wasn't *judging* her.

He wanted to *fight* for her. Even now when it was too late to change what had happened.

"He broke me. I didn't have it in me to fight for any kind of justice. I wanted it all to go away. I wanted to bury it in the past and forget it ever happened."

"That's not something you can forget," Matt said. From what he'd shared, he'd lost enough in his life to understand.

She shook her head.

"But it's part of what makes you you. Part of what brought you here and into my life. I'm sorry you had to go through that, but I'm not sorry that you're here."

Matt is different.

She'd thought Frank was, too. Thought Frank was worth the

risk to her career, never expecting the havoc it would wreck on her life.

By the way Matt was acting, he wanted more from her than she thought she could give.

And definitely more than she deserved.

"Matt—"

"Don't say it, Mia. I'm not asking for a chance. All I'm asking is you keep an open mind."

That he asked so little, meant so much.

He stuck his hand out. "Deal?"

Mia put her hand in his. "Deal."

His grin slowly spread as his cheeks reddened. He climbed out of the bed. That his simple joy in their agreement embarrassed him, she found endearing and cute as hell. It reminded her of another expression she wanted to see on his face.

One of satisfaction and ecstasy.

Matt shrugged into his coat. "Let's go check on Pepita, make sure she hasn't burned the place down or invited all her friends over to party."

Mia stomped into her boots. "Somehow, I don't think you have to worry about Pepita and her friends. They don't seem like the type to cause a lot of trouble."

Matt held open the door as Mia zipped up her coat and preceded him outside. "Don't be mistaken. It's the quiet ones who will fool you."

———

"WHAT THE HELL ARE YOU DOING?" MATT SAID AS HE STOMPED the snow off his boots on his way up Boomer's porch steps. The cabin door stood open, and Dink, Jenna's old cattle dog, sat shivering on the far side of the threshold.

Pepita stood on a porch chair, one arm wrapped around the

porch post, her phone in her outstretched hand pointing it at the heavy gray clouds.

She barely glanced at them when she said, "Trying to get this text to go through."

"No text is worth getting frostbite over." Mia held out her hand. Pepita took it with great reluctance and hopped off the chair.

A trench formed between Pepita's eyes, deep enough for a hiker to fall in and disappear.

Matt knew Pepita well enough to know something was off. "What's wrong?"

"Nothing's wrong." Pepita glanced at her phone.

"Wanna try that again?" Mia asked, "Because I'm calling bullshit on that."

A breeze kicked up, and Dink whined as a flurry of snowflakes blew in his face. Matt ushered them all into the cabin and closed the door behind him. He stalked over to the fireplace and stoked it, adding more logs for good measure.

Satisfied the people weren't going anywhere, Dink jumped on the couch and burrowed under a throw blanket until only the tip of his muzzle lay exposed.

Matt turned to find Pepita's nose buried in her phone again. Mia caught his eye and jerked her head toward the hiking backpack, bedroll, and pair of snowshoes near the front door that he hadn't noticed in his haste to warm up the cabin.

Glancing from the camping equipment to Pepita, dressed in snow pants, snow boots, and an extra heavy coat, he asked, "Where were you headed?"

Pepita lifted her eyes from her screen. The guilt on her face told Matt everything he needed to know.

With what must have been a similar read on the situation, Mia caught Pepita by the hood of her coat and deposited her into one of the seats at the kitchen table.

"I can't fucking believe this," Mia said.

"It's a dollar a curse word." Pepita inclined her head to the glass jar nearly full of bills in the center of the table. "I'm thinking from the way this talk has started, you might want to put a twenty in and pay up front the way my dad does."

"She doesn't have the kind of cash on hand she'll need for this conversation," Matt said. "She may have to PayPal it to you."

Mia thumped Matt in the chest with the back of her hand, and he swallowed down the grunt of surprise, not wanting to give her the satisfaction. "Can you be serious for half a second? Boomer and Sidney are at the hospital on the other side of the mountains, and we almost lost their kid. Pretty sure I'd get kicked out of the program after that, no matter how many times I shared my feelings."

"You weren't going to lose me." The petulance crept into Pepita's tone. Or was that just normal teenager? "I was going to leave a note and let my parents know where I went. But I figured with the snow, I would have made it back before the pass had cleared and they made it home."

Mia sunk into the chair across from her, and Matt took the chair between them in the very likely chance he had to play referee. Where was a damn whistle when he needed one?

"Let me guess," Matt said. "This has something to do with a boy."

By the surprised way Pepita blinked at him, he'd nailed it on the first guess.

Mia glanced behind her at the camping gear. "Make that two boys."

"You were going to meet Charlie and Zach and go on that camping trip, weren't you?" At that moment, Matt was ecstatic that he didn't have kids. And especially glad he didn't have a teenage daughter.

"Wait," Mia said, "I thought the camping trip was canceled

because of the weather. It's supposed to dump a bunch of snow over the next forty-eight hours."

Pepita unzipped her coat as a bead of sweat trickled down her temple. The cabin had warmed up since he'd added more logs on the fire, but Matt figured that sweat had more to do with the internal battle waging inside her than the ambient temperature of the room.

"You going to come clean or are we going to have to resort to extreme measures?" Matt asked.

"Like water torture or breaking my fingers one by one?"

"I was thinking more like calling your parents," Mia said, "but finger breaking works for me, too. Keeps us from having to brave the cold to find a landline."

Pepita slumped in her seat, and Matt knew she would come clean. "Promise not to tell my parents?"

"Absolutely not." Mia's tone held zero room for negotiation.

Though Matt had seen Mia's softer side, if it had been him sitting across from Mia, with that uncompromising expression on her face, he'd probably talk, too. Good thing Mia wasn't his therapist.

Pepita grumbled, "Fine. I was supposed to be meeting the boys. We didn't want to miss out on the camping trip. We've been looking forward to it for so long."

"The camping trip your parents already told you you couldn't go on. The same trip that had been canceled because of bad weather, the same—" Mia stopped talking, probably because her tone lost all semblance of calm. Stopping just short of shouting.

"It's only snow. It snows here all the time. I don't see what's so different about now."

"Besides the fact you don't have permission?"

Matt almost chuckled at Pepita's roasting. He kinda felt sorry for the kid even though she totally had it coming.

"Okay, okay, I get that it was a totally stupid thing to try to do, and that my parents will probably ground me until I'm twenty—"

"I'm thinking more like thirty, but you're getting the general idea," Matt said.

"But still… We were only going to be gone two nights."

Mia slapped a palm to her forehead. "And likely gotten hypothermia in the process."

"You taught us how to start a fire. And we were bringing food, and water filtration units, and—"

"Starting a fire with dry kindling is much easier than starting one when everything's wet from the snow," Mia said.

A fire wouldn't have been the kids' only challenge. "Do you know how to use a map? A compass?"

"Kinda."

Mia bit her lower lip, probably to keep from having to populate Pepita's PayPal account. He'd gladly loan Mia some money. He had quite a bit socked away. The markets had been good to him while he'd been deployed.

"But I don't need a map. I know the way. Charlie and Zach were supposed to have been by an hour ago to come get me."

Mia cut Matt a look, and he knew exactly what she was thinking—if the boys had been on time, Pepita would have run off with them, and Boomer would have taken Mia and Matt out. No question about that.

"Everything looks different when it's covered in snow. It's easy to get lost and turned around out there." Even for a bunch of Marines who'd had survival training. Christ that had been one FUBARed mission.

"I'm not completely stupid," Pepita said. "The ranch has a satellite phone. I was going to bring it in case of an emergency."

"Great." Mia's sarcasm bled through. "How do you think rescuers are going to reach you if the weather is so bad they can't send a rescue helo? Quinn would be grounded during a snowstorm."

Pepita sank further into her chair, her chin nearly level with the table top, her voice small when she said, "Does it count for anything that I'd tried to text Charlie and tell him I'd decided not to go?"

"Maybe." Mia motioned for Pepita's phone, needing, like Matt did, to see proof.

Dragging her cell phone out of the pocket of her snow pants, Pepita thumbed in her lock screen code and showed Mia and Matt the message. "I can't get it to send. That's what I was trying to do out on the porch when you guys came over."

Matt stood. "I think we should go up to the Big House. You can try calling them from there. We'll also see if we can get hold of your parents and get an update on Mac and the babies."

Pepita stood with reluctance. "Are you going to tell them about... you know." She gave a toss of her head toward the camping equipment.

Mia stood as well. "I think they have enough to worry about right now. Don't you think, Matt?"

Mia had this expression on her face, one that said, *come on, let's give the kid a break.* From what Mia had shared of her own experience, she'd been in a few scrapes in her life and probably could relate to Pepita's reckless escapades more than Matt could.

"For now. But as soon as everyone is home safe, you need to come clean. Deal?" Matt held out his fist for Pepita to bump.

They knocked knuckles and got geared up to brave the cold on the long walk up to the Big House. At the last second, Pepita stuck her head back in the door and called for Dink. He wagged his tail and whined but refused to leave the warmth of the cabin.

Matt closed the door. "At least one of us has good sense."

8

———

THE TWO RESIDENT RANCH HANDS, ALBY AND SANTOS, MET UP with Matt, Mia, and Pepita as the men came out of the barn after finishing the evening chores.

Alby was tall, thin, blond, and irreverent. Santos had dark hair, a slighter build, and was one of the hardest workers Mia had ever known. If she had half of Santos' energy, she'd be set for life. As it was, just watching him tirelessly work exhausted her.

"You boys done for the night?" Matt asked as they all climbed up the steps of the Big House's wraparound porch and entered the house through the back door by the kitchen.

It wasn't really that big of a house, but it was the original house on the property with a second story added on some years ago, making it bigger than the foreman's house as well as any of the cabins.

The five of them toed out of their snow-dampened boots, brushed the snow off their jackets, and hung their coats on the hooks by the back door.

"Everyone is tucked up tight in the barn except Eli. We left the door to his run open, since he'd find a way to escape anyway." Santos dropped his cowboy hat on one of the hooks. "Any news on Mac?"

"We were just about to call," Pepita said. "We can sit at the table and put Dad on speaker phone."

A long bar separated the kitchen from a dining table that could sit ten, even if it were a little cramped. Pepita gabbed the phone off the wall and sat on the far side of the table between Alby and Santos, her de facto 'uncles' since the men had been working for the Lazy S since before Pepita ever came along.

Matt and Mia settled across from them as Pepita punched in her dad's number. Right when Mia thought it would roll to voicemail, Boomer picked up, sounding breathless and harried. "'Lo."

"It's me," Pepita said.

There came a hesitation before Boomer said, "What's wrong?"

Pepita sent a furtive glance at Mia and then Matt. Alby and Santos didn't miss the quick exchange, and Alby mouthed, "What?"

Mia shook her head but bumped her chin toward Pepita.

"Hello, hello," Boomer said, "You still there?"

"Um... yeah, sorry. Nothing's wrong." Pepita's voice climbed with the lie as if she expected Mia or Matt to call her out on it over the phone. When they didn't, Pepita's shoulders relaxed, and the furrow between her eyes eased.

"We were calling to see if you had an update on Mac," Mia said.

Alby leaned toward the phone laying in the center of the table. "Are we uncles yet?"

"Babies are here. The nurses swept them off to the NICU. Mac's still in surgery. Something about a complication. I don't know. I'm trying to find Hank and get more info. They kicked him out of the surgery suite right after the babies were born so the doctors could tend to Mac."

Mia's stomach went into free fall, and the air in the room somehow became thinner and harder to breath.

They are going to be okay. They have to be.

Matt must have sensed her distress, because he reached a hand beneath the table and gave her thigh a light squeeze. That simple touch grounded her, keeping her mind from spinning out of control and going into worse-case-scenario mode. Mac and the babies were in the best place they could be. The doctors wouldn't have flown her to the other hospital if that weren't the case.

Pepita started to ask a question but was cut off by Boomer and a lot of voices in the background.

"I found Hank." The other voices became muffled so Boomer must have found a quieter spot. "I've got to go. Everything is good there, right?"

"Never better," Matt said. "Take care, and don't worry about anything here. We'll try to call in the morning."

"And give Mac and the babies a hug for me," Pepita said.

"Will do. Love you, kid," Boomer said. "And thanks guys, for everything."

"We're family," Alby said. "No thanks necessary."

After they'd hung up, Santos glanced around the table, his gaze narrowing on Pepita. "Spill."

Matt didn't hesitate to out her. "She was about to sneak out and go camping with her friends for a few days."

"Hey!" Pepita had the teenaged nerve to be outraged. "You promised you wouldn't tell."

"We promised not to tell your parents before you had the chance to when they got home. This is different."

Alby whistled and shook his head. "Oh, girl, I don't envy you."

"It's not going to be that bad," Pepita said, though it sounded like she was trying to convince herself of that instead of them.

Santos chuckled, his smile warm. "You realize this is your father you're talking about."

"If you survive him, you've got your momma to face next." Alby looked like he was enjoying spinning Pepita up.

The kid did kind of deserve it. Of course, it was better to have her parents pissed at her and ground her for the rest of her life than for her to freeze to death.

Pepita ran her hands down her face. "I'm dead, aren't I?"

Alby put his arm around her. "Cheer up, munchkin, think of all the muscles you'll build when your mom makes you pay with stall cleaning duty."

Groaning, Pepita said, "Don't remind me. My shoulders are still sore from that time I got caught when Charlie talked me into skipping one of my classes."

"Speaking of your friends," Mia said. "Did your text ever go through? It'll be dark soon. I don't like the idea of them running around out there in the dark."

"I told them I got busted and they needed to go home." She held her phone up, her messaging app open. "I got enough service when I got to the top of the hill on the way to the house."

"They haven't answered," Mia noticed. Matt still had his hand on her leg, and she had to admit she didn't hate the continued contact, especially when her emotions were all in an upheaval about the babies and Mac. "That was twenty minutes ago."

Pepita pointed to the screen. "But it's marked as read. Charlie isn't always the best at texting back, and he's especially bad when he's around Zach because Zach teases him every time he texts me."

Santos' stomach growled. "I'm starved. I think there's still some pulled pork in the fridge from dinner the other night. Anyone hungry?"

"I could eat," Matt said. Though there hadn't been a time since Mia had known Matt that his appetite had failed him.

"After that, we'll get some of your stuff from your cabin," Santos told Pepita as he got up and headed for the refrigerator.

"Why?" Her tone said, *have you lost your mind?*

"Because you're sleeping in the house with us." Alby ruffled her hair on his way to the kitchen to help Santos reheat dinner.

Matt couldn't keep the grin off his face, but he didn't chime in.

"I'm not going to run off."

"I know you're not," Santos said. His voice came out even and reasonable as if they were discussing the merits of split reins versus loop reins.

Alby said, "Because I'll be in the guest room at the top of the stairs, next to the creaky floorboards."

Santos unearthed the pulled pork. "And I'll be sleeping on the couch."

Pepita phone clattered on the table when it dropped from her hands. "I'll never get to stay home alone overnight by myself."

———

AFTER DINNER, ON THEIR WALK BACK TO THEIR CABINS, MIA ZIPPED up her coat and ducked her head against the snow flurries and driving wind. More than six inches of snow had fallen. The clouds almost obliterated the moon, and they walked in near pitch darkness with only her far-off muted porch light available to guide them.

She suppressed a shiver, though it wasn't only the cold affecting her. She couldn't get Mac and the babies off her mind.

Had Mac made it out of surgery okay? Was she stable? Were the babies adjusting? Were they breathing okay?

Mia couldn't imagine the thought of Hank losing any one of them. It would crush him.

And she couldn't imagine the emotional tornado he was going through. Hell, her emotions kept her off kilter, her senses dulled, her mind muddled, and she had only known them a few months.

"We're here."

At her cabin door. She shook her head coming back to herself. She hadn't even realized they'd made it back already. "We are."

She didn't make a move to go inside and escape from him the way she would have only a week or so ago. But her brain already wrestled with her most immediate problem, and she didn't have the bandwidth to explore her growing attraction to him.

He took one of her hands in his, a spark of humor laced with an undercurrent of seriousness lay in his eyes. Or maybe that was just the play of the porch light.

Mia had a pretty solid idea of what was coming next, so she decided to beat him to it. "And this is where you tell me not to sleep out tonight."

"It is."

"That it would be irresponsible to risk leaving the cabin on a night like tonight."

A slow grin spread across his face, but there was a sadness to it as well that she couldn't quite place. "Look who has learned to read minds."

"I'm not sure it's a mind-reading thing as much as an *I've heard it all before* kind of thing."

He leaned in closer, and where she might have taken a step back were he any other person, she found herself leaning in as well. The condensation in their breath mingled, their lips nearly touching. It wouldn't take anything more than shifting her weight for her to kiss him. Or him to kiss her.

"Stay inside, Mia. Where you're safe." He cupped her face and brushed his thumb across her cheek. Her face heated with the earnest way his gaze grazed her features. In her head, she heard the unspoken part of his statement as if he'd said it out loud. The part that said, *do it for me.*

If she could do it for *anyone*, she would do it for him, but she couldn't even do it for herself, much less another person. The drive to be outside when darkness fell was invariably too strong to control.

"I'll do my best." It was all she could think to say, even though in the past, her best had never been good enough.

A second passed, two. He nodded, the doubt clear in his eyes. "Goodnight, Mia."

"'Night."

She didn't move to go inside until he dropped his hand. She wanted to let her guard down and lean into his gentle touch. But that wouldn't make anything better, or the long, sleepless night ahead any shorter.

Only after she'd let herself into the cabin did she hear the clump of his boots recede as he left.

You should have invited him in. For cards, or conversation... or sex.

Maybe, but it wasn't his job to babysit her and help her pass the time. No sense in getting used to having him around. In a week or so, if she managed not to flunk out of the program, they'd both be looking at the Lazy S in their rearview mirror.

If she were ever going to destroy her demons, she had to conquer them alone.

But even with all of her cabin's lights blazing, the music app on her phone playing, a deck of cards in her hands as she played hand after hand after hand of solitaire, the walls inched inward, the beat of the drums in the songs sounding more and more like the thump of heavy mortar rounds raining down.

Her abdominal muscles clenched, involuntarily bracing for an impact that wouldn't come. Mia's head knew that, but she couldn't get that message to the rest of her body.

The adrenaline that had been slowly seeping in as the night wore on dumped a load into her veins with enough heat to keep a small town from freezing, much less keep one woman warm out in the snow. Her heartrate jacked up, a fluttering pace that left her lightheaded and nauseous.

And the walls. Closer and closer still.

She had to get out.

Get out!

She stood abruptly. The chair skidded out from beneath her and tumbled over, clattering on the wood floor. Striding to the pegs by her bed, she shoved her arms through the sleeves of her coat and stamped her feet into her boots before the incessant drive to be outside sent her out before she could get properly dressed.

At the last second, she grabbed her pack, always at the ready beside her door, and stepped out onto her porch. The slap of the cold air stole her breath and froze her feet in place before she could run. She shrugged into her backpack, the weight of it feeling as if she'd come home.

She took a step before she caught movement in her peripheral vision. *Matt.* Mia watched through the window as he walked to his kitchen, dressed in nothing but a body hugging pair of thermals that did nothing to hide what he packed downstairs. He scratched his hand through his dark hair, mussing it up even more.

He looked like he'd been sleeping.

She didn't know how long she stood there and watched.

Long enough for his pot of coffee to finish brewing.

Long enough for him to lean against the counter and drink from his mug as he stared out his window, unseeing.

Long enough for her incessant compulsion to be outside to wane.

Long enough for her to start to shiver and come to her senses.

Go to him.

He may not be the answer for always. But maybe he's the answer for right now.

Unless you want to go to sleep in the snow and maybe never wake up.

"Fuck that." Mia dumped her pack on her porch and let her internal momentum take her to his cabin before her mind caught up with her body.

She didn't knock.

Once inside, she closed the door behind her and leaned her weight against it as if that would prevent her from leaving as abruptly as she'd come.

"Hey," was all he said as he set his mug on the counter beside him. She appreciated he didn't say much more.

On her way to him, she stripped out of her coat and tossed it over the back of one of the chairs. It hit, then slid to the floor. Matt looked so damn sexy standing there, his hands braced on the counter on either side of him, the muscles in his forearms flexing as if he had a death grip on the laminate countertop.

His eyes locked on her. His gaze followed her the whole way, every foot, every inch, until she straddled one of his legs. Was that her own breathing she heard, or was it his?

Without breaking eye contact, he picked up the mug and held it out for her. His voice croaked, and he cleared his throat. "Coffee? It's decaf."

That she had that kind of power over a man like Matt, power to make his voice weak, emboldened her. Not that she needed much encouragement when she was in the kind of mood she was in. She didn't consider the sex she sought to be self-destructive. Not when seducing someone beat the hell out of freezing to death.

She took the mug and set it back on the counter beside him. "I didn't come here for coffee."

Even without the anonymity of a dark room, she didn't flinch, didn't feel the flush of heat rise in her cheeks as she told Matt the reason she'd come to see him.

Considering their history, she doubt it came as a surprise.

She didn't quite know what she'd expected him to say, but "On one condition" hadn't even made her possibilities list.

Mia cracked a smile.

He didn't.

She should go. Just grab her coat and her pack. Leave while she still had the chance. The way he looked at her, with understanding and compassion, might prove much more dangerous than a couple feet of snow and subfreezing temperatures.

But she didn't leave, and even though she feared Matt's clarification, she said, "Now you're starting to worry me."

She offered a half smile to let him know she wasn't entirely serious, but that lick of apprehension remained.

"You let me drive."

Narrowing her eyes at him, Mia said, "You didn't like me being in control?"

He spread his legs and settled her between them, locking his hands behind her waist. She should have felt trapped and anxious and restless, but something about his calm energy knocked the edges off her more challenging emotions. Like a human Xanax.

Luckily, he didn't have the power to dull *everything*. In fact, that hum low in her belly, heating her core, made her want to get him naked.

His warm chuckle brought goosebumps to her arms and sent a luscious shiver down her spine. He leaned in and whispered, "It was hot as hell. But now it's my turn to bring you pleasure."

As much as the proposition excited her, it also amplified her anxiety. Ever since the building had collapsed on her, she needed to not ever be that helpless again. Not that sex and being trapped under the rubble of a crumbled building were the same things, but the thought of making herself physically that vulnerable again scared the ever-loving crap out of her.

What about your emotional vulnerability?

Men taking from her wasn't anything new. She was just wholly unaccustomed to a man *giving*.

Which may have been more a function of who she'd allowed herself to be with.

Matt isn't like other men. His demand *was one of the many ways he's demonstrating he's different.*

Wasn't it Jenna who'd said she needed to learn to open up?

Yeah, well, Jenna probably wasn't talking about sex.

Mia sucked in a deep breath and blew it out. "Okay."

Fuck. Did that word just come out of her mouth? Could she take it back? Could she—

Matt hooked his hands on her hips and gave her a light shake, the amusement lighting his eyes. And fuck if he didn't have the most amazing eyes. They drew her in, an invitation she found impossible to refuse.

"Breathe, Mann. You can even use a safe word. Pick a word. You say it, and everything stops. No questions. No having to talk about it or explain. Just that one word and it ends."

They weren't about to engage in an elaborate role-play scenario, he wasn't tying her up or spanking her or doing anything remotely kinky that reasonable people might need a safe word for, but...

One word would be like having a virtual key.

Or a kill switch.

It put *her* in control, even when technically she would hand that control over to him.

Would that work?

"Pineapple," she said.

Holding her chin between his thumb and forefinger, he pressed a kiss to her lips. "Pineapple it is."

His grin landed somewhere between amused and delighted and proud. Her chest tightened, amazed she could put that kind of smile on his face.

He dropped his hands and stepped away. "Hang on. I'll be right back."

———

MATT WENT TO THE BATHROOM TO FIND ZEALAND'S CONDOM stash. He really needed to buy his own, but he'd had little chance to run to the store in the past week, and in reality, he'd never expected Mia to come back.

Had hoped.

But hadn't expected.

He was up for anything if it meant she didn't head out into the cold. If she'd insisted on taking control, he would have gladly given it to her. If she'd wanted to strip him naked and tie him up and hang him from the rafters, he'd have done that, too. All that mattered was her safety... and his sanity.

And if all Mia wants from you is sex, what then? Because it has been more than sex for you, even from the beginning.

Then it will have to be enough. He grabbed a strip of condoms and slammed the cabinet door under the sink.

"Everything okay in there?"

"Fine. Everything's fine." He closed his eyes and took a deep breath, trying to pinpoint the source of his unexpected anger and frustration.

Bracing his hands on the wall, he stared at himself in the oval mirror mounted above the sink. Worry lines creased his forehead, and the furrow between his brow now more of a constant companion these past few weeks. "Everything's fine," he muttered to himself.

But he knew a lie when he heard it.

How could everything be fine when, he'd likely never see her again after the program ended?

How would he know how she's doing?

How would he know she was safe?

You won't.

That realization only made the worry lines more prominent.

If he didn't get back out there, he feared she'd have second thoughts and leave. He slammed his hand down on the light switch, tilting his head from side to side to work out some of the kinks created by the constant tension before stepping back into the main room of the cabin.

Mia caught one look at his face and said, "If you've changed your mind—"

"It's not that." Matt immediately schooled his expression. His anger and his frustration weren't directed at her so much as at the situation.

"You can't fix this," Mia said as if she knew the dark direction his mind had turned. She took the strip of condoms from his hand, tossed them on the bed behind her, and stepped into his embrace, wrapping her arms around his neck.

"You can't fix *me*." She nibbled at the scruff on his chin. "And as much as it aggravates me sometimes, I also appreciate that you're the kind of person who needs to try." She traced a line from his jaw to his ear with her lips and whispered, "Like I've said before. I don't need a white knight."

He muttered a curse as her lips and tongue continued to tease. "How about a lowly master of arms? Or a blacksmith who exists only to sharpen your blades and prepare you for battle?"

She pulled back to see his eyes. Her soft and sexy chuckle wreaked havoc on the boner building in his pants. He needed to reach down and adjust himself but knew what she said next was infinitely more important. He kept his full attention on her, not wanting to miss any of the nuance of her answer.

"Like a sidekick? Or a medieval emotional caddie, picking up and putting down the tools I'll need to slay my metaphorical demons?"

"Your humble servant," he said, unable to keep the grin off his face. "At the very least you could tame and train the demons and make them heel at your feet."

"Hmmm." Her gaze shifted, becoming unfocused as she considered his words. But now wasn't the time to tame or train or fight, it was time to connect.

"But first... do you remember your safe word?"

"Pineapple."

Taking her hand, he led her to the bed. "Lights on or off?"

She tensed, and her grip on his hand tightened almost imperceptibly. "On. It's never great, but the brighter the better."

Shaking the tension out of her shoulders, a sly smile spread on her face. He appreciated the effort she put in to trying to make him feel comfortable with her anxiety, and he saw a flash of the tremendous effort it took her to try to live in the moment.

"Unless you're too embarrassed for me to see you naked in the light," she said.

He took a step back. Public nudity had never been an issue for him, much to the chagrin of his high school principal when Matt's best friend dared him to streak across the football field at half-time during the crowning of the prom king and queen.

At least he'd been able to talk the cops out of arresting him.

He grinned. "You've still got a lot to learn about me."

He hooked his thumbs into the waistband of his thermal bottoms and swept them down his legs. After his shower, he hadn't bothered putting on underwear. Subconsciously, he might have hoped Mia would find her way to his cabin again.

Her eyes didn't scan his body, instead her gaze zeroed in on his junk. He admired the unabashed way that she eyed him. Kicking his thermals away, he gave his semi-hard cock a few strokes before reaching out to her.

"*Mmmm.* Do that again," she said as she took his hand.

Holy hell, he loved her dirty mind. It took all his inner strength to not reach down and do exactly what she'd said. "Nope. I'm the one calling the shots, remember?"

Her lower lip shot out. Fuck she was adorable when she pouted. But she probably wouldn't appreciate hearing that, so he kept it to himself.

Reaching for the hem of her sweatshirt, he raised a brow at her and waited for her nod before continuing. He may have been the one ostensibly with the control, but she was the one who'd granted it to him. Slowly, he pulled the soft material up and over her head. Then he went for the next layer and the layer after that.

She'd dressed to spend the night outside.

Undefined emotions swirled in his head, threatening to kill the moment. He slammed and locked the hurricane door in his mind trying to remain present and not dwell on what she'd been prepared to do.

After nearly as many layers on her lower half, she stood before him in nothing more than her panties and bra. She reached behind herself to flick the clasp of her bra, but he stopped her. "This isn't a race. No one is in a hurry here."

She closed the gap between them and reached for his dick. "Speak for yourself."

He jumped back when all he wanted to do was step into the touch. "Ah, ah, ah."

This night would be about giving, and teasing, and building desire until everything else in the world faded to black—the fear, the anxiety, the uncertainty.

All those negatives blotted, erased.

For a moment at the worst.

For a night at best.

With his hands on her hips, keeping her at arm's length so she couldn't put her hands on him and derail his plans. He turned her and stepped her back until her calves hit the mattress and she dropped onto the bed.

"On your stomach," he ordered.

She rolled over, and he crawled onto the bed and stretched out beside her, his back to the wall and his head resting in his upturned hand as he gazed down at her body. She turned her head toward him.

The fleeting apprehension in her eyes quickly turned to heat as he laid his bent leg over the back of her thighs, his cock brushing against her hip, leaving a smear of precum behind. "Close your eyes."

9

WITH HER EYES CLOSED, MIA CONCENTRATED ON THE SOUND OF Matt's breathing, the creak of the bed as he shifted, and the light gasps of what sounded like amazement as they escaped from his lips.

With a finger, he drew a feather-light line down her side from the ball of her shoulder to the pinch of her waist. She expected him to go further, down her ass, the crease of her thigh, but if the last few months have taught her anything about Matt, it was that he never did the expected, at least not where it concerned her.

She'd come to him for release, to forget, to distract, to fuck and run...

But he wasn't having any of it. At least not on her schedule.

You ceded control. Now allow yourself to be present in that decision.

She blew out a breath and released the tension she'd been holding, giving in to Matt's gentle touch.

"There you go," he said, placing a kiss on the ball of her shoulder, the nidus of where his touch had started.

His fingers, his hands, his lips explored every inch of skin she possessed. The pressure shifting from light to heavy to barely there. He spread her legs, caressing her inner thighs, but always stopping short of where she wanted his touch most.

As he found erogenous zones she never knew existed, the tension returned to her shoulders. A different kind of tension. The kind of tension that brought goosebumps to her flesh, heat to her core, and made her squirm against the mattress, searching for the pressure and friction to find her release.

A firm hand on her hip stopped her. "I didn't say you could do that."

She wiggled her ass. "You need to fuck me already."

Matt chuckled and scooted her toward the center of the narrow bed before straddling her thighs. He braced his weight on his hands by her head, kissing, nibbling, and sucking on the tender area where her shoulder joined her neck.

His heavy cock aligned with the crease of her ass, and she pressed back against him, trying to shatter his control, and force him to give her what she wanted.

He hissed in a breath, the intake of air a cool rush at the top of her spine. He raised his hips, breaking the contact with her body. Resting his forehead on her shoulder blade he said, "You're naughty."

"I'm horny."

He nibbled on her earlobe. It tickled. Her shoulders scrunched up and she giggled. He dropped his voice and whispered in her ear. "Don't worry, Mann. I'm going to get you off."

"I haven't got all night."

He laughed at the teasing petulance in her voice. "That's where you're wrong. We've not only got all night, but if the snow continues, probably all of tomorrow as well."

Sitting back on the tops of her thighs, he ran his hands down the curve of her ass, giving it a squeeze. She immediately pressed back against his palms, the drops of his precum dripping onto her skin. He seemed mesmerized by her ass. What was he thinking? What was his fantasy?

"Roll over," he said.

He lifted his weight off her legs, and she followed orders. He settled in again at the top of her thighs, the tip of his cock near her belly button. Unlike her heavily tattooed back, the front of her was relatively untattooed, only her flanks, parts of her ribs, and the base of her neck were marked where the dragon and memorial tattoo overflowed.

He drew a hand down the center of her body, his eyes drinking her in, a finger skimming over the flat mole on the point of her hip. "You're flawless."

She tossed him a devilish smile, and before he realized what she planned, she reached down and slid her thumb across his slit and brought it to her lips, tasting him.

"*Fuck me*," Matt groaned, as he braced his weight on his forearms and covered her mouth with his. Her arms locked around his neck, holding him there. "I love tasting myself on your tongue. It drives me mad."

But that's what he'd done to her. Teasing her and taunting her and driving her ever closer to insanity.

Angling his head, he took the kiss deeper. His body caged her to the bed, but she took control of the kiss, stealing his breath and testing his resolve.

He pulled back, his chest heaving as he fought for oxygen. A knowing grin spread on his face. "I know what you're trying to do, but—" He panted and caught his breath. "...it's not going to work."

He shifted off her, and she didn't bother hiding her disapproval. "Seriously?"

She felt the deep timbre of his chuckle in her bones as he stretched out on his side next to her, his finger trailing a line down her sternum from her collarbone, driving her crazy by skipping all the good parts. Her nipples wanted to cry when his hand passed them by without even slowing.

Was Matt even human?

If he were cut, would the skin peel back and reveal the gleaming machinery beneath?

Her abdominal muscles quivered as he trailed his fingertips over them. She laid a hand on the back of his head trying to gently guide him to where she wanted him next.

"Throw a poor girl a bone, Bishop."

He huffed out a laugh but allowed her to guide his head toward the good bits below. Following her direction, he moved between her legs, his shoulders bumping against the back of her open thighs, his breath hot and enticing.

She glanced down at him, at the fire in his eyes, the mischievous slash of his grin. She was in for a good time.

Her eyes never left his as he hooked his arms around her thighs. Partly as a challenge, but mostly because of the positive, affirming energy he generated.

She couldn't take her fucking eyes off him.

He nipped at her inner thigh, the scrape of his dark stubble electrifying her already over-stimulated nerves. Her hands started to shake. His eyes smoldered, watching her watch him, as he stuck out his tongue and swiped it through her slick folds. Her head fell back, her spine arched, and she ground against his mouth.

Wanting, needing so much more.

Her hands fisted in his hair, egging him on. By the way he licked and sucked and nibbled, he needed little encouragement. Then his concentration centered on her clit as he slid first one finger and then two inside her. She didn't hide the groans of pleasure, wanting him to hear how much he turned her on.

Riding his fingers, she felt the first spasms start to build. The tingling in her nerves transformed from zaps to heat. Had short circuited?

She wanted him in her, but she didn't beg, knowing he wouldn't give in to her that easily.

A man on a mission, he clearly had a plan he was determined to execute to pleasured perfection.

Her heavy breathing turned to quick pants and soft cries, her body stiffening with her pending orgasm. He kept up the licking, the sucking, the finger fucking apparently content to let her ride it to the end.

Then he groaned, long and low, the guttural vibration on her clit the fuel for the flesh and bone fire he'd built. She cried out, her fingers fisting in his hair, in the sheets, as she rode out the sensations, her body shaking and quaking.

As her breathing slowed and her body relaxed, Matt crawled out from between her legs with a smug smile on his face. He kissed his way up her midline, catching her eye. "I love the way you taste. I'm never going to get enough of you."

She couldn't imagine a forever, not just with him, but with *anybody.*

Instead of letting his words send her into a tailspin about a future with or without him, for once she forced herself to remain in the moment, focusing on him and his delight at the pleasure he'd brought her.

But truth be told, after that delicious orgasm, and with that talented tongue and those amazing lips working their way toward her neglected breasts, the only thing her mind focused on was Matt's sensuous journey up her body.

The cooling sheen of sweat on her skin brought goosebumps skittering up her torso and skating down her thighs.

Trailing the tip of his tongue across the swell of her breast, he teased her taut nipple and sucked it into his mouth. Those nerve endings that had skipped offline jolted back to life, and she reached for him.

Her fingers closed around his cock, and he stilled. His grunt of pure bliss would have had her reaching for the condoms if it meant she didn't have to let go of him to grab them. Since he didn't move away, or order her to let him go, she took advantage of the situation. Of him.

He stopped his exquisite torture of her breast and rested his forehead on her shoulder, his breath already coming faster as she worked the slick precum over the sensitive head and down his girthy shaft. "I should tell you to stop, but it feels so fucking good."

"Guess you have less control than you thought."

He thrust into her hand, his eyes falling closed before they opened again, his gaze glassy and unfocused. "I don't crave the control as much as I want you out of your head."

She let her fingertips trail up his length. "You put this to good use, I promise I won't be thinking of anything but you."

"Good," he said, and just when she thought he'd reach for the condoms, he pulled out of her reach. "But until then, I'm going to make you come a couple more times."

———

Mia lay limp on the bed beneath him, drops of sweat beading at her temple that he wanted to lick away.

"Half of me wants to curl into a ball and sleep for the next week, the other half wants the dicking you've promised me."

"I would have thought that after the number of orgasms I gave you, you'd be satisfied."

"You'd be wrong."

Her eyes drifted closed as he skimmed a hand across her

belly, the muscles fluttering under his touch. "If you want to sleep—"

"No." She opened her eyes, then reached for a condom, and handed it to him. "You promised... unless you're finished? This isn't all about me. If you want a break—"

He leaned in, pressed a kiss to her lips and went to his knees. "We're just getting started."

Precum leaked from the end of his dick, his balls drawn up so tight that he'd be lucky if he got the condom on before he came. Shifting his mind off the dull throb of his cock, he tore the package open and rolled on the condom.

As much as he'd enjoyed it when Mia had come into his dark cabin and taken what she'd needed from him, seeing her in the light, witnessing the intention in her expression, the focus on him instead of whatever had been in her head that she'd been running from, made him glad to have this time with her. He wanted to see the pleasure on her face when the orgasm rolled through her body with him inside her.

Moving between her legs, he settled over the top of her, bracing his weight on his arms. The intensity of her need for sex seemed banked, but as she ground against him, he knew she wouldn't remain that way for long.

She wrapped her arms around his shoulders and pulled him down until his full body weight pinned her.

"I don't want to crush you," he said as he tried to take some of his weight off her.

"I like you on top of me. I thought it would make me spin out of control, feel trapped and claustrophobic, but instead I feel connected and safe." She hid her face in his shoulder. "I know that must sound crazy or insane, but—"

He rose, just enough to see her face. "It makes perfect sense to me."

He kissed her. Kissed away the flush in her cheeks until they heated with something more than embarrassment. Reaching down, he lined himself up with her entrance and eased inside, loving the tight warmth, the slick slide, and the way her eyes rolled up like a window shade at dawn.

She surged up into him, using her hands on his shoulders for leverage to take him deep. His breath caught, his heart thudding out an impossible rhythm.

But in that space, he also knew he wouldn't last long, not with her legs locked behind his back, demanding more. His heavy balls slapped against her with each stroke. With musk and sex in the air, the potent mix of scent and sensation had the base of his spine tingling with his impending climax.

Rising on his haunches, he hooked his hands on her hips, the new angle making her gasp and her walls clench around him. Her breath came in puffs, and the encouraging grip she had on his thighs made him go faster.

"Harder." Her bottom lip caught between her teeth.

He dropped to his hands, driving deep, giving her everything he had until his strokes got erratic, and he shuddered and came. She continued to milk him, and as he started to return to his senses, he reached between them and sent her falling over the edge one last time.

"Oh, fuck," Mia moaned as her breathing leveled out.

"That felt so fucking good." He kissed her, then pulled out and rolled off her.

There was a softness in her eyes he'd never seen before. A softness he didn't think had anything to do with her sated exhaustion. It was as if she'd seen a side of him that he'd never expected to show her.

Or maybe he was the crazy one here.

Crazy about her.

Suddenly he felt more exposed and vulnerable that he ever

would have if he'd stood naked in the middle of that football field with a thousand friends and football fans staring on.

"I gotta take care of this condom," he said, more as an excuse to give himself some space, than the pressing need to clean himself up.

She watched as he clambered over her and padded into the bathroom. He tossed the condom in the trash. He splashed water on his face. He braved looking at himself in the mirror again. All he saw was a man who was gone for a woman.

Which was nuts. He could have sex without falling for someone.

Yeah, but you've been tumbling for a long time. She just broke your fall.

The sex shouldn't have changed anything, but something inside him had shifted, and inherently he knew everything had changed.

He just had no clue what that meant.

By the time he came out of the bathroom, Mia lay curled up on her side, her hands tucked up under her chin, her chest rising and falling in a slow, steady rate. He wanted to crawl into the bed behind her, pull her up against his chest, and wrap them up in the blanket, but for the first time since he'd known her, she was asleep...

Inside...

At night.

A small miracle.

He wouldn't risk waking her for anything.

Slipping into some sweatpants, Matt took one of the blankets off the top bunk and wrapped it around his shoulders. From a drawer in the kitchen, he grabbed a deck of cards and sat at the table, more focused on Mia sleeping than what cards he drew.

He half-heartedly cheated his way through three games of solitaire, the occasional glance behind him at the unused bed had him wondering how much sleep he might be able to get before she woke. Between his brain rolling on endorphins from the sex, and the past few hardworking days around the ranch, he'd been riding a rollercoaster physically and emotionally.

He gathered up the cards and glanced at the empty bunk again. If he could steal maybe an hour or two of shut eye, more of a short snooze than a combat nap, he'd be good to go for a while longer.

Across the room, Mia stiffened, or maybe it was her whimper that caught his attention first. Her body jerked, and her eyes flew open. Her feet hit the floor before he could make it over to the bed.

He dropped down to his knees in front of her. "I'm here. You're safe."

Through the hand he laid on her leg, her tension zipped through him like a deadly contagion, kicking his heart into a frenetic rhythm. If that's what had been transmitted to him, he couldn't imagine the intensity of the anxiety coursing through her.

The muscles in her leg bunched as if she were about to run. Mia sucked in a deep breath and held it, keeping herself from hyperventilating. The technique worked, but when you were in the throes of a panic attack, reason and logic and training sometimes were too slippery to hang on to.

"That's it," he said with a calmness he flat-out faked. "Breathe in and out. Slow and easy."

She mimicked his breathing and by the time he circled her wrist with his hand and laid a finger on her pulse, her rate started ticking down toward normal. She ran a hand down her face, the short sleep doing nothing to ease the faint bruising under her eyes that only stress and a prolonged lack of sleep could stamp into someone's features.

"Yusef. Do you still think of him?" she asked. He must have

had a confused look on his face because she added, "The boy you couldn't save. Do you still think of him all the time?"

He didn't understand where she was going with that line of questioning, but he went with it, willing to do anything to distract her, even if it meant putting himself in a headspace he generally tried to avoid.

Which is why you should go there. Jenna knows what she's talking about. Maybe after almost three months, it's time to internalize Healing Horses' teachings and not just nod and go along, doing the bare minimum.

Matt pulled one of his T-shirts out of the locker at the foot of his bed and slipped it over Mia's head.

He climbed onto the bed and bunched up his pillow before laying down. Taking her hand, he guided her until she stretched out facing him. He wanted to pull her closer but didn't want her feeling trapped. "Every damn day."

―――――――

"Keep talking," Mia said.

Her heart lived in her throat, and it only by focusing on Matt's face, the compassion in his eyes, and his thumb circling on her exposed hip that she kept the walls from crashing in.

Mia shivered, and he adjusted the blanket over her legs.

All softness left his expression, and her heart skipped, fearing what he'd say next. "On the bad days..." His throat worked, and his eyes got glassy. He ran his finger down her jawline, not to arouse it seemed, but more as a grounding touch. "On the bad days, all I see are his last moments over and over and over again. And I dwell on the unfairness of life, on how evil licks at the edges, taking bigger and bigger bites until one day I fear we'll all be consumed."

What little he'd shared of his past made her believe that not all his memories of Yusef were bad. Taking his hand, she pressed a kiss to the center of his palm, to the hand that had brought her so much pleasure and comfort. "And on the good days?"

Clearing his throat, Matt said, "On the good days, I can see his mischievous smile, hear the peel of his infectious laugh, see him dodging away from one of my teammates as they snuck in a game of tag."

His gaze drifted away. Unfocused. The way gazes do when people are buried deep in their thoughts, reliving a moment. The upward curve of his lips made her want to smile at the memories along with him.

Gradually, her heart relocated to her chest. If she listened to his words closely enough, she could mostly ignore the erratic thrum of her pulse, the buzz of anxiety beneath her skin, her heightened anxiety, and the need to run that being indoors at night always brought.

"Sometimes I wish I'd never befriended him. Other times, I feel so fortunate to have had a chance to care about him."

"A double-edged sword can cut just as deep from either side."

The skin around his eyes crinkled, and he smiled.

"What?"

"Where did you get your philosophy degree?"

"Asshole." Chuckling, she skimmed a cold foot along his shin. He hissed in a breath. But he shifted enough for her to slip her foot between his calves to warm her toes. Goosebumps erupted on her arms, but she didn't want to cover herself and risk feeling trapped.

She tried hard to ignore that it was the middle of the night and somehow, she was still indoors. Of course, trying not to think about it made her think about it, and—

"*Mann*," Matt said, with a tone that indicated he'd been

unsuccessful in drawing her attention. "Tell me about your urban climbing. Was the church your first?"

"My first? It was a transmission tower." No wonder her parents still questioned her choices and found them all lacking.

He slapped a hand to his forehand and ran it down the length of his face, his scruff making a scratching sound as his fingers brushed through it. Shifting, her thighs rubbed together and the slight chaff his whiskers had left down there made heat pool, even though her bones and muscles and mind were too fatigued to initiate sex even if she'd wanted it.

A wave of exhaustion overcame her, and she fought to keep her eyes open. Not so bad that she needed toothpicks to hold them open, but close.

"How high did you climb?"

"Almost to the top. I don't know how high it was, but high enough that the hum of the lines drowned out the sounds of the birds. The static electricity raised all the hair on my arms, and the wind made the top slightly sway."

"All without safety equipment, I'm assuming?"

"I was fifteen. I didn't have the money for stuff like that, even if I'd have had a way of getting it. Besides, the climb had been a spur of the moment thing. And I've been trying to free climb higher and higher ever since."

She inched closer until her knees bumped his and their elbows on the pillows touched, as she tried to steal body heat from a man who felt more like a furnace than a human.

"Were you always a daredevil?"

"I don't know. Maybe? I don't feel like I'm taking uncalculated risks, but my mom tells about how she found me on top of the refrigerator when I was three. I don't think I could determine a reliable risk/reward assessment at that age."

"Mia?" She opened her eyes to find Matt smiling down on her. "Go to sleep, you can't even keep your eyes open."

But she couldn't sleep. Knew she wouldn't. And she'd just gotten over the one panic attack. She didn't want to wake to another. Though bone weary, it seemed less tiring staying awake than risking sleep.

"I'm just going to close my eyes. But I'm not going to sleep."

"Then, neither am I." He kissed her forehead. "Let go, Mia. It's okay. I've got you."

But she couldn't let go. "You keep talking. Tell me about your favorite memory from your days in the service."

Matt huffed out a laugh. "Fuck. Okay. There was this time early in basic training, all of us guys didn't know shit, and the kid in the bunk beside me..."

The words Matt spoke faded in and out, too soft for her to catch their meaning, but the gruff tones, the warm chuckles, the calm circles he drew on her hip all had her sinking deeper into her pillow and a mattress so narrow that part of her ass hung over the edge, but—

She jerked awake, and one of Matt's strong arms tightened around her waist.

"I'm here. You're safe."

The blanket only covered her legs, but she was almost too warm. She must have shifted when she'd dozed because she found herself laying partially on top of him, one of her legs between his, her arm folded across his chest, her chin on her hand as she looked up at him. Red infused the whites of his eyes as if he'd stayed up all night.

His morning wood lay trapped beneath her hip, but he was ignoring it, so she did too.

Morning.

She shifted and stared out one of the front windows. The black night had grayed out to early dawn.

He kissed her lips, just a light brush. "You did it."

The pride in his voice made the backs of her eyes sting.

Stupid. It wasn't like she'd cured cancer or was the first woman to take a step onto Mars. She'd just managed to spend a few hours in a cabin with the lights on all night.

So little.

So monumental.

If she squinted hard enough, maybe she could catch a glimmer of her path forward. One that didn't have her sleeping the rest of her life under the stars.

A grin spread across her face until the balls of her cheeks started to ache. "I did. Thank you."

"I'll always have your back, as long as you'll let me."

Could she let him? Did she dare? The last time she let herself depend on a man...

Stop. It.

Matt hasn't let you down.

Yet.

Not 'yet.' Period.

He gave her a light pat on the ass. "Let's get up. I have a feeling today is going to be a great day."

10

<hr>

THE STOMP OF A BOOT ON THE PORCH STEP WARNED MATT A FEW
seconds before Pepita barreled through the door all bundled up
in her heavy coat and snow boots.

He turned at the last second, putting his back to the door as
he stuffed his semi-hard dick into his pants. Mia grabbed for the
blanket to cover herself.

"Ooops." Instead of heading right back out the door, Pepita
stayed. At least she spun around. "*Awkwaaard.*"

Matt reached for his shirt and tossed Mia her bra and
panties. "Pepita—"

"Don't say it."

"Don't say what?" Mia's voice came out muffled as she pulled
her sweatshirt over her head.

"Don't say 'It isn't what it looks like.' I'm not a kid. It's exactly
what it looks like. And I get it, Mia. Matt's not bad looking if
you're into old guys."

Old guys. Hell, he hadn't even hit thirty-five. He swallowed
his chuckle. "What are you doing here?"

She huffed out an exasperated breath. "Can I, like, turn
around yet?"

He glanced over at Mia who was in the middle of pulling up her pants. She nodded.

"You can turn around."

Pepita had a flush on her face, but by the wideness of her eyes and the way she kept glancing at her phone, it wasn't from embarrassment from walking in on them.

"Have a seat." Mia held out a chair before Matt could think to say anything. "What's going on? Alby and Santos okay?"

"They're fine. I think. I guess. They were already up doing chores by the time I woke up. But my problem isn't with them."

Pepita looked like she wanted to spit the rest of it out, but something held her back.

"Keep going," Mia said.

Pepita sucked in a huge breath of the cold cabin air and blew it out. "I can't get ahold of Charlie or Zach."

Pepita didn't relax into the seat, she sat on one bent leg, the other foot still on the floor as if ready to make a dash for it.

"It's probably just the snowstorm not letting the signal through." Matt leaned against the counter as Mia took the chair across from Pepita.

If anything, the snowfall had only worsened overnight. And with the sky not getting appreciably lighter as the sun continued to rise, the accumulation would likely get worse.

"That's what I thought, too, so I called their cells from the landline at the house and they didn't answer. Last night I'd texted Charlie and told him to let me know when they got home. I never heard back."

Matt exchanged a look with Mia, pushing the heel of his hand to the center of his sternum from where the sudden tightness stemmed.

"What was that look?" Pepita glanced between the two of them. If anything, they'd only made Pepita more worried. "That's not a good look."

"Nothing." Matt stepped over to the table. "I'm sure everything is fine. We'll call their parents—"

"I already talked to them. Charlie's parents think he's at Zach's, and Zach's parents think he's at Charlie's. Which means that they aren't at either and their parents have no idea that they took off camping and now I have no idea where they are or if they are okay or—"

Pepita's sentences ran together, and Matt had a hard time keeping up. That, and if she didn't calm down, she would likely pass out from oxygen deprivation.

"Take a breath." Matt laid a steadying hand on Pepita's slim shoulder, the red dissipating from her complexion after taking a few gulping breaths.

Tears filled her eyes. "I don't know what to do. We'd made a pact not to tell our parents and… they're my friends."

"Their parents need to know," Mia said. The utter calm with which Mia spoke had Pepita nodding, and her freak-out factor appeared to ratchet down to merely near-freak-out levels. "This isn't something you can keep from them. I'm sure the boys are fine, but we need to make sure."

Pepita deflated in front of them, her shoulders sagging as she slid down in the seat. "They're going to be so mad."

Matt wanted to say, 'better than dead,' but caught himself in time. He patted her shoulder. "Come on. We'll help you notify their parents."

"And the sheriff," Mia added, more to him than Pepita. He caught the look in her eyes and knew as well as Mia did that those boys could be in serious danger if they hadn't already frozen overnight.

As soon as Matt and Mia layered up, they followed Pepita up to the Big House and started making phone calls.

The sheriff called back shortly after they'd eaten breakfast. Charlie and Zach's parents had been unable to locate the boys, so the sheriff was organizing a search party. He wanted Matt and Mia to bring Pepita in for an interview to gather more information.

Matt tracked down Alby and Santos, explained what had happened. Then Matt, Mia, and Pepita loaded up in one of the ranch vehicles. Luckily, the truck Dale and Lottie had left behind when they'd fled to Florida for the winter came equipped with four-wheel drive.

Matt drove, and Mia sat beside him. Pepita settled in the back, leaning forward with her arms draped over each of the front seats.

"You need to sit back and buckle up," Mia said.

"We're not even going ten miles an hour. And we haven't even made it off the ranch yet."

Mia cut her a look, and Pepita slunk back. The telltale click of the seatbelt told him she'd buckled up. He glanced at Pepita in the rearview mirror as she swiped her frazzled hair out of her face and worried her lower lip with her teeth. If she weren't careful, she'd make herself bleed.

"This is all my fault." The guilt in Pepita's voice made Matt's heart ache for her. She wasn't the only one responsible for the boys, but she must feel like she was. "I should have talked them out of it instead of trying to go."

"They wouldn't have listened." Matt knew that deep down in his marrow. He'd been a boy like them once. Determined to prove himself. Pride and ego and testosterone got in the way of clear thinking too many times in adolescence, and the boys weren't immune. "You did the right thing. You stayed home. You kept tabs on them. You got help when you needed to."

"I should have called their parents last night. Maybe if they knew then—"

"You thought they were headed home. You had no reason to think otherwise."

Pepita's hands fisted in her dark hair, her skin mottled red as she held back her fears. A sound escaped her, part exasperation, part defeat. "I'm so dead. When my dad finds out, I'm going to wish he'd ground me for the rest of my life. Maybe you two can take me with you when the program is over. I don't eat much. I'll do my homework without you having to get on to me about it. I'll clean up your place. I can do dishes, and I can cook some amazing Mexican food if you like that kind of thing—"

Matt knew Pepita wouldn't run. It was just her fear and anxiety talking.

Instead of giving Pepita reassurance that she wouldn't have to leave home, Mia said, "Matt and I aren't going to the same place after the program."

Pepita's hands dropped into her lap, the utter confusion on her face would have been comical in almost any other situation. Matt did his best to keep his own expression neutral. Why couldn't he and Mia leave the program together? Nothing was stopping them.

"Well that's stupid," Pepita said.

Agreed.

He left the ranch road and slid onto the unplowed highway. The falling snow came down in sheets cutting the visibility to nearly zero. If he could have risked taking his hands off the wheel, he would have given Pepita a fist bump.

"We're not together," Mia said.

"But—"

Mia didn't let Pepita finish her thought. "It was... what you saw... it was nothing."

"*Nothing?*" The word escaped Matt's throat, and he wanted to throw a grappling hook at it and yank it back, hating the stark vulnerability in that one fucking word.

Nothing.

If what they'd shared the night before was nothing, it was

the most *something* a nothing had ever been before in his entire life.

Did Mia feel *anything*?

Matt chanced a quick glance at Mia, a *what the fuck?* rise to one of his brows.

In the back seat, he heard Pepita's softly mutter, "*Awkwaaard.*"

———

MIA FOLLOWED MATT AND PEPITA INTO THE SHERIFF'S OFFICE. A deputy immediately took them back to speak with Sheriff St. John. The whole time, Mia couldn't get that look Matt sent her before they'd left the truck out of her mind, his 'nothing?' a hollow echo in her head, that arched brow mocking, disbelieving, and *hurt*.

But it hadn't been anything but sex.

Ha. If it had only been sex, you wouldn't have stayed. You wouldn't have wanted his heat, or needed to hear his voice, or craved his touch. Lie to him all you want, but you can't lie to yourself.

Stop it.

Kids were in danger, their safety infinitely more important than a status she could update on social media.

Does this mean you're acknowledging that there is a relationship, however fragile and fucked-up it might be?

Maybe.

But that was as committed as she was willing to get for the time being. There would be plenty of time to dwell on it later.

The hum of activity in the bullpen area of the small station brought Mia out of the thoughts she'd rather not be thinking. In the center of the room, two long tables had been pushed together, a map spread out on top.

A tall man glanced up.

"Pepita Wilcox is here," the deputy who'd led them back said.

"Hey, Sheriff," Pepita said, her voice shy, almost embarrassed.

Apparently, no stranger to Pepita and presumably the rest of the clan at the Lazy S, he pulled her in for a quick side-hug. "How you holding up, sweetheart?"

"I messed up," she said. The tears she'd held back all morning fell.

With a hand under her chin, the sheriff looked down at her, the compassion in his eyes not what Mia had expected to see. "Don't beat yourself up. We're going to find them. Okay?"

Pepita nodded, and another deputy caught St. John's attention. "Sheriff, we don't have the manpower for the search. Morris called in sick, Roberts got trapped on the other side of the pass on his day off, and—"

"Call over to Bison County. Get Sheriff Day on the phone, see if he's got some people he can spare."

"On it, Sheriff." The deputy picked up the phone on her desk.

With a hand on Pepita's shoulder, St. John led them away from the small group of deputies, doing their best to organize a search when they had no idea where to even begin.

The four of them squeezed into St. John's office, and he closed the door behind him, keeping the activity behind them to a dull roar.

The Sheriff took the seat on the far side of his desk. Mia and Pepita took the two chairs across from him, and Matt leaned against the large window overlooking the rest of the station, crossing his arms over his chest.

"Why don't you start by telling me where the three of you had planned on going." St. John didn't waste any time.

He had a quiet, trusting authority, and Mia appreciated that he kept his calm and didn't put undue pressure on Pepita even though every second that ticked by played against the boys' survival.

Pepita told him of the boys' plans to pick her up and then go to one of the hunting cabins past some place called Eagle Point. "We were only going to be there for two nights."

"You talking about Green Meadow cabin?"

After hesitating, Pepita said, "I guess?"

"You can't guess," Mia said. "You have to know. Otherwise you could be sending the search party in the wrong direction."

"I heard that it's the one past that curvy creek and… that one tree that got knocked down but kept growing."

"You *heard*?"

Pepita glanced behind her at Matt and said, "I haven't actually been there."

This after Pepita had told them she knew the way. The frustration on Matt face was as quick to read as a kindergarten primer with all the pages ripped out.

"Pepita, sweetheart." St. John's patience seemed limitless considering the circumstances. "That doesn't help narrow anything down. Here."

He pulled out a map and spread it out on his desk. It didn't have the same detail and topography of the map spread out in the bullpen, but it would probably do. St. John pointed out the Lazy S, Charlie's and Zach's homes, as well as the trail leading up to the Green Meadow cabin.

"The reason I ask," St. John said, "is that there are four cabins up that way."

Pepita's voice squeaked. "Four?"

After circling Green Meadow on the map, he circled the three other, mostly abandoned cabins. "Once you're past Eagle Point, the trails split off."

The prospect of finding Zach and Charlie in a timely

manner, looked worse and worse, especially with the sheriff's department so shorthanded. Mia had a very bad feeling. "There's no telling which way they could have gone."

"Maybe they aren't even in the mountains." Matt pointed to the trail the boys would have most likely taken to get to the Lazy S. "They were supposed to pick Pepita up yesterday afternoon, but never showed. They could have gotten stuck somewhere along this trail."

Which still would have been bad considering most of the country along that trail consisted of rolling hills with little place to hole up once the weather turned bad. Mia would know. She'd walked a lot of that area over the past few months.

"Can't you just get a helicopter to fly over and find them?" Pepita asked.

"Lieutenants Powell and his co-pilot are grounded in Idaho, from what I've heard."

"That was because Quinn flew Mac to the hospital. She and the babies were having some kind of problem. Mom and Dad are there too. And Hank and Jenna."

St. John glanced between Mia and Matt. "Is she okay?"

"Last we heard, the babies were in the NICU, and Mac was still in surgery with complications. We haven't had a chance to get an update." Mia's stomach churned. With all that had happened since Pepita had stormed into their cabin, Mac and the babies had momentarily fallen off her radar.

They needed to call Boomer for an update as soon as St. John released them.

St. John turned his attention back to Pepita. "Anything else you can tell us?"

"They only had the one snowmobile, but we'd planned on taking snowshoes, so I assume they had theirs with them."

"What about any kind of protection from wildlife?"

Pepita shook her head. "No. Zach said his dad would notice

if his rifle was gone, and Hank and my dad keep ours locked up. The boys have hunting knives, but nothing else. I was supposed to bring the satellite phone in case we got into any trouble."

St. John slowly shook his head as he took in all the pertinent information. He stood at last and held his hand out for Matt and Mia to shake. "Okay. I appreciate you coming in. As soon as I know anything I'll let—"

"We're searching, too, Sheriff." Matt shot Mia a quick glance for confirmation.

Mia nodded. Their helping in the search was never in question. All they needed were orders of where to go. That she and Matt thought the same went far in her book.

Pepita stood as well. "Great. The ranch has a snowmobile. It's old, but it works. My stuff is still packed and—"

Matt clamped a hand down on Pepita's shoulder, not enough to hurt, but enough to get her attention. "Not so fast, kid."

"You're not going anywhere besides home," Mia said. "Your dad doesn't need anything else to worry about right now."

"But—"

"You're staying at the ranch even if Alby and Santos have to lock you in one of the stalls." By the expression on Matt's face, he was only half joking. "Tell us where you want us to search, Sheriff."

At St. John's hesitation, Mia said, "You need our help. You know that."

A muscle ticked in St. John's jaw as he considered their offer, which had actually been more of a demand. "It's dangerous out there. The weather will only get worse."

"Which is why we need to get out there and bring those boys home." Matt wouldn't be put off. "Show us where you want us."

"Fine," St. John said, as if it had taken everything for him to agree. "Follow me."

IT WAS ALMOST NOON BY THE TIME THEY'D GOTTEN AN UPDATE ON Mac and the babies—who were all doing as well as could be expected. The snow made the drive an excruciatingly slow crawl back to the ranch. Despite the snow falling harder and faster as the day wore on, the clouds only darkened.

So much so that Matt considered searching for the boys by himself. He didn't like the idea of Mia out there on the trail with him in a snowstorm. If things went well, they could search the area between the ranch and the boys' homes and the near cabin and get back before dark.

If things went well.

Which was why he wanted Mia to stay, because it likely wouldn't.

Alby and Santos met them at Pepita's cabin with a freshly fueled snowmobile and provisions from the Big House.

Pepita came out from her parents' bedroom, her arms loaded down with snow gear. "These should fit you, Matt. My dad's about your size." To Mia, she said, "You sure you don't need anything? My mom has snow pants and stuff."

"I've got my own gear, thanks."

Santos spread a topo map out on the table. "This is the area you're going to search, but I wanted to show you something." He pointed to a spot on the map where the topographical lines stacked up, indicating a steep incline and a narrow passage between two plateaus. "With all the snow, it's easy to lose your bearings if you don't know where you're going. This spot here, it's a few miles past Eagle Point and it can be mistaken for the trail up to Bear Tooth pass.

"It doesn't really have a name, but we've found some of our cattle up that way. There's a dilapidated cabin up there. I don't even know if it's still standing since last year, but you can only get there on foot. If the boys aren't at Bear Tooth pass, you should check there before heading back."

"Will do." Mia folded up the map and stuck it into the inside pocket of her jacket.

Matt headed for Boomer's gun safe in the corner of the room. Boomer had given Matt the code after relaying the update on Mac. The safe about equaled the size of Fort Knox, and Matt couldn't help his low whistle of appreciation upon opening it. Boomer had a thing for guns.

Something the two of them had in common.

Mia peered around him. "I know all these weapons must make you hard, Bishop, but we gotta get on the trail."

He chuckled. What made him even harder was her talking about his dick and thinking of what they'd done with it the night before.

There's nothing between us.

Those words Mia had spoken rattled around in his head, and he lost his smile. Now wasn't the time to think about what they weren't. Or what last night had meant. Or what, if any, future they did or didn't have together.

He grabbed a rifle and the ammo to go with it. He wouldn't expect to have any problems in this kind of weather with bears or moose or wolves, but he wasn't taking a chance. Again, he thought about trying to get her to stay behind. "Hey, Mia, maybe you should—"

There must have been something in his tone that gave his thoughts away because she stripped the ammo from his hand and said, "Don't say it."

With a guiding hand on the back of Mia's neck, he said to Santos, Alby, and Pepita, "Give us a minute, will you?"

The three nodded, and he practically heard Pepita's unspoken 'awkwaaard' lay clear in her eyes. He ushered Mia into the master bedroom and closed the door behind him.

Mia made it as far as the bed before spinning around. The rustic room was compact and only a couple of feet separated them.

"*What?*" she said.

"I was waiting for you to lay into me."

"I was waiting to see if you had the balls to say I should stay here before I did. You know, give you the benefit of the doubt."

He laid the rifle on the bed and took her hand, the fierceness and the fight never wavering in her eyes. He wouldn't win the argument to keep her back on the ranch. She wasn't that kind of woman, and he supposed he wouldn't love her like he did if she had been.

Fuck. *Love*

He didn't fight the realization. It just… was.

"It's dangerous, Mia."

"You don't think I fucking know that? Or that we're standing in here fighting while those kids could be out there freezing."

It was hard to argue against her point, but his heart—

A knock came at the door, and through it Pepita said, "The Sheriff is on the satellite phone. He wants to talk to you guys."

Matt turned and opened the door. Pepita handed over the phone. "I've got you on speaker, Sheriff. Mia is here as well."

"I received an updated weather report, and with the mess that's moving in, I can't in good conscience send you two out there. We've got some guys from Bison County trying to make it over. We'll do what we can with what we've got."

"We want to go," Mia said. "We're packed and we're ready."

"Sorry. I can't send civilians out there."

Matt wanted to roll his eyes. "Sheriff, we're not your regular civilians."

"I'm sorry," St. John said again. "I need you two to step down, the power of the storm—"

Matt hit end on the call, cutting St. John off mid-sentence.

He was going. And there wasn't anything the Sheriff could do to stop them. He tried one last time with Mia. "I can do this alone, Mia."

"I'm not letting you white-knight this, Bishop. Not by yourself."

During the phone conversation with St. John, Pepita had backed out of the room, though the door remained open. Though at this point, he didn't give a flying fuck who heard them.

"Why?" He didn't know if he was asking why she felt she needed to go, or why she wouldn't let him go alone. A subtle difference, but it was there.

"You've got my back, Matt. What makes you think I don't have yours?"

Maybe the whole 'nothing between us' thing, though Matt didn't voice it. He would be stupid to conflate loyalty with love.

And it was okay that she didn't feel for him what he felt for her. She'd get there in her own time... or she wouldn't.

He took a step back, allowing her question to drop. "Let's go then. While we still have some visibility."

11

MIA HAD LONG SINCE LOST THE FEELING IN HER TOES, AND THE only reason her fingers hadn't gone numb was because she had them wrapped around Matt's waist beneath his warm jacket. There may have been a time in her life when Mia had been colder, but she couldn't remember when.

If someone had told her they were in the middle of another ice age, she would have believed them. And the idea of a woolly mammoth popping up from behind a falling curtain of snow didn't seem too far out of the realm of possibility.

They spent a couple of hours searching the trail between the ranch and the boys' houses. Along the way, there had been no trail to follow, not from a snowmobile, not footprints, hell, there hadn't even been any wildlife tracks either. Of course, with the snowfall dumping down on them, these huge fluffy flakes that built layer upon layer, it came as no surprise they saw no other signs of life.

Besides, no living being was stupid enough to be out in that kind of weather other than the search teams.

As their visibility deteriorated, Matt eased back on the throttle. Not only because they couldn't see where they were going, but because they could easily drive within yards of the boys and not even know it. But what other choice did they have? They couldn't stop until they found them.

Matt pulled the snowmobile off the trail behind a copse of Aspen trees and brambles that blocked a fair amount of the wind. He killed the engine and pushed up the visor on his helmet. She raised hers as well.

"Let's check the map. I think the trail up to Eagle Point is around here somewhere. I don't want to miss it."

Between the wind that made it through the trees, and the snow fall, reading the map proved challenging. Mia glanced around at the foothills that rose toward the mountains and compared it to the map. She pointed to a gap in the trees that looked like it led up toward an outcropping of rock that should be Eagle Point. "That way."

"Agreed." Matt put away the map and pulled out the canteen and offered it to Mia.

She hated to take her warm helmet off, but they wouldn't do the boys any good if they let themselves get dehydrated. She took a few swigs, then handed it over to Matt. Falling snow stuck in his hair, and the tips of his ears turned red from the cold.

"We should shoot off a text to St. John. Let him know we didn't see any sign of the boys on the way here."

Matt sent off the text. A minute or two later, they got a response. The wait took longer than he'd expected. St. John could have been busy as the search coordinator, but it felt more like St. John had stared at their incoming text, shaking his head and deciding what to say two civilians who couldn't follow orders.

He replied with short and sweet: *Copy.*

Matt fired off another, telling St. John they intended to check the cabin up past Bear Tooth pass. As it was, they'd be lucky to get back to the Lazy S before dark.

"Shit," Matt said as he tucked the phone away. "Lost the signal."

"Did your text make it through?"

"Dunno." Matt picked up her helmet and handed it to her. "We need to keep going."

"We're going to find them."

"Damn right." Though the conviction in his voice had bled off from when they'd first left the ranch.

They'd really hoped to find the boys broke down somewhere on their way to the Lazy S. Had they missed them in the low visibility? Had the boys taken another trail? Had they gotten lost? Had they made it to the cabin and were curled up by a roaring fire, playing cards and swapping lies?

What little warmth Mia had regained when they stopped, she immediately lost from the wind chill as they continued down the trail. Even with Matt's body blocking most of the wind. She wished they had helmet comms, so they could talk, and she wouldn't be all up in her head thinking of all the perils facing the boys.

But she had no relief from the biting wind or her brutal imagination.

Higher and higher they climbed, the growl of the snowmobile's engine drowning out all other sound. How Matt found the entrance to the trail, Mia had no clue. She had trouble seeing ten yards ahead of them.

Every lump, every dark patch, Mia scanned, but she found nothing that indicated the boys had been that way.

They navigated a narrow pass, the handlebars of the snowmobile handlebars scraping between some of the trees and rock faces. Matt patted her on the thigh to get her attention and pointed at a dark shape in front of them.

The cabin.

Or at least one of the cabins on the list.

Matt skid to a stop and killed the engine.

The structure in front of them was little more than a single-room log cabin with a crude stone chimney. No smoke drifted skyward, though that didn't mean no one was inside. They pulled off their helmets and called out for the boys.

The cabin lay in a small clearing, protected on three sides with a short outcropping of cliff and rocks. Matt's deep voice echoed off the solid surface.

The thick clouds as well as the falling and accumulated snow dampened other sound. Even the crack of the ice in the tree branches sounded muted as if she'd just descended from thirty-thousand feet and couldn't clear her ears.

Mia climbed off the back of the snowmobile, even though there were no encouraging outward signs of the boys. They had to check inside to make sure the boys hadn't holed up there.

Her quads ached, and she had to work out the stiffness in her joints after sitting for so long. She followed Matt onto the narrow, dilapidated porch, stepping over a rotted board. Matt turned the handle. Unlocked. But he had to put his shoulder to the door to shove it open.

"Watch your step," he said as he went inside.

She stepped over the hole in the floor and spun around in a slow circle. As much as she hadn't expected to find the boys inside, finding the cabin empty still came as blow. Light and wind seeped through the cracks between the logs where the chinking had long since fallen away. Inside, there was little more than a busted-up chair and a balled-up blanket on the floor that the rats had claimed as their own. A piece of a cellophane wrapper got caught in a mini vortex of wind in one corner and rattled around before settling back on the ground. Nothing gave any indications the boys had been there.

"Ready?" Matt said.

The energy wafting off him kept her stomach in a knot as the pressure to find the boys grew heavier. "I need to pee, then I'll be ready."

She made her way around the side of the cabin, as much out of the wind as she could get before dropping her pants and relieving herself. There had been few times in her life that Mia wished she had a penis—driving long-haul transports through dangerous territory and in the middle of a snowstorm were two of them.

As quick as she was, she couldn't feel her ass cheeks by the time she'd pulled up her pants. She returned to the snowmobile as Matt zipped up his fly and kicked fresh snow over the yellow.

He had a grin on his face she didn't expect.

"What?"

He leaned in and pressed his cold lips to hers. "You didn't have to hide around the corner. I've seen you naked."

MATT PRESSED ON, HIS FINGERS NUMB, HIS ARMS, SHOULDERS, AND back sore from maneuvering the snowmobile over rough terrain hour after hour, his body no warmer than a block of ice. The cold didn't just melt into his marrow, it climbed into every cell, numbed every nerve ending, and frosted the lining of his lungs.

Still, they searched on. With each passing hour, his apprehension had grown until it had become this beast bearing down on him, always a step behind, but each swipe of its extended claws coming closer to ripping a bloody swath out of him.

They'd had to double back, check the map, and make several unsuccessful forays down trails that looked promising only to find they'd petered out. Finally, they found the trail Santos had warned them about.

He reached back and gave Mia's leg a pat. She squeezed back, her arms tight around his waist where they'd been most of the day. Having her body pressed against his had been the only bright spot. Then he saw it ahead, the lump of a snow-covered snowmobile, the windshield exposed.

Forget slowing or stopping. He almost leapt from the moving snowmobile. But he contained his eagerness long enough to park and kill the engine. Together, they climbed off and trudged through a knee-deep snowdrift to get to the sled. He kicked up his face shield, and Mia did the same.

"Looks like they rammed that tree hard," Matt said. "The windshield is cracked, and the front ski is smashed."

"The deep snow doesn't help. They probably wouldn't have gotten much farther without getting stuck. Hell, we'll be lucky if we don't get stuck."

That late in the year, the sun set early. With all the cloud cover, it had felt as if they were living through perpetual dusk. Matt didn't have a watch on, but the clouds had thinned just enough for the faint, weak, outline of the sun to appear as it started to set.

"It will be dark before too long," Mia said. "If we were going to head back to the ranch tonight—"

"I'm not going back."

She could take the snowmobile and head home, but he wasn't turning his back when they were that close.

"I'm not saying I want to go. All I'm saying is we need to have a plan before night hits. If you think Mother Nature is going to play along with our little game, you've seriously underestimated her."

The chuckle that escaped came out warm. "I learned early in my life not to underestimate a determined woman. Mother Nature is no different. But we have to keep going. The boys could be around the corner, or the next, or—" Matt ripped his helmet off and ran a gloved hand through his hair, the snowfall had slowed and even the wind had eased, showing them a bit of mercy. "Fuck, Mia, we've got to push on."

"Okay."

He hadn't expected her to say anything else, but it was good to hear her agreement. But there also had been a hesitation in her voice, something bothered her, and he needed to know what before they forged on.

"What's your concern?"

"Besides freezing to death?" If she'd been kidding, it was only by half. "I'm concerned about your mental state. You're all up in your head. Pushing on at night in a snowstorm is a calculated risk, but it could easily be deadly if you don't keep your wits about you."

"I don't understand."

She stepped closer, removing her helmet as well. Whether it was so he could see her eyes, or she could see his better, he didn't hazard to guess. She placed her hand on his arm. It might be crazy as fuck, but he imagined he felt her heat through her glove and the protective layers on his arm.

"Saving the boys… it won't bring Yusef back."

Those words hit like an ax to his chest, splitting him open, allowing the sorrow and pain and guilt to leak to the surface. "You don't think I fucking know that?"

He heaved his helmet. It bounced off a tree trunk and disappeared into a bank of snow. He stormed off up the trail, but the deep snow had him huffing and puffing within seconds. Dropping to his knees, he practically buried himself in the snow. He let out a yell. All rage and denial and self-loathing.

It came back to him on the wind, a sad sound that tore at his heart as it bounced off him again.

He heard the crunch of snow behind him as Mia approached, felt the weight of her hand on his back, saw the cloud of her breath as she knelt beside him. She didn't say anything. She stayed there with him until the tide of emotions washed over him, leaving him tossed and tumbled, the metaphorical sand skinning him raw.

Catching his breath, he pushed to his feet and gave her a hand up. "Sorry." Heat crept up his neck. "I never expected this to hit me so hard."

"You're a fixer. It's as much a part of you as your compassion, kindness, and integrity. It's not so surprising to me. And it's not something you need to apologize for."

She held out her hand, and he took it. "Let's get our gear. We've got a few more miles to hike if I remember the map correctly."

She pulled, taking a step away, but he tugged her back. The momentum had her crashing into his chest. He pressed a kiss to her cold, wind-chapped lips. When she sank into him, opening her mouth and letting him in, he fell even harder for her.

He just hoped he'd survive the impact.

She broke the kiss before they got carried away and jerked her head toward their snowmobile and their gear. They took the time to get out their LED headlamps and shove knit caps onto their heads to seal in the warmth. The snowshoes went on easily. Mia hefted her pack, and Matt took the one that Santos and Alby had packed with food and other gear.

His stomach growled on cue. They'd had little time to eat. The next mile and hilltop always their primary focus. But they couldn't hike without fuel. He pulled some protein bars and beef jerky out of the pack and handed Mia her share. She grunted her thanks and tore the wrapper with her teeth as she started up the trail.

"I think the weather is starting to break," Mia said around a mouthful of peanut butter and chia seeds.

He held out his hand. The snow didn't fill it as if someone was shoveling it onto his hand. Could their luck be turning?

———

"FUCK OUR LUCK," MIA SAID NOT TWENTY MINUTES LATER AS Mother Nature's reprieve now felt more like a slap in the face, or a cruel, senseless joke.

She ducked her head into the wind, her words nearly torn away, so she wasn't sure if Matt heard her or not. The beam of her headlamp stabbed weakly—a short, depressing tunnel into the abyss. Matt hiked no more than a few yards behind her, and all she saw was the pale halo of his own headlamp.

How easy it would be for them to become separated.

She pulled up short, and Matt stumbled into her. He caught her waist and kept her from pitching face first into the snow.

"We have to stop," she said. "I want to keep going as much as you do, but we won't do those boys any good if we get ourselves into serious trouble or die trying."

His hands went to his hips, and when she thought he'd push around her and keep going, she put a staying hand on his chest. "You know I'm right."

Matt took a step back, his head dropping as he absorbed her words and what that meant for them, and more importantly, for the boys.

"This is fucked up," she thought he said, but couldn't be sure, not with the wind whipping and stealing their words.

A long, cold night lay ahead of them. Building a trench shelter in the snow was their best option. They both glanced around. With visibility at a minimum, they couldn't risk getting too far off the trail and getting lost, so they picked the closest depression in the ground that would protect them from the brutal wind.

"This looks good." Matt stepped out of his snowshoes and dropped his pack. Mia did the same. "I'll dig, if you want to find some spruce boughs for insulation."

"Deal." She had a folding saw in her pack she often used for cutting dead branches for kindling.

He caught her arm before she walked off and brought her in for a kiss. "Don't go far, Mann. I'm kinda getting used to having you in my life."

She wanted to laugh it off, but the fierceness in his eyes and his unwillingness to look away made the words land with a truthfulness that made her chest warm. The rest of her wanted to run.

Mia wasn't relationship material. She knew that. And after what she'd shared with him, it should be obvious to him as well.

"Go," he said, "Before we really do freeze."

It didn't take long before Matt had a trench dug in the powdery snow wide enough for the two of them, using the backside of his snowshoe as a makeshift shovel. They laid boughs down to protect them from the cold ground, then covered the trough with small dead saplings she'd cut down to support a roof of more boughs. They covered the roof in snow for added insulation and protection from the relentless wind.

Matt tried to get a text update out to the sheriff but couldn't get a signal.

"Ready?" Matt's breath came in short puffs, mixing with hers as they rested from all their exertion. For the first time since they'd left, her body temperature elevated to a notch above freezing. At least the work had returned feeling to her fingers and most of her toes.

She shined her light on their shelter and shook her head. Her heart rate kicked up instead of settling down, and her unease made it feel like an army of ants marched in double time across her skin. How could she climb in there?

Matt eased closer and flipped up his light so it wouldn't shine in her eyes. "You don't have a choice."

"I could build a fire and lay—"

"Everything is wet. Nothing will burn." He cupped her face in his gloved hands, the outer layer damp from melted snow. But she didn't focus on that. "You spent last night indoors. This is no different."

"This isn't anywhere near the same."

"It's a room, Mia. Nothing more. You can do this. I know you can."

Her words wouldn't come. They backed up in her throat, the near panic weighing them down. She nodded, not because she agreed, but she had no choice.

That, and a tiny, infinitesimal part of her needed to live up to his belief in her, however misguided he was.

She made Matt go first. He got down on his hands and knees and scooted in feet first, sliding in between the blanket they'd laid down on top of the boughs and the unzipped sleeping bag. Inside, he had just enough clearance to roll onto his side.

He held a hand out to her. "Come on, Mann. Show me what you've got."

When was the last time she cared what anyone outside her family thought of her? His approval shouldn't matter.

But it does.

Fuck.

She wanted to be that brave woman he thought she was. Even if she'd only be playing an elaborate game of pretend.

Mia scooted in beside him, and they reached out and pulled their packs in front of the entrance as a wind block. Matt rolled onto his stomach and pulled out crackers and a chunk of cheese from his pack.

Her stomach growled. The protein bar and beef jerky hadn't come close to curbing her hunger. Pulling her gloves off with her teeth, she managed to reach her pocketknife and roll to her stomach. She cut off hunks of cheese, laying them out on part of the blanket next to the pile of crackers. They had other food in the pack, but considering the confines of their space, the cheese and crackers seemed the easiest to deal with.

Mia focused on filling her belly, and not on the tension in her muscles, the twitch of her nerves, all telling her she wasn't safe, that she had to run.

But running would most likely mean death.

What a total mind fuck.

They needed to find the boys, so she didn't have to spend another night reliving her nightmare.

Mia clicked off her headlamp to conserve the battery. In that confined space, Matt's lamp laying on the blanket pointing up at the ceiling of their shelter provided adequate light.

At least they were out of the wind. Cold still infused her body, but with the two of them in the tight shelter, the layers of ice seemed to be chipping off her bones.

They demolished the food within minutes and polished off one of the canteens of water. Hopefully, come morning, the winds would have died down enough so that they could light their small camping burner and melt enough snow to replenish their water supply. If not, their remaining water supply should last them through the next day.

She rolled to her side and faced him. With the food gone, she had nothing else to occupy her mind.

Matt propped his head on his upturned hand, and one of the boughs making their ceiling poked him in the head. He snapped off the offending piece and flicked it outside. "You hanging in there?"

'No. Hell, no. And fuck, no,' were all logical responses, but the words themselves didn't capture the buzz of anxiety coursing through her body like a blast from a taser. It didn't embody the dark images her consciousness could barely keep in that triple-padlocked box in the back of her mind. Or how she thought she'd go insane if she had to stay trapped in the shelter for one minute, one second longer.

So, she ignored the question and asked one of her own. "Tell me something completely crazy that I don't know about you."

Instead of bringing a smile to his face, his features softened, and he skimmed a finger down the length of her jaw. "I love you. How's that for crazy?"

12

———

I LOVE YOU.

Definitely fucking crazy. Mia was sharing space with a raving lunatic.

Yeah, those words had fallen out of Matt's big mouth. What had he expected to gain from that? She didn't love him. Hell, according to her, there was nothing going on between them.

He was a fucking idiot.

A bomb could have exploded in front of her, and her eyes couldn't have been any wider.

"You don't know what you're talking about. I'm broken, Matt. There's nothing here but a shell. Nothing that can love you back or be the person that you want me to be."

Matt shook his head. "That's where you're wrong. You're not broken. A dent or two perhaps, but not broken. And I don't need or want you to be anyone or anything other that what you are."

"Maybe you're the one that's broken, then." She didn't smile, but the lick of humor landed in her eyes.

"If that's the case, then I don't want to be fixed."

He held her chin and leaned in for a kiss. She nipped and sucked on his bottom lip before opening for him. For a woman who claimed she had no interest, she had a peculiar way of showing it.

His recently thawed blood went south, pooling in his cock, and he had fuck-all in the ability department to do anything about it.

Despite the tight confines, Mia reached down, her hand on the fly of his snow pants, his cock screaming 'yes,' while his heart said 'no.'

And it wasn't just because they were practically cocooned beneath six inches of tree boughs and snow, but because as much as Mia equated sex with distraction, he wanted and needed more from her.

He broke the kiss, took her groping hand in his, and kissed her knuckles one by one before tucking it against his chest.

"Can I take a rain check?" he asked.

The sound that escaped her landed somewhere between a huff of exasperation and a growl of frustration. "You're going to make me talk about my feelings, aren't you?"

"I'm not expecting you to tell me you love me back, if that's what you're worried about. You're not there yet. I get that. But you also don't have to run from my truth."

"And what if I never get there? What if I never love you?"

He couldn't tell her the truth, that it would probably destroy him. He'd never felt for another human all the consuming, terrifying, vulnerable, protective feelings he had for her. He didn't subscribe to the notion that there was only one person out there for everyone, but he couldn't imagine a person out there that suited him any better.

"What if you do?"

She chuckled but shook her head. "I'm not convinced I know what real love is. How fucked up is that?"

He didn't answer, not only because it wasn't a real question but also because he didn't think she'd finished talking. As difficult as it was for him to drag anything out of her, he didn't want to interrupt.

"I thought I loved Frank." She grimaced as if the asshole's name had turned to vinegar on her tongue. "Clearly, that wasn't love. I don't even know what you could call it, besides twisted, misguided."

"Undeserving," he added. "It wasn't your fault you fell for him. It sounds like he did a good job of hiding his true self."

"Hmm," she grunted noncommittally.

"What about your parents? You love them."

She stiffened, and in that tiny space with the cold all around them and the wind whipping through the tiny cracks in their makeshift fortress, she could have been in outer space and not been farther away from him than she was now.

Time to backpedal. "We don't have to talk about them."

"It's complicated. And messy. And ugly."

"Okay."

If she wanted to drop it, he'd drop it.

"And fuck... I know they love me. But the way they do..." She let her words drift away, and he wasn't going to be the asshole who pointed out that she was doing what she said she wouldn't. *Talking.*

"...I don't know. In some way, I think that everything that happened with Frank didn't gut me the way my parents' behavior has."

"Their approval means something to you." It wasn't a question. Knowing Mia, it was something he knew to be true. If her parents had meant nothing to her, she'd have been able to pack their relationship into a box and ship it back to them.

No return address.

"Isn't that the stupidest thing you've ever heard? I'm not a kid. What they think of me and my life shouldn't matter."

"What's stupid is thinking you don't have feelings like everybody else on this planet. You're human, Mia. Stop acting like you aren't."

"Fuck feelings," Mia said, but the words didn't have any bite to them.

"You may not feel love up here," Matt said, tapping her temple. "But I know it lives here." He put his hand to the center of her chest over her heart. "Maybe not for me, but for others. I see it in the way you connect in your own way with Pepita, Zealand, the others, the horses. You're gruff on the outside, but gooey in the middle where it counts."

She swallowed hard as the words he spoke hit, but she either couldn't or wouldn't acknowledge the truth. Instead, she curled up against him. He wanted to put his arms around her and hold her but didn't want her feeling any more trapped than she must already feel.

He called it a win that she'd stayed in the shelter as long as she had.

Her breathing evened out, though the tension didn't leave her body.

"Thank you," she mumbled, half asleep.

The simple, sincere thanks wormed its way into his heart. It wasn't a profession of love, but those two words meant she'd absorbed what he'd said, trusted in their truth, and maybe, just maybe, in time, meant she would come to believe them as fiercely as he did.

He'd take that.

For now.

He cupped the back of her head and kissed her temple. A shiver went through her, and she burrowed even closer as what little heat their bodies had generated from building the shelter leached out of their bodies.

They weren't in danger of freezing, but it was going to be one hell of an uncomfortable night.

———

Mia woke with a start, adrenaline dumping into her already stressed-out system. Taking in her surroundings, she tramped down on her urge to run. Matt's headlamp remained on, but the battery had grown weak, casting their shelter in a soft, warm glow.

The urge to escape the confines of the shelter gnawed on her bones, but something inside her had shifted. Having Matt beside her didn't make everything better, but his energy, even when he slept, kept her from spinning out of control. And knowing he had her back, that she wasn't alone, mattered.

She didn't need him to slay her demons, but knowing he stood in the wings, assured she could fight her own battles, gave her a confidence and inner peace she hadn't known she'd been lacking.

Maybe that's what love is.

Had he really said that he loved her? Or had she dreamt the whole thing?

He grunted beside her, his arms fighting an invisible enemy. She shifted away, giving him what little space she could. He cried out, a searing, heart-wrenching cry. One that convinced her Matt hadn't processed Yusef's death nearly as well as he led others—and himself—to believe.

She shook his shoulder to wake him, and he exploded out of the shelter, boiling for a fight that lived only in his head.

The boughs and snow that had made up the roof of their shelter came crashing down, burying her beneath a pile of sticks and snow.

"It's okay, it's okay," Mia said as she, too, scrambled out from the debris and stood.

Matt came back to himself, his breath sawing in and out,

harsh, heated. He doubled over, resting his hands on his knees while he gathered himself and caught his breath.

"Nightmare?" *Stupid question.*

His dark chuckle had a lightness around the edges, and he had a ghost of a smile on his face when he stood and held out his hand to her.

She took it and stepped into his embrace, his hold so tight, so enveloping, she thought he'd never let go.

Which didn't seem like a proposition that totally sucked.

I love you.

Fuck. Could he really mean that? And what did that mean for her?

He buried his face into her shoulder as his adrenaline induced tremors eased.

"Yusef?"

He nodded. He pulled back and stared down at her. His face mottled red in the low morning light.

The wind had died overnight. And the air temperature no longer stole her breath away.

He pulled her in for a kiss, their lips dry and chapped, but she didn't care. The sweet, softness of the kiss brought tears to her eyes.

What the hell? Why are you so emotional? It's just a kiss.

But deep down, it represented more than that, and she knew it, felt it, treasured it.

What was Matt doing to her?

As the kiss deepened, Mia wanted nothing more than to crawl under his skin and live there forever. Finally, Matt broke the kiss and eyed the utter destruction of their shelter.

"If we'd been taking bets on who would bust out of the shelter first," he said, "I would have lost my entire savings."

"Same." The fact that she'd stayed in the shelter all night

and actually had fallen asleep amounted to nothing short of a minor miracle.

He kissed her forehead and pulled her in tight. "I'm proud of you."

Until Matt had uttered those validating words, she hadn't realized how few times in her life she'd heard them or known how profoundly she needed to hear them.

"You say shit like that and you're going to make me cry, and then I'll have to end you."

"I'll take my chances."

Her heart climbed into her throat and plopped down in a La-Z-Boy, content to stay there and clog her airway forever.

She had to blink back the building moisture before her eyes froze shut.

He jerked his head toward the pile of boughs and snow. "I'll clean this mess up, if you want to heat us up some coffee. I could use a good jolt to get me moving."

"When you excavate the phone, you should try to get a call or text through to St. John and let him know we found the boys' snowmobile." She glanced up at the sky. Sometime in the night, much of the low cloud cover had lifted. If they were lucky, the sheriff would be able to launch the search and rescue helicopter soon.

"I'm on it," Matt said.

Not long after, they had their gear repacked, a can of hot beans in their belly, and a canteen full of hot coffee that they passed between them. Matt got a busy signal when he tried to contact St. John. He texted him though, with the rough coordinates of the snowmobile. He called the ranch next and let Alby know their status.

Mia and Matt had just stepped into their snowshoes and started up the trail when the phone beeped with an incoming text.

Matt pulled up short and dug the phone out of an outer packet. "St. John is sending more searchers this way and said as soon as it's light enough they can send up the helo. Looks like we have a narrow window of reprieve before more cloud cover moves in sometime early this afternoon."

He replied to the text and tucked the phone back into his jacket.

"I guess that means we need to start hiking. I don't want to let this break in the weather go to waste."

They were two hours into their hike when they stopped and brushed snow off a boulder to give them somewhere to sit and rest. They plopped down beside each other, trying to catch their breath. The steep climb in elevation mixed with the deep snow and decreased oxygen made their going slow.

They'd called out for the boys as they hiked but encountered very little signs of life besides a few birds and some rabbit and deer tracks. Definitely no other sign that indicated the boys had been that way.

Matt handed her a protein bar, took a few swigs from the canteen, and handed it to her. She finished off the dregs of the now-cold coffee and tore into the bar. It was dry and chalky and had no taste, but her belly wasn't too particular. She stared down the snow-covered mountain, the brutal beauty enough to steal her breath again.

She choked down the last of the bar and shoved the wrapper into one of her pockets. "Shouldn't we be getting close to the cabin by now?"

It felt like they'd been hiking for miles and miles, and she wouldn't have been surprised if they'd popped out the other side of the Rockies and stumbled into Idaho.

"I think we have a mile, maybe two."

Mia grunted and slipped her arms through the straps of her

pack, standing on legs that had already grown stiff. "Let's go then. We need to find those boys before it's too late."

———

Matt used a thick branch he'd found it as a walking stick. He wasn't sure how much it really helped, but it gave him a mental boost if nothing else.

Mia trudged up the trail in front of him at a relentless ground-eating pace, her urgency to find the boys paramount.

Yet something else he loved and admired about her.

If only she could see herself the way he did, then maybe she'd believe more fully in her own worth. But it sounded like her parents and her ex had done a number on her psyche.

"We made it." Mia's pace only increased as they came to the top of the rise where the ground leveled out. She began to run as best as she could, considering they were wearing snowshoes.

"Zach! Charlie!" Matt called out, his vocal cords already shredded from calling out all morning.

If the boys yelled back, he doubted he'd hear them over his panting and the crunch of snow beneath his feet.

Even as they approached the cabin, Matt had a bad feeling in his gut. Just like when they'd found the other cabin, this one had a stillness to it, and he knew without opening the door that the one-room structure lay empty.

Mia didn't even bother removing her snowshoes before shoving her way into the unlocked cabin with Matt only a few steps behind. The snowshoes *clunk chunked* on the rough-hewn wood floor. This cabin showed a minimal improvement over the last one. It had a twin bed and a couple of homemade chairs that looked like they would hold a person if they didn't wiggle around too much.

"Fuck," Mia said. "Look around, maybe there's a sign they were here."

Matt stepped to the fireplace. No smoke emanated from the pile of ash, but he took a stick and poked at the pile.

Were those embers?

He sat on the stone hearth and ripped one of his gloves off and held his hand above the ash.

Warmth.

"They were here," Matt said, his excitement and relief leaching out into his words.

Mia scrambled over, pulling a glove off with her teeth. The smile that bloomed on her face shined as brilliantly as a rising Caribbean sun.

"They can't be that far away. Maybe they went for a day hike and are planning on returning."

Matt glanced around. Besides some ruffled bedding, there were no other indications the boys had been there. If they'd planned on returning, they certainly hadn't left any of their unnecessary gear behind.

"I think they moved on," Matt said, as much as it pained him to voice his concern.

Mia ripped off her beanie and scratched at her itchy head. "I think you're right. But if they left this morning, there has to be a trail. There hasn't been any new snowfall since last night."

And there hadn't been any fresh prints out the front of the cabin. But this cabin had a back door. Could it be that easy? Would they find the boys' tracks and have them lead them straight to the boys?

Mia beat Matt to his feet and clomped over to the back door. She opened it, and Matt said, "Well?"

She glanced back, a huge grin on her face. "They went this way."

In their excitement to track the boys, Mia had forgotten her glove and had to double back to get it. Matt waited by the edge of the clearing and placed a call to St. John. The sheriff answered on the second ring.

"St. John." He must have recognized the number because he said, "Tell me that you found them."

"Not them. But we found a cabin we think they stayed in overnight." Matt gave St. John the general location. "It looks like they might have left again this morning. We're following their tracks."

"I know the area. I'll redirect the helicopter that way. Stay in touch. We need to find them before we lose our window of opportunity."

"What are the chances of getting extra searchers up this way?"

Mia had retrieved her glove and had almost made it back to him.

"The closest pair are miles away. They were searching another area. I wouldn't bet on them getting to you before the weather turns, but we'll do our best."

"Copy that." Matt hung up and leaned in for a quick peck on Mia's lips. "You ready to find these boys?"

"Like yesterday."

They followed the boys' tracks that led them higher and higher, the terrain growing more rugged and dangerous with each passing step. They called out, stopping to listen for any voices in return, but... nothing.

Sometime later, their reprieve from the wind met an untimely end just as a cloud covered the sun. Within seconds, the nice brisk day became frigid.

Matt shivered. The ominous turn of the weather dampened his bright optimism.

He pulled up the hood on his jacket and zipped up the collar to keep the bite of the wind off his neck. They'd survived on water and protein bars, not willing to compromise their search for the sake of their stomachs. The boys were alive now. But if they had to stay out in the elements one more night, their luck might change.

"Who would have thought these boys would have this kind of stamina," Matt said as he drew to a stop next to Mia.

The tracks ended in a bunch of rocks that continued higher. The path the boys had taken clear in the disturbance of the otherwise flawless snow.

The rocks went up for forty or fifty feet. Not so steep you needed a rope, but steep enough you'd be using your hands to help climb.

"You've got to be freaking kidding me," Matt said as he stared up at the path of ascent. "Is there an easier way around?"

"Don't think so. One side is a drop off and the other is a sheer cliff. Only way through is up and over. If I ever get my hands on these kids..." Mia said, not finishing the threat.

"You'll have to beat me to them. Though I think I'll let their parents have first crack."

"Generous."

"It's not all about me. Except when it is."

Mia gave him the eye roll he'd expected. "Stop wasting time. You're not getting out of this climb."

They stepped out of their snowshoes as the wind whipped at the snowdrifts, making it appear as if it was snowing even though it wasn't. After strapping the equipment to their packs, they started the climb.

Between the two of them, no doubt Mia was the more skilled climber, so Matt took up the rear, following in her handholds and footholds. Besides, if he slipped and fell, he didn't want to risk taking her down with him.

A heart-pounding, quad-shaking, hand-cramping climb later, they reached the top.

He sucked in a lungful of air, but it didn't seem to alleviate his oxygen deprivation. "If the air... gets any thinner up here... I'll—"

The wind shifted, and Mia's raised hand shut him up. Her eyes went wider, and she stuck her nose in the air like a hound on the scent of fresh blood.

"What is it?"

"Do you smell that?"

Matt tried to breath in through his nose, but the cold air had made him too congested to smell anything. "No. I can't even breathe through my nose."

She sniffed the air again, her hand grasping his jacket as a smile bunched her wind-chapped cheeks. "I smell smoke."

They called out, but with the wind swirling, their voices wouldn't carry. They didn't bother with their snowshoes. They just plowed through the shin-deep snow following the boys' broken trail. Matt was only a few steps behind her when she skidded to a stop.

He put the brakes on when he saw the crevice splitting the trail, afraid he'd knock Mia right over the edge.

"Watch out," he yelled, but there was nowhere for her to go. He went into a feet-first slide, but instead of slowing him down, he took Mia out at the knees like David Beckham taking out a striker in the final seconds of a World Cup match.

He grabbed for her hand, her arm, her jacket, her hood, anything he could get his hands on.

The woosh of blood in his ears went silent. His heart must have stopped. It probably couldn't beat after lodging so tightly in his throat.

The momentum of his skid turned him on his stomach as he grappled to maintain what little grip he had on Mia as he accidently shoved her over the edge.

"Mia!"

Her body lurched to a stop, and Matt took the brunt of her dead weight in his shoulders, the strain nearly ripping her out of his hands.

"Hold on. I'm going to pull you up."

How the hell he would do that, he had no idea. The wet, slick ground didn't provide any leverage.

"Don't let go," Mia said. "If I can reach this rocky outcrop, I can pull myself up. Don't drop me."

"Never." Matt tightened his fingers, but the fabric slipped as his shoulders screamed for relief.

Then he lost his grip, the excruciating pain in his shoulders vanished as the weight fell away. He scrambled to look over the edge and came face to face with Mia.

"Give me a hand." She reached up to clasp his arm.

He locked onto her wrist and helped pull her up, rolling onto his back as she flopped over his body.

"Fuck that was close." Mia's words came out with a laugh, equal parts relief and exhilaration.

He just lay there, Mia's weight pinning him down as he willed his heart to kick back in. She shifted to her hands and knees, straddling his body, her face inches from his.

"I may not need a white knight in my day to day life," she said, "but I have to admit they come in handy on occasion."

He cupped the back of her neck and brought her in for a kiss. He appreciated her humor, but it would take a few minutes for him to find it himself.

Her lips were cold, but the kiss tasted sweet.

And ended too quickly.

Mia scrambled to her feet and held out a hand to help him up. His legs felt like rubber, and it had nothing to do with the physical exertion of the hike and everything to do with the spike of adrenaline that didn't seem to know where to go now that the danger had passed.

A quick, painless death would be preferable to all these nicks and cuts Mia kept inflicting on his heart.

She eased over to the edge, and he caught her bicep in case she slipped. From where Mia had gone over the edge, there was a twenty-foot drop and no viable way down that wouldn't end up with a broken leg or neck.

"Over here." Matt pointed to his right at the line of disturbed snow. Except now it became painfully obvious only one person had made those tracks.

"That's not good." Her statement tantamount to *Houston, we have a problem.*

"Zach? Charlie?" Matt called out again, but still no answer. The wind blew straight at them now, and even through his congestion, he smelled the smoke. That was a good sign, right? It meant the boys were alive.

Or one of the boys were alive.

He didn't dwell on that thought. He couldn't and still function. Yusef flashed in front his eyes, bright and full of life. Matt braced for the next image that would come, it always came without fail—the one of Yusef's lifeless, bloody body in a dirty street on the backside of hell.

Mia placed a hand on his arm, drawing his attention to her. "You with me?"

"Yeah."

"We need to find a way down there."

"It's too dangerous to go that way."

Overhead, they heard the distant *whomp whomp* of a helicopter's rotors, but the dense tree cover made it impossible to spot. If they were lucky, the boys would hear it as well and find an open area so they could be found.

Unfortunately, with the sky going gray again with the incoming cloud cover, any smoke from a fire would blend in with the surrounding sky.

In their search for a way across the crevice, precious seconds turned into long minutes. Those long minutes stretched out until the constant unease Matt had in his belly coated every nerve, driving him harder and faster.

"Over here," Mia called from a little farther up the trail.

She'd found a downed tree spanning the cut in the earth. A disturbed blanket of snow covered the top, and icicles hung from the bottom side. Any other time Matt might have reached for a camera to capture the raw beauty.

But in this moment, it was nothing but deadly. One foot wrong, one misstep, and it would be a disaster.

"I don't see where we have much of a choice," Matt said. "We could waste a couple of hours hiking to find another way around."

"We don't have that kind of time." Mia placed one foot on top of the fallen tree, then the other, bouncing in place, testing its structural integrity. "Feels solid."

She inched along the trunk, her arms extended to her sides for balance.

"Easy," Matt said when what he really wanted to do was push her aside and make her let him go first, but they didn't have time to stand there and argue about it.

Especially when he knew he couldn't win.

How could he find the same qualities in a person both frustrating and admirable?

Get used to it if you ever want to make a life with this woman.

Is that where this was heading? Hell, he still wasn't completely convinced she liked him.

Mia whistled from the safety of the other side, the sharpness slicing the air. "You're not chicken, are you?"

Not chicken, more like in the middle of a mini existential crisis. He didn't reply, he just stepped onto the tree and started across.

He kept his stride short, the bark slick and icy beneath his feet.

Don't look down, asshole.

Mia reached out a hand, and they locked wrists. When he made it safely to the other side, she said, "Thanks for not falling and killing yourself."

He leaned over and kissed her. "I love you, too, Mann."

It took another hour of hiking before they found a navigable route down to where they thought the boys might be, and even more hiking to get back near where the crevice opened up.

All the while, the helo continued its search pattern sometimes growing near, other times the pattern taking them farther away. Then Matt realized he couldn't hear the engine and rotors any longer.

"You think they're searching another grid?" she asked.

"Either that or they had to go back and refuel."

The scent of smoke grew stronger. The boys had to be close.

Then their trail opened onto a sloped area about the size of a baseball diamond at the base of the crevice. A thirty-foot sheer cliff ran in a semicircle on one side and a nearly sheer drop off on the other that would make a beautiful waterfall come spring.

But the most beautiful sight was the boys.

13

"Charlie, Zack!" Mia called out. The spike of adrenaline propelled her forward on exhausted legs. Her quads complained, but she didn't listen. There would be time to rest later.

Zach turned and stood, a relieved smile on his face. Charlie sat up, the emergency blanket over the top of him falling to his waist.

Mia caught Zach up in a hug as Matt continued past and dropped to his knees beside Charlie.

She held Zach at arm's length. He had a few cuts and scrapes on his face, his cheeks and lips were red and wind chapped, but his eyes were bright.

"We gotta get Charlie some help," Zach said. "He won't stop shaking, and his color's not so good."

Mia didn't bother chastising the boys for leaving the way they had. They'd hear enough of that from their parents.

Taking him by the shoulder, they worked their way over to Charlie and Matt, sticking close to the cliff wall to avoid the scree field of loose rock. One false step on that, and they could slide right off. No telling how far they'd fall.

"What have we got?" Mia asked.

Charlie grimaced, his complexion a pasty white. Matt had pulled up the bottom of the emergency blanket, exposing the lower half of Charlie's right leg.

"I think he has a compound fracture of the tib-fib. Sure as hell wish Zealand were here."

A fractured tibia and fibula were no minor injury, but at least Charlie was awake and conscious. All in all, the kids were fucking lucky.

Now all they had to do was get them off the slope.

She knelt on the other side of Charlie. Zach pulled another dead branch from the crevice. The steep walls had protected the fallen branches, keeping them relatively dry. Zack stoked the small fire as a few fat flakes of snow started falling, and the clouds grew more ominous.

"Finish checking him over," Matt said. "I'll try and get a message to St. John."

As best she could, she checked Charlie out. Much like Zach, the boy had cuts and bruises on his face. The sleeve of his jacket had a tear, and a goose egg had popped up on the back of his head.

"Ow," Charlie complained as she felt all over his skull.

"Did you lose consciousness?"

"I don't think so." The upward inflection of Charlie's voice made it sound more like a question.

That didn't sound convincing.

She glanced at Zach for conformation.

"I had to hike around like you did and crawl back up into the cut. He was awake by the time I got there."

Mia glanced at the crevice, no more than a jumble of rocks at the bottom of a deep cut. It would be extremely difficult to navigate while healthy. "How did you get him down here?"

Zack shrugged that careless shrug that teenagers have. "Just did. We would have never been found stuck in there."

Mia assessed the crude splint Zach had applied using Charlie's snowshoes as splints and the straps from their hiking packs as bindings. She'd certainly seen worse splint jobs.

"Miss Mia," Charlie said, the pain and exhaustion had stripped his voice of its vibrancy, "How are we going to get out of here?"

Fuck if she knew.

She patted his good leg and tacked on as confident of a smile as she could muster. She sure as hell didn't want to give the kid anything more to worry about. "Don't worry, kid. We'll get you out of here in no time."

Even if they had to figure out a way to pack him up and hike him out. Another night out in the elements wouldn't do him any favors.

"They're sending the helo around," Matt said as he hung up from his call and came back over to them. "I was able to give them rough map coordinates to narrow the search."

Charlie slumped back to the ground, his head resting on one of the packs. The wind made the emergency blanket flutter, but Zach had done an admirable job securing the edges under rocks to keep it from being ripped off Charlie's body.

Zach plopped down on his pack, the relief and worry etched in every pore of his young face. "My dad's going to kill me when he finds out I wrecked his snowmobile, isn't he?"

"No doubt." Matt didn't soften the blow.

"It will take me all summer to make enough money to pay him back."

Charlie chuckled. He tried to roll on his side to see Zach better but hissed in pain. "More like all year, if you're lucky. I guess that means we can probably kiss them letting us go to summer camp goodbye as well."

Mia didn't bother to add that their parents would probably be so glad that the boys were alive that the snowmobile was probably the least of anyone's worries. But maybe if the boys stewed in their trouble for a bit, they'd never do anything this asinine again.

The way you learned?

Yeah, well, they weren't talking about Mia's lifelong rash of bad decisions.

The *whomp* of the approaching helo came as a welcome sound. It approached then disappeared.

Zach eased a few steps out from the cliff, trying to find the helo through the canopy cover. "Why did they fly right by us."

"They can't see us." Matt's comment came out casual, but Mia detected the underlying tension in his tone.

Mia eased away from the cliff face, venturing out past Zack to try to get out from beneath the cover of the trees, taking careful steps as the slope of the ground got steeper.

"Don't be stupid," Matt said as the helo approached again.

If she could get out there another twenty, thirty feet, maybe then she'd be spotted. With each step, her feet slid a half foot, the scree field of flat rock piled on top of each other, along with the ice and snow, made each footfall perilous.

She took one more step. The rocks slid. Her foot went out from under her. She landed hard on her ass and slid a couple of terrifying feet before catching herself.

"Don't move," Matt said from the relative safety of seven or eight feet away.

The helo passed overhead again, this time from the other direction. How many passes would they make before they gave up?

Matt stripped off his coat and flung one sleeve at her while he held onto the other. She wrapped it around one hand to help her grip and allowed him to pull her to safety.

Behind her, she'd started a mini rockslide. The rubble hit far below with muffled thumps.

That could have been her.

Matt caught the waistband of her snow pants and tugged her to him, pressing his forehead to hers. "You're gonna be the death of me."

"We've got to get these boys out of here." Mia kept her voice low, not wanting to scare the boys. "Charlie won't be able to take the pain of us packing him out of here. He sure as hell is in no condition to stay out overnight. And if the cloud cover or wind gets any worse, they're gonna ground the pilots."

"I know." He gave her a quick peck on the lips that stupidly did wonders for her flagging morale.

He pulled the phone out of his pocket and called St. John again, putting him on speaker. They eased closer to the cliff face and turned their backs to the wind. When St. John answered, Matt said, "They've flown over us twice already."

"They haven't seen a thing. Lieutenant Powell said he has fuel for one more pass before they need to refuel. And from the reports we've received from the weather service, it will be unlikely they'll be cleared for takeoff again before morning. You have to find a way to make yourself visible."

"It's more than an hour hike back to any ridge from where they might be able to see us," Matt said. "I don't—"

"I've got an idea, Sheriff." Mia glanced behind her at the sheer face of one of the cliffs, mapping an ascent to the top in her mind. Thirty feet up. Forty max. She could do this. She'd been training her whole life for it. "We'll be ready for him on the next pass."

Because she didn't have a second to waste, Mia stepped away from the call to prepare for the climb. She nodded to herself as each handhold and foothold appeared in her mind. It wasn't nearly as difficult of a climb as the one by the hot spring. No part of the climb went beyond vertical, and the first ten or twelve feet were so basic a toddler could do it.

If she had her climbing shoes and chalk, it wouldn't be too challenging, but without them, it could prove to be one of her more difficult climbs.

She stepped to the base where she'd start her route and stripped off her gloves, boots, and jacket. No way could she make the climb in the bulky gear. But she also didn't want to be stuck at the top without her warm clothes. She'd freeze.

Fuck the wind and the cold.

She could barely stand on the freezing rocks in her bare feet. She shifted from foot to foot as she stuffed her boots, socks, and gloves into her zipped-up jacket, pulled the drawstring at the waist tight, and tied the arms around her waist.

She had to climb before she lost all feeling in her fingers and her toes.

Matt caught her bicep as she reached for the first handhold. "No. You're not doing this. We'll find another way."

"There is no other way. We both know it."

In the far distance came the now familiar *whomp* of helicopter rotors. They were running out of time.

"Let me go."

"*Fuck, Mia.*" Those two words encompassed a thousand.

I love you.

Come back to me.

You amaze me.

I can't make it without you.

His hand fell away as the lump in her throat threatened to strangle her. She couldn't speak with the jumble of emotions twisting, twirling, swirling inside her.

Then everything she felt for this man, suddenly came untangled. But she couldn't think about that now.

The rotor beats grew nearer, matching the whirlwind beat in her chest.

She turned to the cliff, blew a warm breath into her hands, and started her climb. At about ten feet up, the wind knifed through her, stealing every molecule of heat she'd ever generated in her life.

Keep climbing.

By fifteen feet, she had to watch each handheld and foothold because she couldn't feel her fingers or her toes. Her muscles started to quake from the exertion, the cold, her low blood sugar. One or all of the above.

Keep climbing.

Whomp. Whomp. Whomp.

The helicopter bore down on them. She only had a few more minutes to get to the top. She had to hurry, but she also couldn't rush.

Slow is smooth. Smooth is fast.

One foot, one hand. Repeat.

She neared the top as the helo grew from the size of a fly to the size of an eagle.

With a final surge of energy, she made grab for the top edge, getting a firm solid grip. She gave herself a mental high-five.

She did it. She *fucking* did it.

Reaching up with her other hand, she grasped the edge, prepared to pull herself up. The rock broke away without warning. Her body swung freely, but this had happened before.

Only this time you don't have water to break your fall.

But she did have more of a reason to try.

She got a small dump of adrenaline, and her heart spiked above its already revved rate for a beat or two before settling back down.

Her shoulder strained, but her handhold stayed solid. All she had to do was swing her body back up and—

Mia's swing landed too short and her fingers missed the top by mere inches. A fissure of doubt crept in. On her subsequent swing, she missed by even more.

Now her arm shook with the stress and strain, and the only reason she knew she hadn't lost her grip was because she still dangled in the air.

"You've got this." Matt's calm, steady voice drifted up to her. "One more time."

What if she *didn't* have this?

She knew her body.

Knew she couldn't hold on much longer.

Knew she only had enough strength for one last try.

She glanced down. Matt was out of her field of vision, but she felt him in her heart. He filled in all the nooks and crannies, a flood of light to shed the darkness, bringing a featherlight weightlessness, a freedom from all the demons dragging her down.

How could she willingly walk away from a man like that?

Of all of her foolish stunts, walking away from Matt would be the most sensationally stupid.

Had anyone ever loved her unfailingly. Without condition? Bias? Judgment?

What had not allowing herself to be vulnerable accomplished? Not protection. She still *felt*. She still *hurt*. Her high shield had robbed her of connecting and letting the people she loved know how she felt.

That shit has got to change.

Sweat beaded on her forehead despite the impending hypothermia.

"Don't let yourself down. You've got this."

How she heard those words ringing so loud and clear over the whip of the wind and the turn of rotors, she'll never know.

"Feel it, Mann. Like I feel it. Like I *know* it."

Taking a deep, clearing breath, she tried one last time. She might fail, but she refused to fail by giving up.

Kicking her legs back as much as she dared, she swung her body, reaching up up up.

"That's it," Matt hollered, "You're there."

If it weren't taking all of Mia's strength and concentration to latch onto the ledge and hook her ankle over the top, she would have laughed.

She was close, but by no means *there*.

———

"She made it." Charlie's words confirmed what Matt had seen.

Matt might have thought it was a figment of his imagination otherwise as if his mind had willed him to see only what he wanted.

Zach whooped as Mia disappeared over the top. Matt's heart continued beating in triple time, refusing to settle until he saw her stand.

Matt stared at the spot at the top of the cliff where she'd climbed over. She had to be exhausted, but all her valiant efforts would be for nothing if she couldn't flag down the helo.

The helo slowed, flying low, slow circles, knowing they were close but not able to pinpoint their exact location. The boys started shouting and waving their arms over their head even though there was no way they could be seen or heard.

Then the helo started a slow turn away from the mountain.

And still no sign of Mia.

Had she collapsed? Was she okay?

"They're leaving." Zach sounded deflated. No... *defeated*.

Matt squeezed the boy's shoulder and turned him back toward Charlie and the relative safety of the cliff base. It wouldn't do any of them any good to watch the helo disappear into the sky.

That's it.

How was he going to get these boys through another night? And where the hell was Mia?

He squeezed Charlie on his good leg. "It's all right, dude. They'll come back first thing in the morning. Promise."

The tears Charlie had been fighting, finally fell. He swiped at his cheeks, but the tears kept coming. "It hurts so bad."

"I know, buddy. You're doing great. Just hang in there."

Charlie took another swipe at his cheeks. His eyes went wide about the same time Matt realized the sound of the helo's rotors had grown nearer.

Zach turned away. "They're coming back. Look, they're coming back!"

Charlie started crying for real, big gulps and body wracking sobs.

Matt couldn't blame the kid. With the lump in his own throat, it wouldn't take much for Matt to do the same.

"Over there," Zach said. "Near the point of the cliff."

Matt followed where Zach pointed. There. On the edge. Mia wildly waved her jacket over her head as if trying to catch flight herself. She pointed in their direction, and the helo slowed and descended.

She was okay.

Matt doubled over, the relief a physical hit that almost brought him to his knees. And fuck, now he was the one wiping moisture off his cheeks.

But he didn't have time for a reprieve. Now came the hard part. Getting a basket down in windy weather with a bunch of tree cover. It would take a damn miracle to keep the basket from tangling in the branches.

The pilot did a slow circle. A little reconnaissance, Matt

assumed. Matt caught a flash of the helo's underbelly in a gap in the tree cover. The next thing he knew, a basket threaded through that gap, a flight paramedic riding it down.

One wrong move, one gust of wind, and it could get snagged and perhaps take the whole helo down with it. They had to work fast. Every second counted. Get Charlie in the basket and get him out of there.

Matt cleared Zach away and steadied the basket as the helmeted paramedic stepped onto the ground. She unclipped her safety harness and held her hand out to him. "Rayne."

"Matt Bishop," he said, shaking her hand.

"You're not an easy person to find."

Understatement. But they didn't have time for idle chatter. And Rayne didn't wait for his answer. She quickly assessed Charlie while Matt filled her in on what he knew.

Since Charlie was stable, she didn't need to provide immediate treatment. She radioed the helo. The two of them carried Charlie to the basket and strapped him in. Rayne stayed below as the helo winched Charlie into the sky. He vanished above the limbs and leaves. Her radio must have gone off, because she pressed the button on her mic and said, "Copy."

She turned to Matt. "Quinn says he's got just enough fuel to get Zach on board. You and Mia will have to walk out or wait until morning.

"We'll walk."

The cable came back down, this time with a harness instead of a basket. Rayne quickly strapped Zach into the harness and then attached both of their tethers to the cable. "See you guys around," she said before giving Quinn instructions to pull them up.

Matt plopped down on one of the packs and watched until he couldn't see them any longer. Within minutes, the sound of the helo's rotors fell away

Fuck. They'd done it.

Matt stood, a life-affirming, cliff-echoing *whoop* tore from his lungs. Mia appeared at the cliff edge in the same spot where she'd climbed over. She'd put on her jacket and the rest of her warm clothes. Her arms wrapped around her as if holding in the heat.

He walked to the base of the cliff and stared up at her. "You were amazing."

He didn't get a smile. In fact, he didn't get much of a reaction at all. "I'm so cold."

Matt read her lips more than heard the words. She had to be nearly hypothermic after that climb. And if she was already hypothermic, she may not be thinking too clearly.

"I'm going to hike over and meet you at the tree," Mia said, this time a little louder, indicating the tree that spanned the crevice.

The last thing he needed was her getting confused and lost. "Stay there. Start a fire if you can. You have your fire striker with you?" As if dazed, she slowly patted one of the side pockets of her snow pants. "Good. I'll be there as quick as I can. Stay put. You got me?"

Even though she nodded, he wasn't convinced she had truly digested his words. But he couldn't sit there and babysit her. He had to pack up what he could and get to her as fast as possible.

With reluctance, he left her at the top of the cliff. He didn't bother with any of the boy's gear. He had his and Mia's packs to worry about. The boy's parents could always come back and get the gear later.

He shrugged into the biggest pack and strapped the smaller one to his chest. It wasn't the lightest way to travel, but he'd hauled much heavier packs on top of carrying his guns, ammo, and body armor. This would be a walk in the park.

It took longer to get back to the tree crossing than it had to get down to the boys. The heavy load didn't help. And truth be told, the cold, the long hikes, and the serious lack of calories he'd consumed over the past day were taking their toll. But he couldn't stop now. Not until he had Mia safely back at the cabin. They'd have a chance to build a fire and put something hot in their bellies.

With his legs shaky, he didn't trust his balance or want to risk crossing the tree with both packs. He stripped them off and tossed them to the other side. Snow had already started to build back up on the tree. He trudged across, the new snow covering up some of the ice, making it less slippery. If he had his bearings correct, he probably only had another fifteen or twenty-minute hike to get to where he'd left Mia.

He pictured her behind a wind block, a little roaring fire keeping her toasty.

But the closer he got to the cliff, the more worry ate at him. Even congested, he should be smelling smoke by now. He practically broke into a run—as much of a run as a man could manage with two packs, noodle-y legs, and a pair of snowshoes on his feet.

The cliff came into view. He spun in the spot where he'd last seen Mia but couldn't find her anywhere. "Mia!"

The shout didn't travel far, not with dread clogging his throat and squeezing his chest. He whistled next, but no sound came in return except the twitter of some birds holed up in the trees somewhere.

Spotting her tracks, he fell into step. At least he knew which way she'd gone. Her path took her farther and farther away from the cabin. Mia had a good, innate sense of direction—if she were going this way, something was wrong.

He pressed on, ignoring the burn in his quads and the bruising beat of his heart against his sternum. Matt didn't stop until her tracks stopped. He glanced around. She couldn't have just disappeared.

Then he noticed the disturbance in the snowbank, and the tuft of blue material. Her jacket. *Mia.*

Dropping the packs, he fell to his knees, digging her out of the snowbank. She must have collapsed into the snowdrift, practically disappearing beneath the pile of snow. He crawled to her head, her face bright red from the cold. He patted her cheek, leaned in, and listened for the sound of her breath. He shook her, and her head fell back.

No.

No. No. No.

He patted the side of her face, lighter than he dared, but harder than he wanted. She grunted, and her eyes fluttered. *Oh, thank fuck.* But she wasn't out of immediate danger.

"It's okay," she mumbled, her eyes closing again. "I'm warm now."

Jesus Christ. Severe hypothermia had set in. You didn't get to the stage where you felt warm until the hypothermia got really serious. No way could she pack herself out of there. He'd have to carry her out.

How can you do that when you can barely carry yourself?

He had no clue. But he had to get her somewhere warm and get some food into them both.

Strapping the smaller pack to his chest again, the one with the food and water, he lifted Mia onto his back in the classic fireman's carry. He paused and braced his weight against a tree, shifting her and catching his balance.

Then he started walking.

A little farther up, Matt stopped and leaned against another tree, his breath billowing in and out of his lungs, his head light, his legs heavy. He needed to put Mia down. He needed to rest. But he feared he'd never be able to pick her up again if he did.

Keep going.

The sound of laughter rent the crisp air. Matt turned toward the sound, his world swirling as if it couldn't spin fast enough to keep up with him. The laughter came again, this time from his other side.

Laughter. Light. Loud.

Yusef.

Catch me. Catch me. The laughter came again. From behind him this time. Matt spun, his legs tangled, taking him to his knees. The pack on his chest kept him from faceplanting into the snow.

Mia grunted on impact, but otherwise didn't move.

Maybe if he just rested a few minutes, then he'd be good to go again. Just a few...

Yusef stood in front of him, that gregarious, infectious smile on his face. His laughter tore Matt's heart apart and put it back together all at the same time. The boy held his hand out to Matt. "Come, come. This way."

But Matt needed to rest. Right here, where it was warm.

"Come, come." The boy took his hand and pulled and pulled.

Matt struggled to his feet and followed the boy.

Yusef was alive. It had all just been a bad dream after all.

A nightmare that Matt had finally escaped. He cried and laughed. It was okay. Everything was going to be okay.

Yusef led him onto a porch, the hollow sound of wood echoed beneath Matt's feet. Yusef grabbed for the knob of the door. "Come, come."

Matt fell to his knees, the sharp pain jarred him as Mia slipped off his back and onto the porch beside him. The laughter came again, but somehow Matt knew when he turned that no one was there.

Matt fought his way out of the pack and crawled over to Mia. This time when he patted her cheeks, her eyes fluttered open and focused on him. "I love you," she said. Her eyes drifted, looking all around. "And Disney is so pretty this time of year."

What the actual fuck?

He stumbled to his feet, shouldered open the door. Hooking his hands under Mia's arms, he hauled her into the cabin and closed the door behind him. Matt leaned against the door and sank to the floor. He had a fire to start, and a woman he needed to warm. But his heart hurt.

Yusef *was* dead.

He hadn't woken from his dream.

He was still living his nightmare.

14

———

THE CLOMP OF A BOOT WOKE MIA FROM A DEAD SLEEP. SHE opened her eyes and stared up at the roughhewn rafters and tin roof overhead. The cabin door opened, and Matt stepped in, swinging her pack off his back. Bright morning light skipped around him, promising a clear, sunny day.

About damn time.

"Morning, Sleeping Beauty."

"*Sleeping Beauty?*"

He pulled off his snow-covered boots and sat on the side of the bed. Easing the covers from over her chin, he kissed her on the lips and leaned back. "There was a moment there last night when you thought you were at Disney."

She pressed a hand to her forehead, where the dregs of a headache lingered. Her tongue felt fat, and the roof of her mouth felt dry and parched. Matt must have read her mind because he reached for a canteen on the floor and held it to her lips. She rose onto one arm, drank a few sips, then collapsed again.

Now that he said that, Disney did sound familiar. "What else did I say?"

His half smile held more warmth than the fire he must have stoked before he'd left the cabin. "You don't remember?"

His tone still teased, but there was an undercurrent there that Mia couldn't put her finger on.

Had she said something important? Something she needed to remember? "It's all pretty fuzzy."

His smile fell, and her heart tumbled with it. If she knew what he wanted to hear, she'd say it, if only to see him smile again. "What did I say?"

"Nothing important. You were pretty out of it."

He patted her leg and went back to the fire, poking it and adding another log. The dry wood caught, popping and hissing and lighting up the room.

"Where were you this morning?"

Matt turned around. Whatever had dimmed his smile seemed forgotten. "I had to leave one of the packs behind to carry you here. It had all your gear, so I didn't want to leave it out there. Now, I'm starving."

"Me, too."

Mia sat up and swung her legs over the side of the bed. Sometime last night, Matt had stripped her to her thermals. She'd rather stay all day in bed wrapped up in a warm blanket and preferably wrapped up in Matt, but nature was a bitch and she was calling. "I really have to pee."

Matt handed over her clothes and boots and helped her dress. Her hands shook with the effort, and she couldn't remember a time she'd felt so drained.

"You need some help?"

"I'm only going to step out back. I should be fine, but thanks."

It almost seemed a shame to put all her clothes on only to have to pull them back down to pee, but going out there in only her thermals, even if it was only for a minute, wasn't an option in her current state.

By the time she made it back inside the cabin, Matt was heating water over the fire in a pan he must have found. She sat on the bed, and he blew into a dusty cup and filled it with hot water. He added instant coffee from their supplies and stirred it with a plastic spoon. They hadn't brought any plastic spoons. She tried not to think about that when he handed her the cup and started making his own.

She blew on her coffee but didn't wait long, not caring that it nearly scorched her tongue. The hot liquid burned a trail down the back of her throat and settled in her stomach, adding warmth from the inside out.

She stretched her neck and her back, her muscles sore in a way that didn't account for all the hiking they'd done. "Why do I feel like Tyson used me for a few warm-up rounds?"

"I had to carry you part of the way," Matt said. Like no big deal, like he'd done nothing more than haul her groceries in from the car.

"How far?"

He shrugged as if he didn't know, when she knew for certain he did since he'd just gone there to retrieve her pack.

She would have died out there. Mia knew that. If she had been so out of it that she couldn't walk, that she thought she was at *fucking* Disney...

"I—" That's all she got out before the words lodged in her throat.

Matt glanced over at her, a brow raised, ever patient.

She took another swallow of coffee and waited for a few milligrams of caffeine to spark up her system. "I'm sorry you had to carry me."

Matt's eyes narrowed. He dropped the fire poker and sat

down on the bed beside her, setting his cup of coffee on the floor. "You say that like you were a burden."

"Out there, in weather like this, half out of my mind… I was."

"Not to me. And if it weren't for you, we'd all still be out there freezing our asses off, waiting for a rescue. You risked your life for those boys. Besides that, I love you. I'd carry you halfway around the world if I had to."

She glanced away. Would hearing 'I love you' ever get any easier? Would she ever feel worthy?

Hooking a finger under her chin, he made her look at him. "Why is it so hard for you to hear me say 'I love you?'"

She shook her head. She didn't have any of the answers.

"You are the bravest, fiercest woman that I know, yet you're terrified of letting someone love you."

He saw so deeply into her soul. It was if he'd tipped a ladder against her shield and peeked over the top, seeing all her insecurities, her foibles, frailties, her *sins*. It made her want to run.

But out there on that cliff, she'd realized her shield hadn't protected her. It had imprisoned her. Mentally, she took a sledgehammer and took a hefty swing at that shield. "No one has ever loved me the way you do. It's humbling. And scary. And exhilarating. And…"

Could she say it? Did she dare?

"And what, Mia?"

"And I think I might love you, too."

Matt grinned, bumping her in the shoulder with his. "You don't seem too happy about that."

"I'm happy. I think." She blew out a breath, her heart beating faster than it had when she hung there at the top of the cliff. "It's somewhere under the terror and the uncertainty and the disbelief and—"

Matt chuckled. "Okay, okay. I'm getting the picture."

Taking her coffee from her hand, he placed it on the floor

next to his. He traced his fingers down each side of her face, from her forehead, along her temple, and across her jaw. Her eyes fluttered closed at the gentle, healing touch. When she opened her eyes again, he leaned in for a kiss.

His lips brushed hers, tender and too fleeting. When he went to break the kiss, she wrapped her hands around the back of his neck and pulled him in for more. *This,* she understood. The want and the need. She shifted and pulled him down on top of her.

He took the kiss deeper as he settled between her legs, taking his weight on his forearms. He tasted of cheap instant coffee and smelled of fire smoked pine. And she wanted more. More of him.

She poured herself into the kiss, all the intensity, all the doubt, all the swirling of emotions she couldn't quite decipher.

Somehow, he took it all in, made sense of it, and reflected it back to her, all entwined with his own emotions, his love. Had she ever felt so full, so seen, so *known*?

She fumbled with the snap on his snow pants, but he reached down and covered her hand with his. "As much as I want this, I don't think I'll have the energy to love you the way I want to *and* climb off this mountain. But I promise as soon as we get home, I'm going to make it up to you."

He slid to the side and stretched out beside her. He had to be exhausted from hauling her and their packs over half of the Rockies. Matt's arms slid around her waist and snugged her up against him, his eyes already drifting closed.

"Didn't you get any sleep last night?"

———

MATT DIDN'T KNOW WHETHER TO TELL THE TRUTH OR LIE. THAT

he hadn't slept. He didn't want her to feel bad, but dishonesty, especially with someone he loved, didn't sit well with him.

"Not so much," he said.

He forced his eyes open as she rolled onto her side to face him. They really should be focusing on getting something to eat and getting back home, but those things didn't seem like a priority right then. The boys had been evacuated to safety. Now he and Mia could take a little time for themselves.

"Neither one of us was in very good shape by the time we made it back to the cabin. It took a while to get a good fire going, get you stripped and under the covers, and..."

He wanted to tell her the rest, but now in the light of day, the sun shining and the birds singing, he wondered how much of any of it had been real. If he told her about Yusef, would he sound crazy?

"What aren't you telling me?"

Sucking in a breath, he blew it out and vowed to tell her what had happened even if it made him look certifiable.

"On the way back to the cabin, I heard laughter." Her brows rose but she didn't interrupt. "I think... I think I was delirious, because one minute we were alone, and the next, Yusef stood in front of me."

He told her the whole story, about how Yusef had taken his hand, had encouraged him to follow, how Yusef had led Matt right to the cabin door. "He seemed so real. I thought I'd woken from my nightmare and that he was alive."

"Sounds like he saved our lives. Like he's your guardian angel."

Matt chuckled in disbelief. "I don't believe in guardian angels."

"Then what would you call what happened?"

"My mind playing tricks on me."

She made a noise in the back of her throat that sounded noncommittal. But did she have a point?

"It was weird though, when we'd both finally stopped shivering, when I felt it was safe to drift off to sleep, I dreamt about him again. Only this time it was different."

She took one of his hands and entwined their fingers, curling their joined hands against her chest where he felt her heart beating true. "How so?"

"For the first time, the smiles and the laughter remained. There was no shift in the dream. Yusef didn't turn from this bright, vibrant boy into that lifeless, bullet-riddled body. He was just a boy." Matt swallowed down the jagged lump in his throat. "Forever a boy."

"That's a gift."

Even if there were no such things as guardian angels, Matt warmed to the thought of Yusef being his.

He squeezed her hand, wanting to shift the focus away from him. "When we get back, we should celebrate that you've spent three nights under shelter."

"Yeah, well, last night I was only semi-conscious. I'm not sure that counts."

"In my book it does."

Her smile reached her eyes and did a number on his heart. If he didn't already love her, that little smile would have made him fall for her all over again.

Giving her a pat on the ass, he said, "We should get some food in us and hit the trail. I want to make it back to the ranch with plenty of daylight ahead of us."

They didn't talk much as they ate, packed up, doused the fire, and hit the trail. The hike to the snowmobile was more pleasant than the hike to the cabin. Not only did they not have the boys to worry about, but the sun shined bright, and the wind had died.

Mia drove the snowmobile with a heavy hand on the throttle. They made it back to the ranch with a couple of hours of daylight to spare.

Mia parked the snowmobile in front of the barn where Zealand was working one of the gentled big bay mustangs in the round pen under Sidney's watchful eye. At the sound of the engine, Jenna came out of the barn, and Pepita came running over from the Big House.

Zealand climbed up and over the round pen and was the first to greet them. He gave Matt a back-slapping hug and pulled Mia into his side, planting a smacking kiss on her temple. "How you doing, beautiful?"

Mia groaned. "Stop calling me that."

Zealand chuckled and let her go.

Pepita rushed her, jumping into Mia's arms and wrapping her in a bear hug. How Mia remained standing was the real miracle of the past few days. "Charlie and Zach said you were fricking amazing. You saved their lives and—"

"I wasn't the only one there." Mia set Pepita back on the ground. "Matt had a hand in it, too."

"I know." Pepita gave him a hug that felt more like a condolence prize. "But he didn't scale a cliff."

Matt stood back and enjoyed watching Pepita fangirl all over Mia. Hell, it was hard for him to not do the same.

Jenna and Sidney joined the hug fest, their faces getting all blotchy as they tried to rein in their emotions.

Jenna pulled her phone out of her pocket. "I have to call St. John. He wanted me to let him know when you guys returned."

"No need." Zealand pointed down the ranch's long drive at the sheriff's pickup truck as it slipped and slid in the mud and snow. "He's here."

Pepita bounced on the balls of her feet beside Mia, holding

her hand, not letting go, her excitement at their return both adorable and infectious.

As a group, they walked over to the sheriff as he parked near the barn and climbed out. There were greetings and handshakes all around.

"How are the boys?" Matt asked.

"Grounded," Pepita piped in.

They all laughed, and then St. John said, "Charlie had surgery this morning, and is expected to go home tomorrow or the next day. Zach was checked out at the hospital and released last night. All in all, a couple of very lucky boys."

"Not when their parents get done with them," Pepita muttered.

Matt barked out a laugh. "Well, it will give them something to tell their grandkids someday."

"I wanted to come by and thank you two personally," St. John said. "And I wanted to tell you that I put you two in for a commendation from the city. There's going to be a press conference the day after tomorrow at the station. Five o'clock. Be there."

Mia turned green. Matt knew Mia hated that kind of attention. She preferred to blend into the background. But it was hard to do that when you were a hero.

"That's not really necessary," she said.

"Tell that to the mayor." St. John hitched his thumb toward his truck. "I've gotta go. Kleb Clayhorn's bull jumped the fence again and Mitchell is threatening to shoot it if Kleb can't keep him on his own property."

They said their goodbyes, and everyone returned their attention to Mia and Matt.

"I've never met a real hero before," Pepita said.

"Sure, you have," Mia deflected. "Your mom and dad and just about everyone on this ranch are heroes. All in their own way."

"You're right, but they still didn't climb any cliffs. I wish I'd been there to see it."

Sidney clamped her hands down on Pepita's shoulders. "I, for one, am very glad you weren't. And so is your father."

"And me," Jenna said.

Zealand gave her a soft punch in the arm. "Ditto, kid."

"Why don't we call it a day, guys," Jenna said to Zealand and Sidney. Then to Matt and Mia she said, "Lottie and Dale are home. Lottie's making a big dinner to celebrate being back and the babies being born. We'd love for you two to join us tonight."

"How are the babies?" Mia asked.

"They're expected to be able to come home at the end of the week. They're small, but mighty," Sidney said.

"Just like their mom." Pepita reached down and zipped up her jacket. In her rush to greet Mia and Matt, she'd run out in nothing more than her jeans and a pair of flip-flops.

Mia pasted one of those smiles on her face, and Matt knew, after seeing that, Mia would decline dinner. Big crowds weren't her thing, and to be honest, he'd like nothing more than a quiet night alone with her.

"I'm pretty tired. I think I'm just going to take a hot shower and call it a night."

Matt took her hand. "Same."

"We get it." Sidney steered her daughter toward the house. "Get back inside before you freeze."

"See you two in the morning," Jenna said as she started for the house herself. "I'll take barn duty so you guys can sleep in if you want."

"Thanks." Matt reached for their packs.

Zealand brushed Matt off. "You guys go. I'll bring your things down when I've put the horse away."

Matt would be a fool to argue. And he was too damn exhausted for that. "Thanks, man."

With an arm around Mia's shoulder, they walked the short distance to their cabins. He led her to her door, hoping for an invitation, but not expecting one. He leaned one shoulder against the wall to the left of the door. "You did a good thing, Mann. You should be proud."

For the first time, instead of deflecting a compliment, she accepted it. "Thanks. I kinda am. Who would have known my misspent youth would come in handy?"

"Anything that brings you joy isn't misspent."

She didn't have a smart-ass retort for that. She pushed her door open a few inches. "You coming?"

"You asking?"

"Sounded like it."

Matt slid a hand around her waist and kissed her. He wanted to take it deeper, but with his invitation, he'd have plenty of time for that. "I'm going to catch a shower, make us some sandwiches."

He left her with another kiss and a promise he'd be back. Once inside his cabin, he left a trail of clothes as he stripped on his way to the shower. He just hoped the hot water lasted long enough to scare the chill out of his bones.

Zealand returned to the cabin as Matt finished making Mia's sandwich. Matt stuffed the sandwiches along with the two apples and a bag of tortilla chips into a grocery bag. He reached back into the fridge for some of Zealand's contraband beer.

He held the bottles up. "Do you mind?"

"Take them all if you want."

"Naw, if I have more than one, I'm going to pass out."

They stood there awkwardly looking at each other, each feeling like they should say something, but neither one of them knowing what.

"Are you two okay?" Zealand finally asked. Clearly, they were both alive and in one piece, so Matt knew Zealand expected more than a casual, "I'm fine."

Matt set the beer on the counter beside the food and crossed his arms over his chest. He scrubbed his hands down his wind chapped face and shook his head. "Fuck me, Zee. She scared three decades off my life. She'd made it to the top, then a handhold broke away. She hung there by one arm, and all I could see was her falling and me not being able to do a damn thing about it."

"It's not a good feeling." The king of understatement. "But these women we love don't need saving. They can save themselves."

"And everyone else, apparently."

Zealand clapped him on the shoulder. "You've got that right."

Matt slipped the handles of the grocery bag over his arm, grabbed the necks of the bottles in one hand, and headed for the door. He held the beer up and said, "Thanks, again for these."

"Oh, hey, hold up. I've got something else for you." The smile in Zealand's voice had Matt turning at the door.

Zealand grabbed something out of his footlocker and stuffed it in Matt's bag.

"What's that?"

"Your own box of condoms. Now stay out of mine."

Matt laughed as he opened the door. "Then you should have bought me the jumbo pack."

MATT WALKED INTO MIA'S CABIN WITHOUT KNOCKING, WHICH WAS perfectly fine with her. At this point, they really didn't have many personal boundaries. She finished pulling her heavy sweatpants over her hips and slipped a fuzzy sweatshirt over her head, sans bra.

She'd cranked the heat up in the cabin as soon as she'd walked in, but she still couldn't quite get warm.

Matt had a bag on his arm, two beers in one hand, and an irrepressible smile on his face. She met him at the kitchen counter and pulled everything out of the bag. Ham sandwiches, apples, chips, and… condoms? She held up the box. "What are these for?"

"Should I start with the birds and the bees, or—"

She elbowed him in the ribs. "That's not what I meant, and you know it."

"It's a gift from Zealand."

Good Lord. Mia laughed. She should be embarrassed, but she couldn't drum up any emotion besides gratitude. "Cheapskate. He should have bought the big box."

Matt grinned at her. "That's what I told him."

He leaned against the counter, took her hips in his hands, and settled her between his strong legs. She locked her hands around his lower back. He smiled down at her as if she was the most brilliant star in the sky, the funniest joke, the wisest word, the kindest soul, the prettiest view.

He smiled down at her as if she was his world.

She tried to breathe in. Her chest refused to expand, wrapped up in the best emotional bondage.

"We make a really good team," he said at last.

"Agreed."

She thought back on their three days in the mountains. It had been trying, frightening, primal, but also exhilarating, life affirming. Despite the cold, the harshness of the environment, and the high stakes, she couldn't get past the feeling that out there, in the hills and the valleys, was where she belonged. She didn't know what that meant for her moving forward. Her life after Healing Horses was so high up in the air, the space station would have to dodge it.

He tipped her chin up. The emotion welled in his eyes and made his face blotchy. "I almost lost you."

Matt pulled her into his chest, holding on tight as he buried his face into the crook of her neck, his breath coming in shudders. She held onto this man who'd looked over her shields and had the guts not to run screaming.

When his arms loosened, when his heart no longer thumped erratically against her chest, she pulled away, having to clear her throat when she said, "You ready to eat? All this sappy shit makes me hungry."

Matt laughed and placed a smacking kiss on her temple. "I'm starved."

They got out plates and divvied up the food. Matt twisted off the tops on the beer and took a long swallow from one before setting them on the table. Matt turned his chair around, sitting in it backwards across from her and dug into his food as if he'd been hiking across the Rockies for three days.

It only took minutes for the food to be demolished. Matt chewed on his apple core until only the seeds and stem remained.

"I could make us something else," Mia said, "if you're still hungry."

"I'm good for now."

Mia felt that creeping feeling under her skin as daylight began to fade. She went through the cabin turning on all the lights to stave off the encroaching walls. She may have managed to avoid sleeping in the open three times, but that didn't mean she was cured.

Though having Matt as a distraction didn't hurt.

She helped him clear the table, and she hopped up on the

counter next to him as he washed their plates. "So... what are your plans after Healing Horses?"

He stopped sponging the plate mid-swipe. "I'm not sure. What are your plans?"

"What does that have to do with me?"

Mia jumped when the plate Matt dropped clattered in the sink. With what looked like extra care, he shut off the water and dried his hands on a dishtowel, taking his time folding it and laying it on the counter next to him.

He turned toward her, leaning a hip against the counter that, by the tension in his entire body, was more calculating than casual. "It has everything to do with you."

"Why?"

"You're fucking kidding me, right?" The smile on Matt's face was deceptively cool, hiding the nuances of his anger.

He stared at her.

She stared back.

"Because I love you, Mia. Why the hell else do you think?" He didn't give her time to answer before continuing. "Because... I don't know... because maybe I want to see where this can go, see if we've got something that will last? What I feel for you doesn't come along every day, and I'm not willing to throw up my hands and walk away from it like it's something I can find around every corner or under every stone. It's not, Mia. This—" he gestured between the two of them, "is something special."

"I don't even know if I'm graduating yet. I could be going to jail for a year for all I know."

"Then I'll fucking wait." Matt paced away from her. She'd never seen him this agitated before.

"You can't wait."

He stormed back, settling his hands on the counter on either side of her, his face inches from hers, his complexion red, and a vein throbbing at his temple. "Oh, yeah, Mann? Who's gonna stop me?"

"Maybe you should leave."

He straightened and went for the door, his hand on the knob when he glanced up at the ceiling. He took in a deep breath and blew it out. He would walk out. Because that's when they always left, when they got frustrated and mad and angry and disappointed and realized she was too much. That she wasn't worth the effort.

She braced her hands on the counter and stared down at the floor, knowing it would tear out her heart if she had to watch him leave.

Mia didn't hear his approach until he was close enough to reach out and take her hand. He wrapped it in his, and brought it to his lips, kissing the back of her hand.

"Look at me." All anger had drained from is voice. "I don't want to leave. But I will if that's what you *really* want."

Mia's eyes stung, and she sniffed back the tears before glancing up at him. "You're mad."

"Yeah, but that doesn't mean I want to go."

"That's when they all go." She couldn't hold his gaze anymore. It hurt too much. This love shit? *Highly* over-rated.

"Oh, baby." Matt wrapped her up in his arms, holding on tight and kissing the side of her head. "Just because I'm mad, or frustrated, or infuriated, doesn't mean I don't love you anymore. All it means is we need to talk things through until we're on the same page."

Mia pulled back, her breath hitching. "W-what if we can't get on the same page? What if we aren't even in the same fucking library?"

"Then that would be the real shame. We don't have to have all the answers tonight, Mia, but it would be great if we could at least agree that whatever we face next, we face it together."

"I think I'd like that."

Matt stepped between her legs, holding her face in his hands as he kissed her. He hadn't apologized, but neither had she. They let their lips, their tongues, their passion, do the talking for them.

Hitching his hands under her ass, he lifted her off the counter, and she wrapped her legs around his waist. He carried her to the bed and laid her down, going back for the box of condoms. He crawled over the top of her so she could be on the outside of the bed.

Matt slipped his fingers under her sweatshirt, his hand spanning her abdomen as he nipped and kissed his way across her jaw.

"How are the walls?" He slipped his hand under the waistband of her sweats. "No underwear. Jesus, that's sexy as hell."

"Holding. For now." Mia's eyes drifted closed, and she arched up into his touch, wanting his hands in all the places that brought her pleasure and made her forget.

"I'm pretty sure I can find a way to distract you, if you want." His fingertips brushed through the short curls between her thighs, teasing and taunting.

"I don't want you to distract me, Matt." He glanced up at her, the slightest confusion on his face. She dug down deep for the words, the vulnerability welling up almost choked her. "I want you to love me."

He rolled between her legs, nipped at her chin, and kissed her on the lips. "I can do that."

For the first time in as long as she could remember, she let a man take the lead. She didn't want control. She wanted to hold up the white flag and surrender.

Matt took his time removing first her sweatshirt and then her sweatpants. It took a lot of kisses and nibbles and licking of hard nipples to get her stripped, but by the time he did, she'd lost all sense of where she was or which dimension she existed in.

Maybe she was somewhere in between.

Somewhere where the stars came within reach and the galaxy spread out all around her as she drowned in her pleasure. Inch by inch he made his way down her legs, kneading the sore muscles in her calves, kissing a trail up the tender flesh on her inner thighs.

Her hands fisted in his hair as his tongue traced the seam where her leg joined her body. Her hips rose, and she cried out in frustration when Matt skipped over the good bits and traced the seam on the other side.

Matt chuckled and drew back. "What's the matter, baby?"

She gripped his hair tighter and stared down at him. "You know damn well what the matter is."

The innocent rise of his eyebrows said he was clueless, but the mischievous grin on his face gave him away. He nipped her inner thigh and licked the erotic sting away. "Maybe you should tell me what you want, clear and slow, like I'm a grunt on my first day of basic training."

Who was she not to give a man what he wanted?

"I want you to suck me, then I want you to fuck me. That clear enough for you, soldier?"

"*Jesus Christ*," Matt muttered, his eyes lighting with delight. "You keep talking like that, and you'll make me come without even touching me."

She scrubbed her hand over his head and got a better grip, tugging his head back so he could see her face and not misinterpret her words. "You have your orders, soldier. Don't make me tell you again."

"Yes, ma'am."

He shook off her hand and dove in, his tongue tracing up her center before landing at her clit.

Angels sang.

Fireworks exploded.

A rift formed in the space-time continuum.

With her hands on the back of his head, she held him there, never wanting him to leave. Hips arching up, she ground against him as he licked and sucked.

Pulses of lightning, of liquid fire, raced up and down her arms and legs. Goosebumps erupted like a million tiny volcanoes. She didn't fight the sensations, she reveled in them. Each shudder, each shake, reminding her she was alive.

Reaching her peak, Matt eased off, kissing her inner thigh before she could go over. She moaned her complaint, but that only made Matt chuckle. Wiping his face in the covers, he rolled out of bed and quickly stripped naked.

His cock, with precum dripping from the slit, was the most perfect salute she'd ever witnessed in her life. "I need that over here."

He shook his head. "If you touch me, I'm coming. And I don't want to do that until I'm inside you."

15

Matt climbed back into bed and tore into the box of
condoms. Within seconds, he sheathed himself and resettled
between her legs, scooping his arms beneath her shoulders and
cradling her head.

He kissed her, and she opened for him, their tongues
dancing for once instead of dueling. With his cock between her
thighs, he pressed against her, enjoying the groan of frustration
erupting from the back of her throat.

She grabbed his ears and broke the kiss. "If you don't put
that thing in me now, I'll have to discipline you for insubor-
dination."

God, he loved this woman.

Matt laughed and nipped at her jaw. "That fucking sounds
like fun."

"*Matt.*"

Reaching down, he took hold of himself and gave her what
she wanted. What they *both* wanted. He buried himself balls
deep, the long, slow slide into her slick warmth made her buck
up and her eyes roll into the back of her head with a satisfied
moan.

He had to hold himself still and take a calming breath to keep from immediately climaxing. Though the thought of what she'd do to him as punishment almost had him spilling himself. But that was for another time.

For now, he wanted her to know she was cherished, know that his love was unconditional, know that no matter what, they could get through anything as long as they were together.

He didn't know if he could convey all that with his body, but he would give it his damn level best.

Her moans got longer, and her breath got shorter as he thrust into her with slow, fluid strokes. Mia's head thrashed from side to side, her eyes squeezed shut as she met each stroke, driving him deeper.

His balls drew up tight, and as much as he wanted this to last for now and forever, it wasn't going to happen. He consoled himself with the knowledge that with his short refractory period, he could be up and running again for round two in a very short period of time if she wanted.

Mia grabbed his ass, encouraging him to increase his speed, to lose herself in the fucking, in the sounds of flesh on flesh, in the smell of musk and sweat. But he didn't want her lost.

He wanted her to know she'd been found.

"Mia," he said, slowing even more, drawing her attention. "Look at me."

She opened her eyes. She may have only told him she loved him once. She may not have known if she'd really meant it. But in her eyes, he *saw* the words laid bare before him.

"There you are," he said.

"Here I am."

His heart beat fast and strong, so full of love that it tripped and tumbled and forgot its rhythm. "You with me?"

"Always."

The admission stole his breath, made his head go light, and

pins prick behind his eyes. He didn't blink back the moisture that gathered because it matched her own.

The base of his spine buzzed with his impending orgasm, his once-slow strokes becoming faster, harder, erratic. Mia rode the wave with him, her head falling back and her eyes closing in bliss.

She shuddered in his arms, her muscles clamping down around him. He fell over with her, breaking her fall and catching her on the other side.

He collapsed on top of her, then realized what he'd done. He went to brace himself on his arms so she wouldn't feel trapped, but she held on tight as her breathing slowed and she came back into herself.

"I'd better take care of the condom," he said as he started to go soft. "I'll be right back."

He climbed out of bed and quickly cleaned up. Grabbing a bottle of water out of the refrigerator, he took several long swallows, drinking so fast that it spilled down his chin and chest.

He wiped himself dry with his hand and passed her the bottle.

"Thanks." She sat up and polished off the rest. "I think I'm still a little dehydrated from the past few days."

"Same." He tossed the empty bottle in the trash under the sink and brought another to bed with him. "I think it will take us a day or two to fully recover. Especially with all of our extracurricular activities at night."

"It's worth it."

Matt crawled over the top of her and lay down beside her. With the heat turned up in the cabin, they didn't need to get under the covers as the sweat on their bodies dried. He rolled up onto one arm and looked down at her, his fingers tracing all around her torso and the bits and pieces of her tattoos that curved around her sides with a light touch.

If the walls had started closing in on her, she hadn't said, but by the way she lay there, her body relaxed and free of tension, he had to believe that for now, the walls stayed at bay.

He could get used to this, lying in bed, a sated Mia beside him with nothing more to worry about than if the box of condoms Zealand had bought them would last the night.

As much as Matt had enjoyed their first time having sex, back when she'd sneaked into his cabin in the dark, taking him in near silence... as hot as that had been, the disconnect had left him wanting.

This time... *This time* she'd been all in, whether she'd known it or not. He'd felt it. Cherished it. Would the two of them make it? He didn't know. He only knew that he'd give it his all, that he'd try to show Mia every second of every day that she was worthy, that she was loved, that she was his world.

"I DON'T UNDERSTAND WHY WE HAVE TO DO THIS," MIA complained as she pulled on the dress pair of jeans and the fancy pair of cowboy boots she borrowed from Jenna. Mia hadn't brought anything to Healing Horses nice enough for the ceremony, the press conference, or the cash bar reception after.

"I think it's nice that the town wants to show their appreciation," Matt replied from the bathroom.

Mia found him and bumped him aside with her hip as he slapped on the last of his aftershave. At least she didn't have to worry about doing her hair because it still hadn't grown in sufficiently to do anything with it. She looked like a recruit who had gone AWOL and missed their regular haircut. Not that she really cared that much. Besides, Jenna had also provided a crisp, black cowboy hat, which would cover her head.

She squeezed a bead of toothpaste onto her toothbrush and started brushing. "Ah fink ah wud uh—"

Matt stilled her hand and pulled the toothbrush out of her mouth. "I can't understand a word you're saying."

"I said I think I would have left the boys up there if I'd known they'd punish us with this silly ceremony."

He released her hand, and she resumed her brushing.

"We did a good thing here, Mia."

"I know. I just—"

"Don't like being the center of attention. Yeah. I know." He gave her a swat on the ass as he scooted by her. "You're just going to have to suck it up, buttercup. I'll buy you a stiff drink at the reception. It will make smiling at all your admirers that much easier."

She spit into the sink and rinsed out her mouth.

Too bad she couldn't have that drink before they left.

By the time she and Matt walked up the steps to the small stage set up in the annex of local VFW hall, Mia's stomach had tied into a convoluted knot. There were mics and reporters and... *people.*

"Why are there so many people?" Mia whispered to Matt as they took their assigned places at the back of the stage to one side of the mayor.

Mayor Jenkins was a broad, black woman who looked like her hard angles had been softened by time. But she had a way of talking to you that made you feel seen, much like Matt, and Mia didn't know what to do with that. Not when most of the time she tried to go unnoticed.

The United States and the state of Wyoming flags flanked them on either side. St. John stood on the far side of the mayor, all buttoned up in his dress uniform. Poor guy. Mia caught his eye and mouthed the word, "Sorry."

She didn't see or hear his response because Matt elbowed

her in the ribs, as the mayor's microphone buzzed with feedback.

"Welcome everyone," the mayor said. "We are here..."

Mia rocked back on the heels of her borrowed boots, tuning the mayor out. She knew what she and Matt had done. She didn't need to hear the recounting. On the floor in front of the stage, about fifty or sixty folding chairs had been set out with an open aisle down the middle. A few reporters sat in front with Charlie and Zach and their parents while the locals filled the rest of the chairs. Some people lined the walls as late arrivals found all the seats taken.

Mia wasn't so convinced they were all here to celebrate her and Matt as much as enjoy a town gathering and heavy hor d'ourves on the town's dime.

Charlie gave her a little wave, his injured leg resting on a chair with his crutches on the floor next to him. She waved back. And fuck if seeing the kids smiling, with healing scabs on their now-clean faces, didn't clog Mia's throat.

Matt was right. They'd done a good thing here.

After the mayor spoke, St. John gave a short but sweet speech, and then the awards were given. Brass plaques on a walnut base. What the hell would she do with it? She didn't have a home, much less a place to put it.

Then photos were taken, thanks given, and hands shook.

Just when she'd thought she'd survived the worst of it, she stepped off the stage with Matt at her back, and Zach and Charlie's mothers wrapped her in hugs. Their tears of thanks enough to make Mia emotional all over again. She caught Matt's eye over Charlie's mother's shoulder and gave him a look that said, 'Where are those drinks?'

He smiled back at her and mouthed, "Hang in there," as Zach's dad shook his hand.

When the mothers released her, the boys came in for a hug.

That was what she'd needed. Not all the flash and ceremony. Just seeing the two boys safe and happy.

"You boys look a damn sight better than you did the last time I saw you."

"I'm just glad to be warm," Zach said. "I'm trying to get my parents to move to Florida, but I don't think it's going to work."

Mia laughed and to Charlie asked, "How's the leg?"

"Still hurts, but I got to fly in a helicopter and ride up in the basket, so it was worth it."

"You have plans to move to Florida with Zach?"

"Nope. I think I wanna go into search and rescue now. I think here's a great place to do it."

Charlie's mother put her hands on his shoulders. "I think you need a career in padded-room resting. I don't think I could take it knowing you were out there on the mountain again."

"*Mom*," Charlie said in that way kids do when their parents are being unreasonable. "It's not like—"

Movement by the open double doors leading into the annex caught Mia's eye. She did a double take.

No.

Who invited *them*?

Zach waved his hand in front of Mia's face. "Are you okay? You're as white as Charlie was."

"I—I'm fine." She glanced around. Where was Matt?

He must have seen the color drain from her face because he excused himself from one of the reporters and came over to her, his hand on her elbow. He glanced around, searching for danger, but no way he'd know danger came wearing a box store suit or fake pearls. He leaned in and said, "What's wrong?"

"Get me out of here."

———

MATT DIDN'T KNOW WHAT THE HELL WAS GOING ON, BUT HE deftly made their excuses to the small crowd around them and ushered Mia through a swinging on one side of the room. Turns out it led into the kitchen.

There were baking sheets filled with food that made his stomach grumble. He maneuvered past a couple of the caterers dressed in black pants and white shirts who were more concerned about the filling in the pastries than their quiet domain had been invaded. Matt found a door to the supply closet, tugged her inside, and closed the door for privacy. It smelled of bleach and musty old mops.

"What happened out there?"

"My parents are here."

"Who invited them?"

"That's what I want to know."

He turned over a couple of empty five-gallon buckets and sat her down on one while he took the other. "I guess it doesn't really matter who. The only thing that matters is what you want to do about it."

"Run."

Matt raised his hands as if surrendering. "If that's what you want to do, Mann, say the word. I'll drive you out of here right now. And we can keep on driving for all I care. If we can't drive far enough, I'll get you a boat. If that's still not far enough, I'll find you a rocket. Name it. I'll do it."

"Fuck." She curled in on herself, her hands clasped behind her head, her elbows on her knees. She wasn't hyperventilating, but Matt kept a close eye on her just in case things turned.

She muttered something he didn't quite catch. Hooking a finger under her chin, he lifted her eyes to his. "What was that?"

"I'm so tired of running."

"Then we won't run. The reception should have started by

now. We can get lost in the crowd and if we can't do that, I'll be there to face them with you."

"You don't have to do that. This is my mess of a family. I don't need to drag you into it."

"What did I tell you before about dragging me into things?"

"It's not dragging if you volunteered to go."

"Exactly." He cupped the back of her head, his thumb grazing across her cheek. "I love you. I'm all in. And I'm not going anywhere. I keep telling you that. When is it going to sink into that stubborn, beautiful head of yours?"

The half-smile she gave him made his heart light when it reached her eyes, her visible tension easing. "I don't know, but I think it's starting to sink in."

Matt stood and held out his hand. "Are we going or are we staying?"

She blew out a breath and took his head. "We're staying, but I'm going to need that drink you promised me."

He squeezed her hand. "Deal."

By the time they made it back into the large hall next to the annex, the reception was in full swing. Even more people were there than had been at the ceremony. He kept a tight hold on Mia's hand as she glanced around the room, her senses on heightened alert.

Matt was all for Mia standing her ground, but maybe this wasn't the time to do it. Maybe he should pack her up and take her home. Live to fight another day sort of thing.

But then Quinn Powell walked up, Jenna's husband and the helo pilot who had flown the boys to safety, his hand outstretched to the both of them. "I haven't seen this kind of buzz in the town for a while. You two know how to make a splash."

Matt shook Quinn's hand. "Couldn't have done it without that fancy flying of yours."

Mia started to relax as Jenna came over as well, sliding under the protective arm of her husband. Matt leaned in and whispered in Mia's ear. "I'm going to get those drinks, okay?"

"Sounds good."

He left her and waited in the long line. At least she had people she knew and trusted standing with her. Though he'd caught a glimpse of her parents when they'd arrived, he hadn't seen any sign of them since he and Mia had returned to the reception.

Maybe they'd taken the hint and left.

But that's not what Matt's gut told him. His gut waited for bomb blast. Hopefully when it did, it wouldn't kick them in the ass.

Finally, he made it to the front of the line and ordered their drinks. A couple of double whiskeys for the both of them. Seemed like the best medicine, considering the circumstances. And if they were lucky, they'd finish their drinks, shake a few more hands, and he'd get her out of there before anything happened.

By the time he turned back to her with their drinks. Jenna and Quinn had gone, leaving her by one of the front windows. Mia stood alone, stiff with tension as an older man and woman bore down on her.

He picked up his pace and narrowly missed taking out a server with a full tray of finger foods. Matt made it to Mia's side just as her parents did.

Mia's father was an average-looking man with an average-looking wife. Cornbread, middle America kind of people. The kind of people who blended into the fabric of the nation. He found it hard to believe that these two people terrified the woman he loved and the toughest person he knew.

"Here you go, baby." Matt said as he handed Mia her drink, subtly letting her father know that Mia was with him.

He hoped it gave the man pause before he spoke. She took the glass, slugging the whiskey down.

"Is that really necessary, dear?" The disapproval in her mother's voice could smother a five-alarm fire. It certainly extinguished the brief spark the whiskey had put in Mia's eyes.

Mia exchanged her empty glass for Matt's full one and drained that glass as well.

"Answer your mother."

Matt expected a fiery comeback, if not a down right 'fuck you,' but Mia shriveled in front of him as if her parents had sucked out her life force. A meek, "no, ma'am," came out.

Instead of her bold self, she was beaten.

Putting his hand on her shoulder, he tried to give her as much of his strength as he could. He didn't know much of their history, only that they were estranged, but then again, after what he'd just seen, he didn't really need to know the full story to understand.

He set the empty glasses on the windowsill and stuck his hand out to deflect her father's glaring attention. "Matt Bishop."

Mia's father's cutting gaze lingered on Matt's hand before he locked eyes with Matt. When the man spoke, he aimed his words to wound his daughter. "I have no need to shake the hand of every man my daughter spreads her legs for."

The rebuke Matt expected Mia's mother to give her father never came. Instead Mia's mother hung her head. "I thought you would have learned your lesson, dear."

The 'dear' grated on Matt, setting his teeth on edge. His hand fisted at his side. He'd never hit a woman, but today might be his lucky day.

But Mia's mother wasn't finished. "Being a slut, sleeping with men out of wedlock, it's no wonder the good Lord took your baby and—"

Mia grunted as the verbal hit made a brutal landing.

"And I think we're done here," Matt said, just as Lottie came over.

"I see you found your daughter." Lottie shook their hands. "It's so good that you could come." Lottie glanced at Mia. "Isn't this wonderful? I found their number in Jenna's files under your emergency contact number. I wanted it to be a surprise."

Yeah, it was a surprise all right.

But then again, Lottie and Dale had been in Florida for most of the time he and Mia were in the program. Lottie had no way of knowing that Mia's parents wouldn't be welcome.

"Oh, shit," Jenna said, from off to Matt's right. She hurried over and grabbed Lottie's arm. "Grandma, can I speak with you a moment?"

Jenna hauled Lottie away, but Lottie wasn't the problem. The man and the woman standing in front of him were. Standing your ground wasn't always the right move.

Sometimes the situation required a strategic retreat.

"We would like a word with our daughter, if you don't mind," Mia's father said. Matt didn't even know his name. Didn't care to. After today, he had no plans to speak to the asshole ever again. And neither would Mia if he got his way.

How the man could sound so civil and almost pleasant when such vile, hateful words dropped out of his mouth with such ease, Matt would never understand.

"Actually," Matt said, "I do mind. We *both* mind."

He steered a dazed Mia around her father, leaned in, and whispered into the man's ear. "If I were you, I wouldn't try to contact her again. You got me?"

Matt didn't wait around for an answer. He just hit up Zealand for his truck keys and got Mia the hell out of there.

16

"HOW ARE YOU FEELING?" MATT ASKED AS HE STEPPED ONTO HER porch with a cup of hot coffee in his hand.

She took it, wrapping her hands around the mug. The warmth seeped into her skin as the sun of a new day started to rise.

"Hungover."

It wasn't from the liquor. She hadn't had any more to drink after Matt escorted her out of the VFW hall and whisked her away in Zealand's old truck.

But sometimes emotional hangovers hit harder than the alcoholic ones.

Matt sat down on the porch beside her, his back to the wall. His blanket lay under her and her sleeping bag lay unzipped across her lap. The previous night hadn't been good to her. She'd been restless and unable to settle, and she knew Matt had feared she'd head to the hot spring for the night.

It hadn't been an irrational fear.

Somehow, they'd reached a compromise, and they'd slept out on the porch.

Looked like four nights under a roof was a record that might hold for a while.

You should have jumped on Matt. He was willing. He could have held the walls back and made you forget.

"What are you thinking?" he asked.

"I don't think you really want to know."

He smiled. God, she loved that indulgent smile. "Try me."

She let her head fall back against the wall with a light thud and turned toward him. "I was thinking that you're not just an anonymous dick and that I shouldn't jump on it just to keep my past from barging into my life."

Chuckling, Matt said, "Then what am I?"

"My white knight."

His mug stopped half-way to his lips. "I thought you said you didn't need a white knight to save you."

"I did yesterday."

"Yeah, well, your parents are a piece of work. I don't know how you came out so normal after being raised by the likes of them."

It was her turn to laugh. "I'm not exactly normal."

Matt shrugged and took a sip of his coffee. "'Exactly normal' is over-rated."

Maybe. Then came the admission she didn't want to voice, but if she'd learned nothing over the last three months, it was that sometimes you needed to reach out and let someone in.

After all, 'help' wasn't a four-letter word.

"I don't know what I should do about my parents."

Matt didn't hesitate. "Cut them out of your life, Mia. They're toxic. You don't need those kinds of people in your orbit even if they share your blood."

"It doesn't feel right, shutting out the only family I have."

"What's not right is them treating you like you're grime under the mat they wipe their dirty boots on. Maybe someday they'll come around and apologize for all the hurt they've caused, but until then, you've got your friends here at the ranch, and you've got me."

And she couldn't have asked for a better man for her than Matt. Someone who wasn't afraid to sit back and watch her kick ass but was also willing to step beside her and forge a unified front.

On those rare occasions when she was too wounded to muster the strength to fight for herself anymore, he would pick up her sword and fight for her.

She leaned in and kissed him. "I guess if I can't shake you, I'll have to take you with me."

"I'm glad you're finally seeing things my way." He kissed her back, this one lingering, savoring, promising. "And just so we're clear, I'm not sure giving you orgasms every night to help your mind rest is a sustainable option, but me and my dick are more than willing to let you try."

Before he could go in for another kiss and maybe let her take him up on his offer, she heard the tinkling of Dink's dog tags. They glanced up, and Dink ran down the road ahead of Jenna. The weather had warmed over the past few days, melting much of the snow. In fact, it hadn't even dipped below freezing the night before.

Dink jumped up the two steps, muddy feet and all, wedging himself between Matt and Mia on top of the sleeping bag. His tongue lolled to the side and little clouds puffed out with each pant.

"Get off of there," Jenna hollered out.

Dink ducked his head, refusing to look at Jenna. Mia scrubbed her hand through the ruff of the cattle dog's fur. "He's fine."

"Sorry," Jenna said as she climbed up the steps and leaned

against the porch railing. "He's forgetting his manners in his old age. I think he's getting senile."

Dink lay down, his head on Matt's thigh. Matt's hand dropped automatically and started stroking the dog's head as he took a sip of his coffee. "Were we supposed to do the barn chores this morning? I thought—"

"No. It's the last day of the program. I figure I need to get used to doing it myself again. At least until my new victims—I mean *veterans*—arrive next week. The program's expanding. We're expecting six in the next group."

Or seven. If you fail to graduate.

Then again, if she didn't graduate, it would be hard to do the program from a jail cell. Mia wanted to ask if she'd passed, but she was too afraid of the answer to form the words. One way or the other, by the end of the day, she'd know.

"But I didn't come down here for that. I came because I owe Mia an apology for my grandmother. She didn't know, but she had no business searching through my files and inviting your parents."

"She meant well," Mia said. "I can't fault her for that. She had no idea what kind of shit show inviting them would create. My parents are thoughtless at best, deliberately cruel at worst. And I'm going to take Matt's advice and cut off contact entirely. Maybe I should thank Lottie for helping me see that."

"I don't know about that, but I'm glad you can see their failing isn't yours and that you're taking steps to protect yourself."

"If nothing else, these past few months have shown me it's okay to make myself a priority and that maybe, just maybe, letting a few people in is not such a terrifying thing."

"How does that make you feel?"

Mia wanted to roll her eyes, but she didn't. She'd heard those words so many times in the past few months. She answered as honestly as she could. "I feel like the shield around my heart has a hole so large you could drive a semi-truck engulfed in flames right through. Only now, I'm standing by that wall, a hose in my hand with a tank full of retardant instead of accelerant."

Jenna grinned.

What am I missing?

"What is it?" Matt must not have understood Jenna's smile either.

Out of her pocket, Jenna pulled a folded piece of paper and handed it to Mia. "I got an email this morning. I printed it out for you."

Mia's stomach lurched and churned until and the coffee creamer turned into butter in her gut. Her hand shook, and Matt took the paper from her. "Want me to read it?"

Mia covered her eyes with her hands so she wouldn't be tempted to read it over his shoulder. "Go ahead."

"Ms. Mann, I'm pleased to inform—"

Mia ripped the paper out of his hand and read it out loud. "I'm pleased to inform you that you have fulfilled your obligation to the courts. Risking your life to save two boys is commendable and selfless. All charges have been dropped. You are now free to move on with your life. I hope, for both of our sakes, I never see you in my court again. You've done the hard work. Live your life to the fullest. You deserve nothing less. Judge Fremont, fifth court of the blah, blah, blah."

The paper dropped from her hand, and Matt picked it back up to reread.

Mia couldn't believe it. "How did he find out about Charlie and Zach?"

"The story made national news," Jenna said. "But a little bird sent an email with a link to the story just in case the judge missed it."

"Wait." Mia stood. "Does this mean I get to graduate?"

"I agree with the judge. Honestly, I had my doubts before, but I think you've learned and absorbed more than any of us have given you credit for. Which is the long way of saying, yes, you get to graduate."

Mia blew out a breath, the sting coming to the backs of her eyes. Fuck. She hadn't cried this much since kindergarten. She got to her feet and pulled Jenna in for a hug.

The program hadn't been easy, and she'd fought it the entire time. But Mia wasn't the same angry person who had moved in three months ago. She had hope that she could continue picking up the pieces of her life. She now had reasons to smile. She was loved, and more importantly, knew *she* could love another.

Would she ever be completely better? No clue. And maybe that shouldn't be the end goal. But she no longer felt the drive to endanger herself or to live life on the ragged edge.

Maybe that was enough.

And maybe all that the judge had ever wanted for her.

"Thank you. You and the program have given me back my future. For a very long time, I didn't think I had or deserved one."

Jenna pulled back, using the sleeve of her jacket to wipe the tears off her cheeks. "Now you've got me going."

Matt stood as well, but Dink just burrowed his face under the edge of the sleeping bag. Matt wrapped his arm around Mia's shoulder and pulled her into his body, kissing the side of her head. "I'm so proud of you."

The love in Matt's eyes when he beamed down at her knocked great chunks out of her shield. It wouldn't take much now for the whole damn thing to come tumbling down.

"What are y'all's plans for after the program?"

"I haven't given it much thought. To be honest, I thought I'd be spending my next year in a six-by eight-cell, so my plans are up in the air."

"Whatever it is, we're doing it together." Apparently, it wasn't a question in Matt's mind, and really, it wasn't one in hers either.

"You don't have to leave right away. Like I said, the next group doesn't start arriving until next week, so you're welcome to stay here until you find your next place to land."

"We appreciate that," Matt said. "But we have a few options."

They did? What did that mean?

But before she could ask, Jenna said, "Sidney's wanting to take the horses you three have trained out on the trail one last time for their final training session. Then we're having a party. Hank and Mac and the babies are coming home today, and with the three of you graduating, it's a great time to celebrate."

For the first time since Mia could remember, she was looking forward to the gathering. This gathering of friends. No... of *family.* "We're looking forward to it."

"I'll meet you two at the barn after breakfast, and we'll saddle up and ride out. Can you pass it along to Zealand?"

"Sure thing," Matt said.

Jenna patted her thigh. "Come on, Dink."

Dink got up and trotted down the steps, leaving behind a trail of muddy footprints all over their bedding.

"I swear," Jenna said, "Schultz was thinking of Dink when he made up Pig Pen." She gathered up the bedding and locked her hands around the bulk. "I'll take these up to the house and wash them for you."

Jenna gave Matt a wink before turning on her heel and walking away.

"What was that all about?" Mia asked.

"No clue."

Mia narrowed her eyes at him. Something *was* up, and she had no doubt Matt knew exactly what that was.

MATT, ZEALAND, AND SIDNEY RODE BACK TO THE RANCH, twilight chasing their tails. Matt's cheeks and lips were chapped from being out in the light wind all day, but he wouldn't have missed the day on the trail for anything.

Mia rode the same way she did everything dangerous, without fear and with a smile on her face. She and Jenna had raced back to the barn, galloping ahead of the rest of them. Jenna's massive blue roan, Angel, just edging out Mia in the last few strides.

Matt trotted up to the barn and eased out of the saddle. One thing he wouldn't miss was the saddle sores. He'd ridden a lot over the past few months, but his body still hadn't gotten used to it. But if his plans went the way he wanted them to, his body would have to get the hell over it already.

He tethered his horse to the hitching posts next to Mia and her horse and glanced at his watch. Shit. He was going to be late.

"Wow," Sidney said, as she too, slid out of the saddle. "Maybe I need to keep you three on permanently. All of you did excellent work on the horses. I think if we mix them with a few of the others that haven't sold yet, we'll have a very nice string to sell."

One of the ways Healing Horses helped keep the costs down was by selling the mustangs that the veterans trained while in the program. It was a win all the way around. For the veterans, for the program, and for the mustangs that would otherwise still be in government holding pens.

"Ha," Zealand said. "I've already got my bags packed and in my truck. Taylor's looking forward to having me around full time."

"You have a buyer?" Mia asked.

"I think so." Sidney didn't elaborate. "I should know more tomorrow."

Jenna walked her horse into the barn to untack, and Matt left his horse and followed her inside.

"You excited?" Jenna asked.

Matt glanced behind him to make sure Mia wasn't within earshot. "I think I'm too nauseous to know right now. Ask me again in the morning."

Jenna chuckled. "I think she's going to like it."

"I sure as hell hope so." Matt had never been so unsure of anything in his life. It was a big fucking step, and he didn't know if he was going to slip and fall on his ass or if he would make it safely to the other side. "Is everything set?"

"Lottie and Dale packed everything in the back of the old pickup. The keys are in the ashtray." Jenna pulled her phone out of her pocket and checked the time. "Shouldn't you already be there?"

"Yeah." He hitched his thumb toward the hitching post. "You think you can—"

"I've got the horse. You do what you need to do."

"Thanks." Matt turned to go.

"Hey, Matt."

Matt stopped and looked back. "Yeah?"

"Good luck."

He smiled. "Hopefully I won't need it."

Matt strode out of the barn, his sights on the truck and his mind on what he had planned.

"Hey there, cowboy, wait up." Mia jogged up behind him, her spurs tinkling with each step. "Where are you going?"

"To see a man about a horse," he said cryptically.

Mia put her hand on his arm to keep him from walking off. He really didn't have time to stop and talk. He kissed her on the forehead. "I've gotta go."

"You're not going to tell me?"

He wanted to. But he didn't dare. Not until he'd dotted all the i's and crossed all the t's. "It's just something I need to take care of. I should be back before the party gets started."

Mia let him go. She wasn't the type of woman who demanded answers. And she would know everything all in good time.

By the time Matt finished his errand and returned to the ranch, darkness had fallen, and Boomer had the fire pit in front of his cabin blazing so high that it shed faint light on his cabin. Matt parked the old truck he'd borrowed and pocketed the keys. He'd be needing them later.

Climbing out of the truck, he pulled on his jacket but didn't bother to zip it up. With nightfall, the wind had settled and if anything, the temperature had risen instead of dropped. It wouldn't last, not with winter coming on, but he'd enjoy it until then.

Mud and snowy slush splashed his boots as he walked down to the fire, hoping to catch up with Mia before things got too hectic.

He found her in front of Boomer's grill, scraping the grating clean. Sliding his hands around her waist, he kissed the back of her neck and said, "Did you miss me?"

Mia wiggled her ass against his crotch. "What do you think?"

"Fuck, Mann," he grumbled into her ear. "You keep that up and you won't get to enjoy any of the party."

"Promise?"

He chuckled, nipping at her neck. "We don't have to stay the whole time. We can leave whenever you want."

"Actually, I'm kinda looking forward to it. I haven't seen Gil, Tessa, and Jack for a while. It will be nice to catch up."

Gil had been one of the first veterans in the program and he'd recently become engage to Quinn's former co-pilot, Taylor Foxx.

"Booomerrr!"

"Speaking of..." Matt took the scraper out of Mia's hand and set it aside. He took her hand in his and went to greet Gil and Tessa.

Tessa's son, Jack, sprinted toward Boomer, jumping up into his arms for a bear hug. Boomer fell back a step but caught himself. "Hey kiddo. Long time no see."

Jack scrambled back to the ground. He was only six, maybe seven. "I've been busy. My friend Billy says that next year we're going to have even more homework and I already have some almost every night and how am I supposed to have time to play video games if all I'm doing is math? And it's new math. Mom says the old math was way easier and—"

"Okay, champ," Gil said, a hand on each of the boy's shoulders. "Why don't you see if you can find Pepita. She should be around here somewhere."

Boomer bumped his chin toward his cabin. "She's around back, buddy. Charlie and Zach are back there, too. They're camping out tonight."

"I want to camp out. Can I?"

"Jack," Tessa said, "It's for the older kids, when—"

"He's welcome," Boomer said. "I'm camping out with them, too, so if you're okay with it, it's fine with me."

"Okay." Tessa ruffled the hair on her son's head. "Go help them set up camp, then."

Jack ran off, giving the rest of them a chance to hug and shake hands. Tessa leaned in, but her bump of a belly got in the way.

"How did I not know you were pregnant?" Mia asked.

Matt waited for the darkness to flash in Mia's eyes, a ghost of the hurt and the pain of her own loss that she always carried with her, but her smile seemed genuine.

Tessa put a hand on her belly. "Sorry, I thought everyone knew."

"She's already counting the days," Gil said, tugging his wife to his side. "Me too. Living with a helo pilot who's grounded until the baby is born is—"

"You probably shouldn't finish that sentence," Tessa said.

Gil was a bulldog of a former Marine and undercover DEA agent who turned into a sappy puppy where Tessa was concerned. Gil kissed her cheek. "You're probably right. I'd hate to have to sleep outside with the kids tonight."

"So where are the babies? I came to see babies." Tessa glanced around. "They were coming home today, right?"

"They're in the cabin," Boomer said. "Go on in."

Tessa and Gil headed into the cabin, and Boomer turned back to Mia. "You don't have see the babies if you don't want to. Mac would totally understand if that was a problem for you."

"Actually, I would like to see them." Mia backed a step away and to Matt said, "You coming?"

Matt loved every facet of Mia, the dark parts as well as the light. They were what made her *her*. But he could get used to this side of Mia, the open, vulnerable side. The side learning to accept the joy life still had to give and not just focus on what it had taken.

"Yeah, I'm coming."

————

Mia opened the door to Boomer's cabin, tramping down on the trepidation trudging through her gut. Inside, Mac sat on the sofa, a baby swaddled in her arms while Sidney stood rocking another.

"I'd get up," Mac said as Mia and Matt walked in, "but..."

Mia went over and gave Mac a hug, careful not to squish the baby. "I'm glad you're back."

Mac may not have known how much her own stories had helped Mia frame and analyze and learn to see her own in a new light. Hell, all of them had. Boomer, Mac, Quinn—when he wasn't flying—Gil, Matt, and Zealand. She'd come to the program convinced it had nothing to offer her, only to find that it was an integral part of what had saved her.

A timer in the kitchen buzzed, and Sidney carefully dumped a baby in Matt's unsuspecting hands. "Wait. I don't know what to do with one of these." But he shifted the baby into the crook of his arm and held it against his body, as if it came naturally.

Mac chuckled. "And you think I know what to do with one? With two? I read the books and I read the books and it still doesn't prepare you for the real deal."

Mia eased back the edge of the pink baby blanket of the baby in Matt's arms so she could see the baby's face.

"That's Willow," Mac said. "Willow Grace Nash. And this is Jedediah."

Tiny, red, and wrinkly, Willow had a way to go before she had rolls of fat and chubby cheeks. Her little hand slipped out, grasping Mia's finger, refusing to let go. "She's fierce, like her mother."

"You're telling me," Hank said as he walked in, catching the end of the conversation. "I'm just going to surrender now. There'll be no winning in my house with those two women around."

"That's so cute," Mac said, "You thought you were winning before."

Hank leaned over the back of the couch and gave Mac a kiss. "I've got you, Army. That's a lifelong win."

"You want to hold her?" Matt asked Mia.

Yes. No. Maybe.

Though she had to admit she liked the look of a baby in Matt's arms. Something about the contrast between the white knight and an innocent child made her ovaries squeal. Then

Willow started fussing, and the thinly veiled panic in Matt's eyes made Mia laugh.

"You're not so tough, are you?"

Willow let out another cry, her little face turning red. "*Mia.*"

"I'll warm the bottles," Hank said as he patted Matt on the back on his way to the kitchen. "Hang on tight, buddy. Help is on the way."

"I can hold her if you don't want to," Tessa said.

Matt glanced at Tessa, then back at Mia. "Yeah, sure, if—"

"It's okay," Mia said. "I'll take her for a minute."

With a mild shake in his hands, Matt transferred Willow into Mia's arms. She was tiny and adorable and angry as fuck. This kid didn't like to miss a meal.

Mac patted the seat cushion next to her. "You can sit here and feed her."

Holding the baby was one thing, but for some reason, the thought of feeding her was too much. Old feelings welled up, and Mia knew she had to set herself a healthy boundary and accept the baby step for what it was and not push herself too far too fast. "Um..."

"I've got her." Gil swooped in. Gil didn't know much of Mia's past, but in their brief time together at the start of the program, he seemed like someone who had a lot of intuition. Probably what had made him such a great undercover agent.

Mia smiled up at him. "Thanks."

Hank came back with two bottles, giving one to Gil once he'd settled on the couch. "You need a break, Army?"

"Yeah, thanks."

Hank took his son and stood to feed him. Mia couldn't help but step closer to see Jed. Tess took a spot on the couch next to Gil and Willow.

The front door opened as Mia said, "They're both so fucking adorable."

Pepita hurried through, headed for her room. "That's a dollar for the cuss jar. It's on the table. I'm saving up for a car now, but my dad's getting better at not cussing and I'm afraid the Ferrari is out and I'm going to have to settle for a Fiat."

Gil glanced up, his hand stroking Willow's soft hair. "Not with Mia around."

"You're a fine one to talk," Tessa said. "If we had a jar like that at home, we'd already be able to send Jack to Harvard or Yale."

"I'm pretty sure that kid's already getting a full scholarship, so I don't think we have to worry."

"Burgers are ready for the grill," Sidney said.

Mia needed to find a graceful way to exit the baby situation. As much as she'd wanted to see them, she couldn't hang around too long without her thoughts going places she'd rather not entertain. "I'll take them out."

"I also have a cooler of drinks, and chips and dip that need to go out."

Gil passed the baby to a waiting Tessa and helped Mia and Matt take the food outside. Pepita followed tight on their heels with an iPad in her hand. "We're going to watch movies all night. Or at least until my dad can't take it anymore."

"Poor Boomer," Gil said. "I'd offer to help him with the kids, but—"

"But you're not a masochist?" Matt said, finishing Gil's thought.

"Exactly."

17

———

As Matt, Mia, and Gil returned outside, Taylor walked up after a long evening with an emergency.

"Hey, babe," Zealand said, pulling up a chair for her. "You look dead on your feet."

She gave him a quick kiss and dropped into the chair, not too close and not too far from the fire. "I don't want to complain about having too much business, especially after barely being able to make ends meet for so long, but I could seriously use a night off. Ever since my name got out after the incident with the wild mustangs, my phone has been ringing off the hook."

Mia, Matt, and Gil all found a seat, the chips and dip set on top of a cooler within everyone's reach.

Boomer laid the burgers on the grill as Zealand took a seat next to Taylor. "I keep telling her she needs to think about hiring another vet. It's too much for one person. And with me starting work next week, I won't be able to help as much as I have."

"Maybe you're right," Taylor said as her phone chimed. She picked it up and checked her messages. "I've got to go."

"You just got here," Zealand said.

"A couple of coyotes attacked a sheep."

Zealand stood. "I'll come with you."

Taylor kissed him, then pulled back. "Stay. They only have you for one more night. I've got you for the rest of my life. Besides, it's at the Packard place, and they've got plenty of people who can assist me."

"I'll walk you up to your truck at least."

After they left, Matt turned his attention to Gil. He didn't know Gil as well as he knew Mia and Zealand. "What about you, Gil, what do you have lined up?"

"He could tell you, but then he'd have to kill you." Boomer flipped the burgers, coals hissing and spitting as the fat dripped down.

"It's kind of hush-hush at the moment." Gil dipped a tortilla chip into the bowl of salsa. "But it should definitely keep me on my toes, and my finger on the pulse of law enforcement."

Mia helped herself to some chips as well. "This have something to do with that building project Boomer won't tell us about?"

"Maybe," Boomer confirmed with a grin.

Gil and Boomer could have their secrets and their intrigue, as for Matt and hopefully Mia, they had a much less perilous future ahead of them. That is, if Mia agreed to what he'd planned.

The kids came running around from the back of the cabin, chasing each other and playing tag. For a kid on crutches, Charlie got around amazingly well. Though it looked like he'd duped Jack into being *it* when Charlie inevitably got tagged.

"You kids need to slow down," Boomer hollered. "Charlie's parents are going to kill me if he breaks his other leg."

"Awh, Dad. Charlie's fine. Right, Charlie?"

"Actually, my leg is starting to hurt a little."

Off in the distance, came the rhythmic thump of trotting

hooves, and Matt stared into the darkness until Sidney's Houdini horse came into view.

"Eli's coming," Pepita said. "Let's get some treats from the cabin."

Then came a donkey's bray, a sound that drowned out everything else. It got louder and louder until Boomer's donkey, Donkey, came trotting up behind Eli. "Jesus Christ," Boomer said, "I knew it would be a bad idea to put those two in the same paddock together. Eli is teaching Donkey all his bad habits."

Boomer closed the grill and stepped away as Donkey came up to him. Donkey put his fuzzy chin on Boomer's shoulder, and his eyes rolled into the back of his head as Boomer scratched Donkey's neck with both hands.

When Boomer finished, Donkey trotted off and joined Eli as they scraped their hooves over some of the remaining snow and nibbled the dead grass underneath.

Matt could live that life. The animals. The outdoors. Hopefully, Mia could see herself there as well. His stomach knotted. What would he do if her dreams didn't align with his?

You know what you'll do. You'll follow her to the ends of the earth until she finds whatever she's looking for.

The night wore on. Food was eaten, drinks drunk, lies and a healing helping of truth told. Quinn wandered in at some point, having returned from a night-training mission that Tessa couldn't hear enough about.

Hank and Mac joined them after Lottie and Dale volunteered to babysit the twins, but the last week or so had taken its toll on everyone at the ranch, and instead of the talk going on late into the night, people sank lower into theirs chairs, the stress and sleepless nights having caught up with them.

Except for the kids, who must have fueled themselves on caffeine, sugar, and Red Dye Number 3, because it seemed like they were only getting started. They came out of the house, giggling and laughing, Jack getting a piggyback ride from Zach. In the peals of the children's laughter, Matt thought he heard another.

Yusef.

But this time, instead of the memory pitching him back to a time he hated to remember, it brought him a sense of peace. Maybe Yusef *was* his guardian angel. And if he were, he deserved a few fun hours off, playing with the kids.

A short time later, Hank patted Mac's leg, and she woke with a start. "We're calling it a night. You can't keep your eyes open, and the twins are only going to make that worse." He helped her to her feet. She was slow to rise, her body still healing from the c-section.

They all said their goodnights, and the others gathered up their empties and headed to their beds as well. The kids had settled into the tent to watch movies on the iPad, and even Eli and Donkey had wandered back to their paddock for the night.

"I guess we're heading to bed, too," Mia said, though only Boomer and Sidney remained.

Matt stood and caught her hand. "Not so fast. I've got something I want to show you."

———

THE QUESTION 'WHERE ARE YOU TAKING ME' DIDN'T STRAY FAR from Mia's mind as she and Matt walked up to their cabins, and he helped her up into the ranch's old pickup.

The excitement and nervousness wafting off Matt fueling a few twinges of excitement of her own. But whatever this was, somehow Mia knew it was a good thing. Maybe it was because of the grin Matt had to fight to keep from spreading across his face or the grip he had on her hand, or the way he sang to the old country song streaming through the crackly speakers as they drove down the windy road.

The headlights cut through the darkness, and Matt slowed as a dirt road came into view on their left, the entrance mostly overgrown with vines and once-tamed brush now gone feral.

"Close your eyes," he said.

"I already can't see anything. It's pitch black out here."

"Just do as you're told, soldier."

Mia chuckled. "If you remember, I wasn't a very good soldier." But she closed her eyes anyway. She enjoyed this light side of him and didn't want to spoil whatever surprise he'd cooked up.

The truck bumped and bucked over ruts and potholes, the overgrowth scraping the underside of the truck and down the sides. She had to grab onto the hand grip up by her head to keep from bouncing out of the seat even with her seatbelt on.

"Hang on." Matt gunned the engine and the truck went through a muddy patch, the tires spinning and sliding until they caught again on firmer soil. For a few seconds there, she thought she'd have to push him out of the mud.

Finally, after one kidney was shook loose, Matt accelerated up a hill. At the top he stopped and parked. He didn't cut the engine or kill the headlights. She could see them through her eyelids.

Matt's grip got tighter on her hand. Blowing out a deep breath, he said, "Before you open your eyes, I want to tell you one thing."

"Okay." The trepidation in his voice made her heart skip and slide worse than the tires had.

"This is for us. But if you don't like it, it's not going to hurt my feelings. All I want is for us to be together, however that looks, however that makes us both happy."

The tremor in his voice almost had her opening her eyes

before he said she could, but she squeezed them tight so she couldn't. "Now you're scaring me."

"No, Mann. It's a good thing… I think."

"Can I open my eyes now?"

Matt squeezed her hand again, holding it to his chest, his heart thumping against the back of her hand.

He must be so fucking nervous.

"Open them."

It took a few seconds for what she saw to register. The beam of the headlights shone on a tall structure. It went up four or more stories. Stairs wrapped around the outside. Somewhere around the third level, was some sort of room or something, but the stairs went higher still, until it disappeared into the darkness.

"What is it?"

Matt popped his door and released her hand. "Come on, I'll show you."

He met her at the front of the truck. He'd left it running so they'd have some light, but Matt pulled a flashlight from a pocket of his coat and used that to help guide their way. They had to tromp through knee-high brush that the snowfall hadn't smashed down. "It's an old fire watch station that's been decommissioned."

Fire watch station?

The movement of the flashlight spotlighted a pair of eyes. "What's that?"

Matt crouched, dropping the beam of the light toward the ground. "Come here, boy. It's okay."

Out of the darkness, a hairy gray—or was that white?—form appeared. A wolf? No, it was too large to be a wolf. It crawled out of the darkness on its belly, its tail and butt wiggling. "He hangs out here, apparently," Matt said. "I think he's an Anatolian Shepherd. They're some kind of livestock guard dog I'm told."

The dog was sweet but shy and skinny, only sticking around for a few pets and scratches before skulking back into the darkness.

Matt gave her a nudge. "Let's go see the rest."

With her hand in his, he practically pulled her up four flights of stairs, not even stopping at what Mia thought might be a room. At the top, a metal walk and guardrail went around the perimeter of the glass enclosed tower. That high up, the stars practically came down to greet them. Matt led her to the door, a key in his hand unlocked the door.

He had his hand on the knob when he said, "You ready?"

She still didn't understand what all this meant, so without hesitating she said, "I'm ready."

He pushed open the door and let her precede him inside. It was a large, empty room. Or mostly empty. He laid the flashlight in her hand. "Hold this."

He went around the periphery of the room, lighting a thick, sturdy candle every few feet until he'd made it back to her. Retrieving the flashlight from her hand, he clicked the light off, pitching them into the warm glow of the candlelight.

The scent of burning wax and candle smoke wafted up, mixing with the smell of cleaning supplies and laundry detergent. In the center of the room lay Matt's blanket and her sleeping bag, fresh from the wash. A picnic basket sat on one corner.

"What do you think?"

"It's awesome. I'm speechless." She took a quick spin around the room, the candles not so bright they prevented her from seeing out the windows for the full three-sixty degrees—a vastness that seemed to go on until infinity.

Matt came up behind her, his hands locking around her waist, his chin on her shoulder. "What do you think?"

"Stunning." There was no other word. It took her breath

away and gave it back. It made her heart race and stand still. It opened her mind to the light and closed it to the darkness.

She had never been in a place before that made her feel like all the different pieces of her life could sit together in perfect harmony.

They stood there together, minute after minute, drinking and breathing the magic in.

Leaning back against him, she let her tensions float away. This minute, this moment, with Matt filled her.

"Who owns this place?"

He took one of her hands and placed the keys in the palm of her hand. "You do."

She turned in his arms. "*What?*"

"I signed the paperwork today."

Mia tried to hand him the keys back, but he would have none of it. "I can't accept this."

"It's a gift. No strings. No matter what happens between us, I want you to know you have a safe place to land. You deserve it. You deserve this."

"What do you mean 'whatever happens to us?' Where are you going?"

He pulled her into him, a hand cupping the back of her neck, holding her close. "I don't want to go anywhere. I want to be here with you, but I don't want you to think that me and the tower only come as a package deal."

"I think I might like strings and package deals, if it's you that comes included."

"Yeah?"

She wrapped her arms around his neck, kissing and pouring her gratitude into him. If she didn't want him, he'd leave, and he wasn't the kind of man to pitch a fit about it. She'd learned to not only trust his word but trust the man.

But he had more thoughts, more plans he wanted to share.

She could feel it in his body, in the way he held back, not taking full breaths.

"What else?"

"This is a great base for a guide business. There are corrals and paddocks for a small string of horses. Good, level land where we could build guest cabins. The mountains are only a couple hours ride from here. After the mayor's press conference, people have been calling me, wanting to hire us for their next adventure."

"Holy shit."

She didn't have time to say much else because Matt pushed on, apparently needing to get everything out. Sometimes it helped to say what meant the most to you all at once without thinking about the words as they tripped out. The program had taught her that.

He took her head in his hands, his eyes ablaze as they lasered in on hers. "Build something with me, Mia. A business. A home. A *life*."

The clog in her throat prevented words from sneaking past, even after dry swallowing a few times. She nodded and he wrapped her in a hug so tight that she could barely breathe. But that was fine with her.

When she'd come into the program, she hadn't wanted anything more than a Get Out of Jail Free card, but she'd earned so much more than that.

He finally broke the hug, and they were both busy swiping the tears off their cheeks. Matt blew out a breath, a nervous laugh now free to escape.

"I've got champagne," he said.

"Oh, hell yes."

He pulled a bottle from the basket, the cork hitting the roof, barely missing the floor-to-ceiling banks of windows.

They laid out on the blanket, him on his side, his head

propped up on one hand, while she lay facing him on her stomach, her glass between her fingers, the bubbles going straight to her head as he told her more about the property.

"You have almost fifty acres total, and—"

"*We.*"

"We." Matt leaned in, kissing her. He tasted of champagne and dreams and hope. "Downstairs there's a kitchen, a bath, a small den, and a tiny bedroom. But I don't see us spending a whole lot of time inside."

"And the tower," Mia said. "Don't forget the tower."

"It's the best part. I wanted a place where you were safe, but you could still feel like you were outside. It's not perfect, and if you need to camp out, I'm there. I just thought—"

She pressed her fingers to his lips, and he nipped playfully at the tip. "It's amazing, just like you."

The emotion rolled in, the emotion she'd tried to hold at bay because she knew it would swamp her. She knew her voice would shake, but if she'd learned anything, she'd learned that there was nothing wrong being vulnerable in front of this man.

He would guard her.

He'd protect her.

He'd keep her safe.

"I love you, Matt. I had to live through all that hell to bring you into my life, but I'd do it all again if it meant building the rest of my life with you. So, I'm giving the words you've given me, back to you. *I'm all in.*'"

Matt set his glass aside and took hers from her as well, drawing her into his arms and rolling her on top of him. He was already hard, and she hoped like hell he had a big box of condoms stuffed in that picnic basket.

There came a scrape at the door. A soft whine.

Going to the door, she opened it to find the dog sitting at the threshold. "Do you mind if I let him in?"

"Hold up a sec." Matt clicked on the flashlight and propped it up against the picnic basket. The light shined up in the air to illuminate the room. He went from candle to candle extinguishing the flames. They were a nice touch, but a big dog in a small space with open flame wasn't the best mix.

Matt pulled a hand towel out of the basket and met her at the door with the flashlight. "It's not much, but it should knock most of the loose dirt and mud off."

Together they did their best to clean the dog, knowing nothing short of a full bath would do the trick, but that could wait for another time. When the dog was as dry as they were going to get him, they opened the door. The dog went around the room sniffing the corners and candles.

Matt took her hand, and they lay back down on their bedding. The boards were hard, but there were no rocks, sticks, or bugs underneath, so it was nearly perfect. Laying on his back, Matt tucked a hand behind his head and pulled her into his chest. The dog came over, curling up against her back. He smelled like mud and possibly something dead that he'd rolled in, but it honestly wasn't that bad. They could always open one of the windows if they had to.

Here in the tower, instead of feeling claustrophobic, she felt... whole.

And seen.

"I love you, Mia. I've got the best feeling about this. About us."

She did, too. And as they lay there together, the stars blanketing them, the dog let out a loud, contented sigh.

"And as a bonus," she said, thinking about all the stairs she'd be climbing every day. "I'm going to have a killer ass."

A LETTER TO MY READERS

Dear Reader,

The Lazy S Ranch series has been an amazing, fun world to create. While the series ends here, the thrills continue in my next Romantic Suspense series, **Steele-Wolfe Securities**.

Wyoming Confidential is another slice of the Lazy S world set just before Cowboy, Undercover where some of the Wyoming Confidential crew have cameos.

Your next adventure starts here: www.books2read.com/Wyoming-Confidential

ROMANTIC SUSPENSE

Lazy S Ranch Series
Cowgirl, Unexpectedly (Book 1)
Must Love Horses (Book 2)
Hot on the Trail (Book 3)
Cowboy, Undercover (Book 4)
Cowboy, Unbridled (Book 5)

Cowgirl, Unbroken (Book 6)

Wright's Island Series
Don't Look Back (Book 1)
In Her Defense (Book 2)

Steele-Wolfe Securities
Wyoming Confidential (Book 1)

CONTEMPORARY ROMANCE

Rockin' Rodeo Series
Luck of the Draw (Book 1)
Photo Chute (Book 2)
Reined In (Book 3)
Rockin' Rodeo Series Collection (Books 1-3)

MM ROMANCE

Black Stallion Studios Series
One Shot (Book 1)
Key Grip (Book 2)
Best Boy (Book 3)
Black Stallion Studios Box Set (Books 1-3)

Valley Boys
Art of Love (Book 1 July 2020)

ABOUT THE AUTHOR

Vicki Tharp makes her home on small acreage in south Texas with her husband and an embarrassing number of pets. When she isn't writing, you can usually find her on the back of her horse—avoiding anything that remotely resembles housework—smelling like fly spray and horse sweat.

Join my newsletter at: http://bit.ly/V-W-T
Join my street team and receive free Advance Reader Copies of my upcoming books at: http://bit.ly/S-W-S-T
You can find my website at: www.VickiTharp.com
I love to hear from readers. You can email me at vwtharp@VickiTharp.com

Or you can stalk me at:

facebook.com/VickiTharpAuthor

instagram.com/author_Vicki_Tharp

bookbub.com/authors/vicki-tharp

amazon.com/author/vicki_tharp

twitter.com/vwtharp